Superior Hearts

SUMMER: PAIGE & CONNOR'S STORY

Superior Hearts

OLIVIA HOPE McCARTHY

ISBN (paperback): 979-8-9908446-8-1
ISBN (ebook): 979-8-9908446-9-8

Editing & proofreading by Caitlin Miller
Cover design & typesetting by Benita Thompson

To anyone in need of the healing power of faith and love.
May you find threads of both in this story.

Content Warning

The following story is a kisses only romantic comedy that contains issues some readers may be sensitive to:

- parental abandonment
- references to addiction and gambling
- alcohol usage
- fade to black between married couple (in bonus scene)

1

PAIGE

April Fools is *not* for vampires. It's a regular day that should not involve costumes. But my job as the part-time phlebotomist at Dr Gartinen's pediatric office required me to dress up. I don't know if Dr. Gartinen wanted social media promo photos and thought 'perfect opportunity!' or if he confused April Fools Day with Halloween. Either way, it was actually for the kids. So I did it. I hated it. But I did it, because it made the kids laugh when I drew their blood.

This is why, at 5:17 p.m. on April 1st, I am walking down the street of Viewport, Michigan, I've lived on for my entire life in a vampire outfit, complete with false teeth, and clutching an envelope of forms to my chest. My black cape swirls in the wind, and I kind of love the dramatic flair. But not enough to do this for fun anytime soon. LARPer, I am not.

The whole reason I'm still in this crazy getup after work is because Blaze, my now-eleven-year-old neighbor, who I've babysat for nine years, will get a kick out of it. Phlebotomist, vampire—ha. I thought I was clever too.

I'm on my way to give Blaze's parents my application for working at their pre-teen leadership summer camp. Chet and Ember recently decided to reopen the camp as a way to give back to the Yooper community, and Blaze's mom is the closest thing I have to a sister. So when I told her I felt stuck in my job, stuck in Viewport, and stuck in general, she told me to think about working at the camp for them as a 'nurse' and counselor. Ember gave me a stack of papers and told me the job was there if I wanted it.

Ember's husband, Chet, can be intimidating, but what Ember says goes. His love for her means that, even if I'm not exactly what they envisioned for the position, I'm guaranteed the job.

I hated every moment of being in this stupid costume, and now I feel more stuck than ever. I couldn't take it anymore, and I spent my lunch break in my car filling out these forms. I don't want to take advantage of Ember's kindness, but maybe this is an opportunity to do something *different*. I have to give them to her before I chicken out.

The snow has melted into puddles, and it's misty. The wind has a bite to it that hints at winter weather. I wish I was wearing a hat, but a hat on top of a wig seemed overkill. I'll have to ask Ember if we're in the clear or if we're projected to have any late winter snow storms. We usually get a few in April, with at least one in early May, but with where we're situated right off the water of Lake Superior, the weather isn't small talk. It's life. And as a local meteorologist, Ember is somewhat of a celebrity and everyone asks her about the weather. She never minds.

I dodge a puddle on the walkway of the O'Malley's house, climb the porch steps, and knock. After watching Blaze for so many years, I have a special knock to let him know it's me. We made it up together.

Three sharp knocks followed by six taps of my palm against the door—we even have a rhythm because percussion is fun. I've just gotten to the second tap of my palm when the door is wrenched open and I pitch forward, false teeth and all, into the arms of...*not Blaze.*

These arms do not belong to anyone I know. They are muscular and covered in black long sleeves. I drag my eyes up the arms to a broad chest and discover this man is wearing a henley. The top button is undone. My eyes travel up his neck, across a lightly stubbled jawline, and, finally, his head. He's taller than me by at least six inches. His dark brown hair hangs in perfect coils sitting just above his shoulders, blue eyes, and lips curved into a deep frown. He's wearing a backward baseball cap. I can't. I don't *do* interacting with attractive men. But this one looks like a dark-haired Heath Ledger in *Ten Things I Hate About You,* and goodness knows I have a LOT of notebooks filled with ridiculous fiction regarding that particular no-chance scenario. Since Heath left us, I haven't found a new celebrity crush. But this guy—he could be it.

I straighten and step back, embarrassed at having fallen, and begin apologizing profusely. The fatal flaw in that plan is that my stumble jarred my false teeth, and now my speech is unintelligible. I think I'm spitting. *Great. Now I look like I have rabies.*

"Thowy!" I say as I back away, unsure where to put my hands or what to do with my teeth.

Blaze runs around the corner. "PAIGE!" He gives me what can only be described as a bro high-five. He outgrew hugging me last year, and as his long-time babysitter, I definitely cried. Blaze looks from the man to me. The man glares at my head. "We're learning about shipwrecks in school!" Then, with a crinkled brow, he says, "You didn't do our knock. I would have gotten it if I heard it."

I sigh, then attempt to tell him that I was about to knock, but there's a flaw here too. I can't take my teeth out because where would I put them? Capes don't come with pockets.

I choke on my own saliva. The man in black snakes his hand out and taps me on the back, attempting to clear my airway. My teeth go flying with the impact and land on the floor. My face reddens as both Blaze and the attractive man's eyes follow the projectile teeth.

"Paige?" Blaze asks. "Why are you dressed like that?"

The mystery man scowls deeper.

"April Fools!" I squeak, keeping my eyes on Blaze and trying to ignore the man's disgust. "We…uh…dressed up at work, and I thought you'd like to see it. But that was a mistake, and these are for Ember, and if you could give them to your mom, I'd be really grateful. Ok. Byeee." I thrust the envelope into Blaze's hands and turn to leave. I hustle out of there and am already off the front porch when a deep voice calls out.

"Wait, Alice." I turn around slowly, even though Alice is *not* my name. The man in the black henley stands at the edge of the porch, his hand outstretched. He opens his palm and smirks at me. "You forgot your teeth."

Humiliation burns in my throat as I trudge back to the porch. I grab the slimy teeth and stare at where his black joggers meet white socks. Thanks," I say before walking away as fast as I can without running.

2

CONNOR

The vampiress apparently known as Paige walks faster than an Olympic speed walker down the sidewalk. I ignore the cold and lean against the porch railing. I watch until she disappears up a driveway and through the side door of a house down the street.

My hand is slimy from holding her ridiculous teeth. Growing up as the youngest son of a dentist, I spent a lot of time at the office. I'm immune to spit and teeth, whether real or dentures. Also, do you know how many people forget their teeth, retainers, or night guards at hotels?

I wipe my hands off on my joggers. It's been a long time since I've felt anything around a woman, and that was unexpected.

Yes, the Halloween costume was odd for April, but she had a reason. I can't believe I called her Alice—a nod to the *Twilight* obsession Kaleigh made me endure during our relationship. Paige's flushed face was bright red, but not before I noticed the light dusting of freckles across her nose. Her black hair was pulled back in a tight bun at the nape of her neck, and I wonder if it was part of the costume or if she wears her hair like that usually. Her eyes were wide and blue, and the way she fell into my arms felt…right. Which is bizarre. Because absolutely nothing about that interaction was normal.

Thinking of Kaleigh makes the cold nipping at my face even more welcome. My long-time girlfriend and I always talked about getting married young. I'm a caboose, with a big age gap between me and my next oldest sibling. I guess I wanted to even the field a little. I was tired of being the baby, the last to do everything. And I really do want a family of my own. I love kids. They never mind the goofier side of my personality. My nephew, Blaze, is awesome. If it wasn't for Ember having a baby this summer, I'd beg Chet and Ember to let Blaze come to camp. As it is, I understand they want to soak up time with him and settle in as a family of four. I'm happy for them. But I want what they have. With less drama. I love my brother, but he is a Class-A idiot. Or, he was. He's shaped up and is lucky beyond belief that Ember and Blaze are in his life.

I replay the interaction in my mind. Calling Paige 'Alice' was a mistake. Now I can't stop thinking about *the incident.*

When I proposed to Kaleigh over a year ago, she said no and broke up with me. Adding insult to injury, the whole thing was filmed. I hired a photographer and videographer duo to make us sparkle in the sunshine like the vampires in Kaleigh's favorite scene from *Twilight.* This involved glittering me with stage makeup. It was awful and itchy, and glitter was stuck to my arm hair for months. Because I paid the company, they delivered the footage within a day, just like their super-fast turnaround time promised. They even edited it into a montage. Her coming to the clearing, redwood trees towering in the background, me waiting for her—and we both sparkle. There I am, down on one knee, and I look like I've been dropped in a pool of glitter. She gets away with only having a sparkle filter edited onto her. And the woman who loved *Twilight* sees me, shrieks, puts her hands over her mouth, and begins to say, "NO!" Repeatedly. For eight minutes.

Apparently, we'd been together for too long, and she had bigger ambitions. I'm not sure if that meant the actual Edward Cullen was who she wanted to be with, but it clearly did not mean me.

After that, I watched the video multiple times a day for a week until Chet came to California. And bless him, when he saw it, he did not laugh. He destroyed my video, but I know Kaleigh was sent a copy, too—part of the contract I signed.

Chet's romance with Ember was the stuff of sheer stupidity, but he's good in a crisis. If anyone could understand being a fool in romance, it's him. My brother helped me pick up the pieces of my life without Kaleigh. He helped me sell my possessions and then offered me a job.

He told me about how he and Ember had been playing with the idea of opening Gramps' old camp and hunting property back up and making it a tween leadership camp. The camp needed significant supervision, and since Ember and Chet couldn't be there to handle the day-to-day stuff, and I had experience in hospitality, Chet asked me to be the manager of the camp. My first advice as manager was not to use the word *tween*. Preteen, please.

I finished out my contract with the boutique hotel I managed, packed up my apartment, sold almost everything, and moved to Michigan. Northern Michigan. Technically I was born here, but my family left for sunnier California when I was six. My memories of living here are sparse, but I do have memories of Gramps' property. Every year from ages nine to thirteen, my parents sent me to stay with him for a week in the fall. Every year, I learned all I could about responsible firearm use, hunting, caring for the land, and all of Gramps' tall tales. I miss him.

Gramps is gone now, but Chet is here. I'm crashing at his house for the next week before I head over to the camp and begin preparing for the campers.

The wind whips up, and I can smell the unique scent of Lake Superior. Water shouldn't be so *big* unless it's an ocean. Lake Superior didn't get the memo.

Ember's round belly comes into view before she does. "What are you doing out here, Connor? Blaze was looking for you. Something about needing to finish beating you in a video game?"

I grumble. I might be the worst person to ever touch a video game controller in the entire world. Blaze is merciless in beating me, but I can't blame the kid. He's my favorite nephew, and I'm pretty sure I'm his favorite uncle. A sacrifice to my dignity is worth it.

Ember smiles knowingly, fans herself, and turns her face into the wind. Over the past few days, I've heard her mention the temperature being *hot* several times. It is *not* hot in April in the Upper Peninsula of Michigan, but I'm not going to argue with her. I like my sister-in-law a lot. She's been good to Chet, and she's an amazing mother. She's also pregnant, so *nope*, not arguing.

She leans her hands over the railing and takes a deep breath. "What's bothering you?"

"Kaleigh," I say, and my voice comes out rougher than I expected.

Ember puts an arm on my shoulder, which is comical because at six feet three and a half inches tall, I'm taller than her by a lot. She shifts her weight from side to side and pulls me in for an awkward hug. I try not to bump her belly, but she's seven months pregnant.

She shifts away after a brief sisterly but also motherly hug. "I'm sorry. But why?"

"Uh. I was just remembering the…vampire proposal. The girl at the door earlier was dressed as a vampire."

Ember takes it in stride. I know Chet told her about the vampire proposal. I also know that Ember isn't one to mock. "What girl?"

I shrug and point down the street to where Paige disappeared. "Paige."

"Paige? She was here?" Ember peers around like Paige is going to pop out of the bushes below the porch.

"Yeah, but she left."

"Dressed like a vampire? Why? How?"

"She said it was April Fools. Something for work."

She laughs. "That's actually really perfect for her job, but it probably went over all the kids' heads. Most importantly, was she dressed like a *Twilight* vampire or Dracula?"

I find myself wanting to know what she does for work, but Ember would be like a dog with the scent of a bone if I asked or showed interest. Especially since I just admitted to thinking about Kaleigh, the last person I had romantic feelings for.

I settle for answering her question with details. "Pointy teeth, black cape, red cumberbund." I really want to know if the hair was part of the costume or her actual hair. But I also don't want to give too many details. No hints that my heart stuttered when she was in my arms. Nope. That was nothing.

"Ahh, so Dracula. But that doesn't have anything to do with the *Twilight* vampires, right?"

"It was odd."

"So, other than her boss confusing Halloween and April Fools, what did she want? She isn't babysitting Blaze until we take you to the camp next week."

"She gave Blaze an envelope and said it's for you."

Ember brightens. "She's going to work at camp with you! She's just the sweetest. I'm so glad for her. You have to look out for her.

She's had a rough few years, and she needs someone she can look up to. I think she's twenty-four, only a year younger than you. You finally get the chance to be an older brother! She's practically a big sister to Blaze, so there's a family connection here somewhere."

That's not good. Because the last thing I want is to form a sisterly connection with Paige.

3

PAIGE

Ember asked me to babysit Blaze a few weeks ago. She and Chet need to go to the camp property and open it up for contractors to begin working on updates. Camp is about three hours from Viewport, so they're leaving before dawn and won't be home until late.

I haven't seen Mr. Handsome-You-Forgot-Your-Teeth guy again, and since it's been a week, my mortification has faded a little. He was probably some friend of Chet's and was just stopping by. I'll never have to see him again. The thought both soothes and stings my heart. We could have had such a wonderful future.

I may have let my mind run away with a scenario where I wasn't dressed like a vampire when I met him, where he didn't call me another woman's name, and where I was witty and clearly a catch. *And* in this dream scenario, he was clearly interested in *me.*

My red hair is piled on top of my head in the messy bun I slept in. I'm wearing plaid pajama pants with a long-sleeve *Great Lakes,*

Great Shipwrecks tee under my bulky winter parka. A thermos of hot tea is in one hand, and in the other, a bag with running clothes and shoes. I'll use Ember's treadmill to get my run in today. Since it's still dark out, I strap a head lantern to my forehead. My breath comes out in white puffs of steam as I hurry through the frigid air.

I turn up the walkway to the front porch. In my periphery, I catch sight of a car I've never seen before parked in the driveway. It's larger than Ember or Chet's car, but with the new baby coming, Ember probably wanted a new car. She mentioned that to me the last time I saw her. This one looks very family-friendly.

I don't expect Blaze to be awake at this early hour, so I tap gently on the O'Malley's door. To my horror, Mr. Handsome-You-Forgot-Your-Teeth guy opens the door. He stands there, arms crossed over his chest.

I stand there, staring, because this is clearly a nightmare, when Chet walks by. "Hey, Paige. Thanks for coming by so early."

Handsome-teeth man steps back, and I swallow hard. *At least I'm not a vampire today.* I can keep reminding myself that. It might make it better.

I duck into the house, trying to make myself as small as possible as I pass the attractive man who, for some reason, is staring at me.

"Paige, this is Connor. Connor, Paige," Chet says in his warm, deep voice. One time, Ember called it a weighted blanket voice. I'm not interested in Ember's husband, but he should probably narrate audiobooks because his voice is soothing and comforting, and even though I'm mortified, it feels ok with Chet narrating.

I smile politely as I remove my boots and drop them on the tray next to the door. The mystery man—Connor—smirks at me. He shuts the door but stands next to it with his arms crossed as he looks me up and down. "Bella and I have already met." I can't really call our previous interaction a meeting, but if we change the word from 'met' to something like 'watched as she mortified herself,' it would be accurate. Semantics.

"Bella? No, that's Paige. She's watching Blaze for us today. I'm going to go check on Ember. We should be good to go in a few." Chet disappears up the stairs.

I don't know what to say to this man. He's devastatingly hand-some, but he's also called me weird names twice. At least I know *his* name now. "Hi." I unzip my coat and shrug out of it. Connor's eyes stay on me as I hang it up on the hook above the boot tray. I step into the living room where I can set my tea on the coffee table and curl up under a blanket for the next few hours. I don't think Blaze will wake up until at least seven, and it's only five now.

I settle on the couch and reach behind to grab a blanket from the blanket ladder. My fingers grasp the tassels, but it slips out of my hands and is now in that difficult spot to reach between the back of the sofa and the wall.

"It's too early for this," I grumble and close my eyes in frustration.

"Too early for what?" a deep voice that isn't Chet's asks.

My eyes pop open and I find Connor holding the blanket I was reaching for. I shake my head, my cheeks reddening. Our eyes lock. The blue shirt he's wearing brings out the blue of his eyes. I blurt out the only thing I can think to say when faced with my daydreams turned into nightmares: "Too early for me to not have a blanket."

Connor doesn't say anything in response. He walks around the couch, the blanket still clutched to his chest, and with a snap, spreads the blanket over me. "There," he says roughly before giving me a small head bob, his gaze lingering on my face. His eyes sweep my body and take in my disheveled state before he hightails it out of the room just as Ember plods down the stairs and over to the couch.

"Paige!" she whisper-squeals. "Thank you!"

"No problem," I whisper back. I start to stand, but she motions me back down.

"You know where everything is and how everything goes. Have a great time with Blaze. All of Blaze's favorite foods are in the house today, so that should be easy. I think we'll be home pretty late tonight. Maybe around ten or eleven."

I nod. "Sure thing. Happy to help. I know Blaze is older now, but it's nice to spend the day with someone else. I can use your treadmill, right?"

"Of course, it isn't getting much use from me right now." She rubs her belly. "Oh, and you met Connor?"

I swallow. "Yeah."

"Ember, honey, it's time to go!" Chet whisper-calls.

Ember sets a comforting hand on my shoulder. "I'm so happy you'll be working together. Connor will take good care of you. See you later tonight, Paige!"

Ember treads away, and I try to understand what she means by working together. The side door from the kitchen to the driveway closes with a creak, and the distinct sound of two cars driving away follows.

4

CONNOR

The heated steering wheel of my new car is a balm to my hands even after a brief exposure to the frigid air. I follow behind Chet and Ember's SUV and realize a simple fact. I am in trouble. I spent the last few days ignoring the stutter my heart gave when I first met Paige.

Now I have to face the truth.

Both times I've seen her, it rattled me. I don't *get* rattled by women. I've had one serious relationship that lasted from high school through college. And it didn't end well. Paige is…not my type. Or at least, I'm pretty sure she isn't. Can you have a type when you've only had one girlfriend? To make things worse, my brain is supplying all the ways that Paige is different from Kaleigh, and Paige is *winning* this weird comparison game.

A chill runs down my spine. I echo Paige's sentiment. It *is* too early to be without a blanket. Instead, here I am, driving to my grandpa's old property to run a camp in his honor and put my hospitality degree and experience to good use. But it's also to have a fresh start after Kaleigh's humiliating rejection. So now, when I should be thinking about the *camp*, I'm thinking about women.

Trouble. Right?

The truth is, Paige's crazy hairdo this morning was wildly attractive. Now that I've seen her fiery red hair, I know the black hair was part of the costume. The red hair suits her more than the vampire wig, but I had never imagined her looking like *that*. And yes, I did imagine what she looked like as a normally dressed person, despite my determination not to.

Her shipwreck shirt was ironic in a way that made me want to laugh and get to know her. She's pretty. Gorgeous, actually. Kaleigh was always trying to look effortlessly beautiful. Paige somehow manages it naturally. I know enough to know that Paige wasn't wearing makeup, that she showed up in pajamas, and that she was probably planning on crashing on the couch for a few hours.

I groan. Stupid blanket. What possessed me to foolishly pluck that blanket from the ladder? Was it a middle school urge to get her to talk to me? Have I been spending too much time with Blaze? No, never. Time with Blaze will never be the problem. I could forgive myself for giving in to the urge, but then I went and spread it over her like a parent tucking in a child.

That was weird. I'm a goofy guy at times, but I'm not so totally hopeless around people that I squash every social norm known to man to a pulp.

I adjust the radio, trying to find something to keep me awake on this long, dark drive. The stations bounce between weather reports, soothing jazz music that is entirely too peaceful for this time of morning, and country music. I'm not a huge fan, but I settle on a country station because I know the chorus of the song they're playing. I'm a singer. I don't do it in public, but in the car, or the shower, or alone—when there's music, I sing.

The song ends, and I tap my steering wheel with my fingers as a new one starts. It's a catchy beat, but the lyrics are questionable, and I don't know how this is redeemable. It's a man singing about checking a woman for ticks.

Ticks are one of our major concerns for campers at camp. We have plans in place to cut down on exposures, but really, this guy thinks checking a woman for ticks is *sexy*?

By the end of the song, it has not been redeemed. It is absurd.

My entire mood is soured because of the stupid tick song, and now I'm thinking about the potential tick problem I have to make a contingency plan for.

Chet's incoming phone call appears on the screen. This SUV has all the technology I might need, and is big enough to haul both people and supplies from bigger cities back to camp. It's also basically my only possession right now. Buying something practical after selling everything from my life in California felt right, even if I am a single twenty-five-year-old man who's going backward in his career and love life and had the cash for something more extravagant.

I press the accept button. "What?" I bark. It comes out with more intensity than I mean it to, and I grimace. I blame the ticks. Or the threat of them. And the tick song.

My fingers tighten on the steering wheel.

"Woah! Cool it there, little bro." Chet's good-natured tone sounds through the speakers.

Ember's voice comes next. "We wanted to ask a few questions about—but…maybe now isn't a good time."

I sigh, then make a concerted effort to not sound as terse. "Which one of you is actually calling me?" The line stays silent, and I shove a laugh down. "So, Ember, using Chet's phone, then. What do you need?" Ember is my favorite sister-in-law. At the moment, she's my only sister-in-law, but she'd be number one anyway. She's fun and has never once made my accomplishments feel less than just because I'm the youngest of the four O'Malley brothers.

"Chet was wondering why you weirdly called Paige 'Bella' this morning?"

I stifle a grin. Chet absolutely was *not* wondering. That's all Ember.

Rolling my eyes, I deadpan, "Yes, that's exactly what Chet was wondering."

His voice comes through. "Well now I really am wondering, since it's such a secret."

I sigh and scrub my right hand through my hair, the curls bouncing back. The motion brings back the number of times Kaleigh told me she wished she could have my hair… "Uh. The first time I saw Paige, she was dressed like a vampire. Vampires—*Twilight*." I don't say anything else because I think this is self-explanatory for *everyone*.

"OH." Chet's understanding is audible. "Wait, Emb? You don't seem surprised."

"Yeah, I know about the vampire thing," she says.

"Why was *Paige* dressed like a vampire?" Chet asks.

"Actually, I don't understand that either," I interject. Chet and Ember have a tendency to have lengthy conversations between themselves while others are involved but not actively participating. It's like a ping-pong match, except instead of a tiny ball, they volley words, and the people around them watch.

Ember lets out a pent-up sigh. She's my favorite sister-in-law, but she can be dramatic. "Paige was dressed like a vampire because her boss, Dr. Gartinen, apparently doesn't understand the difference between April Fools and Halloween. And Paige is witty and smart and a phlebotomist."

Chet says nothing. I say nothing. I'm too busy digesting Ember's praise of Paige and also wracking my sleep-deprived brain for *what* a phlebotomist is. I keep landing on the word botanist, but I don't know why vampires would have anything to do with plants.

After an uncomfortable moment of silence, Ember's voice picks up again. "Phlebotomist. You know, the people who draw your blood at the doctor. That's what she does—or *did*—since she'll be working with you this summer, Connor."

"Yeah," I say, my voice gruff. The realization that Paige is going to be an employee I oversee hits me in the chest. A woman I'm attracted to, working under my supervision, at a camp full of kids. This couldn't be any weirder.

"And you called her *Bella*?" Ember prods.

"Yeah. Bella Swan." I grimace just thinking about it. They will know. They can't know. I can't face that type of humiliation again.

I hear Chet murmur a few words to Ember. I hear a muttered "fine," and then Ember speaks again. "Connor, Paige had a really tough past. She needs people to be kind to her, not tease her. Please, promise me you'll be good to her. She's an important part of mine and Blaze's life."

"Hey, mine too! I love Paige. She never gives me the side-eye when she catches me making out with you." Chet's commentary is not helpful. I give him the best side-eye I can from my car. I do not need to know about Ember and Chet's makeouts. I've been subjected to enough of them since I arrived.

"That's my cue to leave this conversation. I'm going to stop for gas and coffee at the next station." I press the end call button with more force than necessary.

5

PAIGE

Ember is economical about heating her house. I suppose it's a side effect of being a single mom for so many years. Every penny counted. When Chet came into the picture, Ember started heating the house a little more, and I could finally stop wearing two sweaters when I babysat. The last few times I've been over, the house has been frigid. Chet texted me a four-digit code and the fire emoji before he left this morning—the code to the thermostat. Chet really is a good guy. I'm happy for Ember. Seeing them get their happily ever after has been sweet, but also tugs on my heartstrings in a way that makes me feel like I might snap.

As soon as the cars are safely out of the driveway, I sneak over to the digital thermostat. Something about changing the settings behind Ember's back seems ridiculous. But it's also ridiculous to have the heat set at fifty-seven degrees when it's twenty-six degrees outside. I don't want to go too crazy, but sixty-eight sounds balmy. And Chet did give me permission to be comfortable.

I snuggle back into the couch with the blanket Connor put over me. It's five thirteen. I try to sleep, but the weird interactions between Connor and me keep replaying on a loop in my mind.

At least this time, I was the normal one. I mean, underdressed and definitely not prepared to see a handsome man at five a.m., but he made it weirder. If I was keeping score, which I'm not, it would be a close match. Vampire Paige: -1. No makeup/bedhead Paige: -2. But Connor calling me weird names twice: -1.

Also, the blanket thing. *What was that?*

The hum of the furnace clicks on and I snuggle in, creating a cozy cocoon. My fingers absently grasp the tassels on the edge of the blanket, and I finally drift to sleep.

"Paige?" I flutter my eyes open and find Blaze standing near my head. "Who's Cobar?"

"What?" I try to orient myself, which is difficult because there's an eleven-year-old eyeing me with suspicion. I was just having a lovely dream about Connor calling me by my actual name and telling me how much he loves *my* red hair.

After being the butt of 'gingers have no soul' jokes for the past decade, being told someone loves my red hair is a fantasy. It's right up there with being cast as the love interest in a movie opposite…literally any attractive man, *and* then him actually falling in love with me in real life and not just on the screen.

The likelihood of that happening is below zero. Blaze would say I have no rizz. He's right. Rizzless Paige, but I do have a hardened heart. I'd like to love and be loved, but Mom leaving left scars. And you know what they say about scar tissue. It's the toughest tissue of them all.

"You were saying Cob-arrrrr." Blaze makes his voice oddly nasal and stares at me accusingly.

"I have no idea." I pivot the conversation to safer waters because I actually *do* have an idea. "Want some breakfast?"

Blaze grins. "Always."

"Pancakes? Waffles? Eggs?"

"All of the above."

I snort. This boy and his appetite. He's a carnivorous pit. "Only if you help."

Blaze would rather go off and play video games, but since we used to cook together all the time, he willingly follows me to the kitchen.

We've done this for many years, so we have a routine. He gets the ingredients as I call them out, and is the chief mixer. I supervise the hot surfaces.

"What game should we play after this?" I ask once the food is all cooking.

Blaze rattles off something about a new football video game. I'm not great at video games, but I've learned enough over the years to be a gnat of annoyance to anyone playing me. I just don't see the point of video games, but I'm being paid to hang with Blaze today—though honestly, if gas wasn't so pricey and I wasn't worried about getting my own place, I'd do it for free. If video games are how he wants to spend his time, then that's what we'll do.

We start eating in a sleepy state of silence as the warmth of the house washes over us and the nostalgic food fills our bellies. Blaze surprises me when he puts his fork down after three bites. "Paige?"

I look at him.

"Would you please help me tell my parents I want to go to camp?"

My heart breaks. I know the reason Ember and Chet won't send him is the new baby coming mid-July. They want to do it all the right way this time. To be a family together. I don't want to tell him no outright though.

"I wish I could, but they want you to be together as a family this summer."

Blaze shifts uncomfortably. I take a drink of water so I don't have to face his emotions head-on. "But you're like family. And Uncle Connor *is* family."

There's a sweetness in his words, but my mind hitches on the word *uncle*. My brain is not capable of processing this so early in the morning.

"Uncle?" I cough after swallowing my water wrong.

Blaze looks at me with narrowed eyes. "Yeah. Uncle Connor. Remember, you met him? When you were dressed up all weird. He left today and isn't coming back until after the camp season is over."

"Hey! I wasn't dressed that weird. It was because I'm a phlebotomist, and it was April Fools..." I sigh. "Yeah, it was weird. I thought you would understand my wit and think it was funny."

"You looked like one of those YouTubers who does stupid stuff for videos."

"Gee, thanks. I'll just take the rest of the pancakes now..." I fake getting up from the table.

"No!" He groans. "Don't take the cakes!"

I get up and put another pancake on his plate, then give him a hug from around his chair. Blaze leans back into my shoulders, and I get a glimpse of the little boy who loved trains and coloring and monster trucks as he looks dejectedly at his food. I understand what's going on better than he knows.

"Blaze? Why do you want to go to camp?"

"Because you're going."

"I know that's not why. I'd love to hang out with you all summer, but why do you really want to go?"

"The new baby," he mumbles. "Dad wasn't here when I was a baby, and what if he loves the new baby more than me? What if Mom does too? What if I'm just a big stinky oaf who eats all the food?"

The level of derision in his words is shocking. There is no way

Ember said that to Blaze. It sounds like something she might have said to Chet in a moment of pregnancy-induced snack searching.

"Blaze," I say with a smile. "You're an awesome kid. Your dad came back and found you. Your mom worked hard for you when things were really tough. They have proved their love for you every day. I know change is scary, but your parents love you."

Blaze flushes, but I know he's pleased—and relieved. I also know how easily someone who loves you can walk away, but I do not say that to Blaze. He doesn't deserve that fear when he's already dealing with his own. It's my burden to shoulder.

Sometimes I look at Blaze and feel jealous—jealous that instead of a parent who left, he gets to have the story of a parent who came back. It's not jealousy in a way that means I want to take it from him. He deserves his happy life. No, it's jealousy in the way that I wonder what it would be like to have *that.*

We finish breakfast in silence. The older Blaze gets, the fewer words he needs to say to me, but I don't mind.

"You gonna play or watch?" he asks.

There's only one answer that will make him smile, so I give it. "I'll play…for now."

"Good. You're harder to beat than Uncle Connor."

"Really?" I ask in a high-pitched squeal.

"Yeah, he's terrible at video games." He eyes me. "That was weird."

I shrug, trying to play it cool. "Well, I'm just excited I might beat someone at a video game for the first time in the history of the entire world." Blaze gives a snort. "I'll meet you in the den after I clean these dishes. Your mom said you should shower this morning. Do you want to do that while I'm doing the dishes, and then we can play?"

Blaze gives me one nod in a perfect imitation of Chet before he leaves the kitchen.

My mind swirls as I rinse the dishes in soapy water. Blaze dropped a bomb on me with the *uncle* comment, and now my mind can't get him out of my head. How can I get information about Uncle Connor from Blaze in a way that's not obvious? Does Connor like redheads, or is he terrified of me after seeing me both as a vampire and completely unprepared for civilization?

And, most importantly, what is he doing at the camp where I'll be working?

6

CONNOR

Northern Michigan air smells different. Viewport has a distinct water smell, while Camp C.G.O. smells like moss, ferns, and quaking aspens. Camp C.G.O. is the name Chet and Ember landed on. It's catchy, if unusual. Most camps have names like Pineview or Camp North Mountain. Not ours. It's a solid acronym—Camp Charles George O'Malley, the C.G.O. being my gramps' initials.

I'm standing at the end of the winding dirt drive with Tom, the jack-of-all-trades, who's been helping me for the past few months with all the little tasks that need to be done before camp opens in four weeks. I should be climbing up a ladder, but right now I'm letting the sun warm my arms and smelling the fresh air. I'm sore from all the work I've done, and yet there's still more to do.

I sigh before opening my eyes and catching a glimpse of Tom's ancient sky-blue, heavy-duty pickup. There's more dirt on it than paint. At the moment, a rope is wrapped around the rusty trailer hitch and coiled neatly on the drive. Like most rural properties, there is a ranch gate between the county and private road. The rope runs over the wooden beam above the drive and attaches to the custom laser-cut metal ranch sign we'll hoist into place.

Chet grunted when I explained the expense, but people being able to *find* the camp with appropriate signs is one way to build trust with the parents dropping their kids off.

I scrub my hand down my jaw, feeling the burn of a beard I hate but haven't had time to shave off. Just because I live in the far north doesn't mean I have to have a beard like every other man up here.

Tom gives me a toothy grin as he straightens from checking the rope knot he tied onto the sign. He pulls the long gray beard he'd tucked over his shoulder down and strokes it. "I'm thinking we're gonna have to go real slow. We don't want the sign to get scuffed."

"Good point." I know what he'll say to the next question, but I have to joke with him a little. "Are you sure you have the horse-power to do this?"

Tom scoffs in response.

I huff. "Ok, then." I did expect his response. Never insult a northern mountain man's truck. And yes, implying a lack of horse-power is an insult.

I move to the ladder as Tom climbs into the driver's seat and starts the engine. The gears strain as they change when he shifts into drive.

I can drive a stickshift, but not well. Tom would have been all about standing on the ladder and securing the chains to the hooks in the beam, but I did not want him to mock me. The past month and a half at the camp property have revealed to me just how unprepared I was for this type of work, in this type of setting. Northern Michigan is a challenging place for a camp. It *is* doable, but the camp's condition was somewhere between dire and apocalyptic.

Ember and Chet surveyed the property with me the first day I moved out here. We made a plan, starting with the most pressing needs, and then, with a business credit card in hand, I began to address them.

I've spent the past six weeks marking trails, cutting swaths through the underbrush, and dealing with contractors. I've tried to save money wherever I can. Ember and Chet are trusting me with the financial responsibility of running a viable business. I managed finances for a boutique hotel in California, so this isn't unfamiliar, but the stakes feel higher. Not only is this entire camp in memory of Gramps, it's also my brother and sister-in-law's dream. I want things to go perfectly for them, especially since they're expecting a new baby.

Thankfully, the camper cabins were in decent shape once they got new roofs. The insides were in need of thorough cleaning, and a raccoon family had clearly nested in one of the cabins. An elbow-length pair of leather gloves, a bucket of bleach, and a lot of elbow grease got me through the first cabin on my own. And then Tom showed up. I don't know how or why he did, but divine intervention is definitely not something I'll rule out as a possibility.

The man and his rusty old pick up truck appeared one afternoon as I was preparing to toss a bucket of bleach water into the thicket of brush to the side of the cabin. The thin older man with a lengthy gray beard and a long ponytail tucked under a ripped and stained Detroit ball cap leaned against the door of his truck. "Son. You have more work than you can handle 'round here." His red plaid flannel and worn blue jeans hinted at the northern lumberjack stereotype. For the most part, it's true. Tom is a true Northwoodsman.

He's been helping me ever since, and I still don't know his last name. All I know is I'm grateful for him, because after two weeks on my own, it was clear I'd never get the camp ready in time.

"Here we go!" Tom hollers as he inches forward.

I climb up the ladder as I watch the sign lift slowly off the ground. My breath hitches as it sinks in that a hundred-pound metal sign is suspended right over my head. The sign finally hangs off the post.

I reach over and grab the chain, hooking the hook into the eye fastener. The rope slackens now that it's not supporting the heavy sign.

Tom leaves his truck idling but meanders back to me. I climb down the ladder and move it a few feet so I can secure the other side of the sign. I shake out my sore arms.

"You look good, boy. Tell me, a young guy like you…got any ladies you're interested in?" Tom asks as I stand there, chilled by the nip of the wind but also sweaty from the exertion and my nerves.

I grin at him after dragging my forearm against the sweat on my brow. Tom does *not* open up about his private life, but this is the perfect segue. We've worked together since the day he appeared, and I still only know that he hunts, grows his own food, and has a really old truck.

"Nope. What about you, Tom? Got any lady friends?" I toss the question over my shoulder before I step onto the bottom rung. I can see him from my periphery as I climb.

He shrugs. "Never needed one." He turns the conversation back to me. "You, on the other hand, do."

I stop four rungs up. "I do?"

Tom studies me for a moment, his brown eyes seeming to pierce my very soul. "You definitely do."

I continue climbing. Tom is exceptionally easy to talk to, but I haven't told him about Kaleigh. I have told him about moving away from California, about managing the camp for Chet and Ember, and feeling like I'm going backward in my career and life. I've just omitted a few details about *why* I feel that way.

The eye fastener accepts the hook, and the new sign makes a creaking noise as it sways. Tom stays where he is, one hand on the ladder, bracing it as I climb back down.

When I'm on solid ground, he doesn't say anything, just looks at me expectantly. Surprisingly, I want to talk about it. I *never* want to talk about it, but something in me says I should, and Tom is right here.

"I had a serious girlfriend. But it ended badly." Tom's bushy eyebrows raise. "I proposed to her. And Kaleigh said no." I draw in a breath, not sure how to explain to a much older man about the *Twilight* thing. "I tried to make the proposal really special. She really liked *Twilight*…"

"Movies or books?" Tom asks as my mouth falls open.

It takes a moment for me to recover. "Both. You know *Twilight*?"

"Yep."

"Ok… is there a story about how you know it?"

"No. But there's a story about your proposal you're trying to avoid telling me."

I sigh, pulling off my baseball cap and running my hand through my sweaty hair. "Yes. It's just that I proposed in an imitation of a scene, and she said no, and it was humiliating."

Tom is silent for a beat. Sometimes older people share deep wisdom with those of us in a younger generation. Other times, they do not. I don't know what to expect from Tom, but the silence builds. "You were humiliated. Why? Because she said no? Because you tried something for her? Why were *you* humiliated when she's the one who walked away?"

I blink in the late afternoon sun. "I guess, it's just that we were together for so long, and I thought I loved her. But then I found out we were more of a habit to each other than anything. And it hurts that I spent so much time with someone who didn't see me as worthy."

Tom has somehow procured a piece of straw, which he puts in his mouth. "Have you considered, Connor, that her saying no was the right thing?"

I stare. That is not usually what people say when you tell them you were humiliated by your long-time girlfriend rejecting you during a ridiculous-themed proposal.

"I know you're the sort of man who would have been faithful to her, who would have done everything to make it work. But you just said you were habits to each other more than anything else. Is a habit love?"

I don't respond because that question is far too deep. It's like Tom dove into the depths of Lake Superior, except it's my inner psyche and not actual lake water.

"Anyways, you'll find the right woman. And she won't be a habit. She'll *be* love and you'll *be* love. Kaleigh was many things to you, but you both deserve what the Good Lord has in store for you. Pray for peace. The rest will come after. Now, what's next on the list for today?"

His abrupt topic change startles me, but I'm happy to leave thoughts of Kaleigh in the past. "I'm going to shower and work on some of the office stuff. Ordering food deliveries for the campers, and making sure we have the insurance coverage we need. Boring stuff."

"Good," Tom says, chewing on his straw. "I'm heading out. I'll put the rope away."

"Thanks for your help today, Tom." I wave as I put the cap back on my head. My hair is too unruly without it.

He waves in response and hops into his truck.

It's only after he's driven off and I'm seated in my office chair that I realize I haven't prayed in days. I close my eyes and ask God for peace.

1

PAIGE

There is one small problem with the backroads of Northern Michigan near Camp CGO: gas stations every few miles don't exist. My gas gauge is off, the needle floating between empty and full at random, but I was sure I had enough to get to camp.

I was overly optimistic.

Things are not going well for me. Intrusive thoughts worm their way into my mind. My car is a piece of junk. I'm not a full nurse, and I'm off to work at a camp doing a job that would be better suited for a college student studying to *actually* be a nurse.

Adding insult to injury, the moment my car sputtered to a stop on the side of the road, I was daydreaming and imagining the witty things I would say when I saw Connor again.

I bite back tears. I haven't seen Connor since April, but I can't get him out of my head. It's just a harmless little crush, right? I don't even know if he has a girlfriend. I couldn't ask Blaze directly, and I really couldn't ask Ember or Chet, so I pried a little. Blaze isn't a font of information, but I found out that Connor is Chet's younger brother by ten years. He lived in California and 'worked something with hotels'. Not exactly the information I was snooping for, but it was something.

The sun is beginning its descent over the Michigan mountains. It will be fully dark within the hour, and I'm twenty minutes away from the camp, sitting alone in my car, on the side of a two-lane county road. All because my piece-of-junk car can't tell me when I need to fill up my tank.

I dig out my phone from where I've stashed it in the console and call the official camp number. It rings. And rings. And goes to voicemail. I sigh and call the only person I can think of who might be able to help. Ember.

"Hey! Made it to camp?" she asks.

"Uh. No. I had car trouble."

I swear I can hear her shaking her head. She's been telling me my car isn't safe for the past year, but I've been saving for something. I don't know what that something is because I might want to go back to school or maybe to move away. The only thing I do know is that I'll need money to do whatever it is.

"Where are you?"

"I'll share my location with you."

"Ok. What kind of car trouble? Are you ok?"

"Yeah, I'm just stranded on the side of the road. My gas gauge isn't reliable and..." I let the sentence trail off because it's so ridiculous. I ran out of gas. I am a responsible woman. I have money for gas, but it's really hard to fill your tank when you don't know WHEN you need to stop for it.

"You ran out of gas?"

"Yes, but it —"

"I know. Your gas gauge needle is floating, right? My old car used to do that too. I'll call Connor. He's the closest person to you." She hangs up.

It would have been weird to have had her give me his personal number. But also, it would have been less weird than her calling *my boss* on my behalf.

I groan and sink a little lower in the well-worn seat. I rest my forehead on the steering wheel. With nothing else to do, I count the good things.

My dad didn't leave.

I have a job. I have some savings.

The power steering still works on this trash heap.

Ember cares about me.

Mom left. Mom left. Mom left. I don't have a mom who wants to be with me. Mom doesn't care. Mom couldn't give up what she wanted for me. I wasn't worth it. I'm not worth it. I'm a failure. I'm alone. I'm stuck. I'm stranded. I'm—

Tears fall, and I make no move to stop them. One time, after Mom left, a therapist suggested that if the intrusive thoughts felt too heavy, I set a timer and think the thoughts. The key was being in control, and being able to come back to the present after the timer went off. What the therapist didn't tell me was how emotionally draining it is to listen to your own thoughts when they're mean.

I haven't listened to my intrusive thoughts in ages, but they are here in full force. I close my eyes, tears furiously streaming down my face and dropping into my lap as the intrusive thoughts take over.

A rap on the window startles my eyes open. I peel my face off the tacky fake leather of the steering wheel and look through the pane. Connor hunches over a little to see through the glass.

Of course he's there. My eyes lock in on his stormy blue ones. I don't know why—it's not like I was expecting anyone else—but seeing him is like falling out of a tree and landing on your back, the wind knocked out of you.

"You ok?" he asks, his voice deep and a little scratchy.

I shake my head yes, my two hands gripping the steering wheel for dear life.

"Do you need me to open the door?"

My eyes widen as I realize I've made a fool of myself, again. It's a common theme for me around Connor.

"No!" I shout, then remember there was no need for me to yell.

I fling the door open, the handle snapping off in my haste. I stare at the piece of my car in my hands. I'm holding it like some sort of short dagger. "This day is the worst," I mumble.

I swivel my body ninety degrees so I can get out of the car without stepping on the rotted-out floor board beneath the pedals. Connor watches my exit with an arched brow and a small smirk.

Once I'm on solid ground, Connor looks pointedly at the car and my exit. "Is that how you get out of every car?"

"Yeah." I'm not in the mood to tell him. I'm not in the mood for anything right now except a hot bath and a cup of tea.

"So…" He lingers on the *o*. I stare at him, the cool air hitting my skin. "We meet again. I'm Connor, if you didn't remember."

"Yeah, I know." I huff. "Ember called you because I can't even get to camp on my own."

Connor cocks his head slightly, his mouth turning down in a frown. He doesn't ask, he simply opens the back door gingerly and pulls my things out. I have two duffle bags, a suitcase full of medical supplies that Ember and Chet wanted me to bring, and Larry, my worn stuffed bear.

I have to hand it to the man, when he gets to the bear, he doesn't say anything. The two duffel bags' long straps are looped over each of his shoulders, the expandable handle of the suitcase in one hand, and in the other hand, Larry Mr. Beary. He carries him as if it's normal to carry a grown woman's teddy away from a car whose only possible purpose in life at this point is to be destroyed in a rage room.

I shake my head to clear the weirdness of that image and turn to the trunk. Opening it involves hitting a specific spot just right with my elbow while I jam my palm under the latch. It always hurts. I grimace thinking of it, but I have a bin of feminine hygiene products and other things that need to come too.

I begin the painful process, but just when I'm about to make contact with my elbow, Connor's voice cuts in. "What are you doing?"

My gaze follows the sound of his voice and my elbow slips, hitting the side of the dent I've put in the trunk from doing this over the past year. It's close, but not close enough to open the trunk. "Argh." I grip my elbow and clench my teeth in pain. "I'm—" I close my eyes, wincing from the pain. "Opening—" I squeeze my eyes as tight as I can. "My trunk."

"I've *never* seen anyone open a trunk like that. And I've seen *a lot* of things," Connor says. The hint of humor in his voice makes me crack open my eyes.

"Ugh. Now I have to do it again," I mutter.

"I'll do it." Connor walks around the back of the car and stands next to me, close enough that when he moves his arm, the long black sleeve of his coat brushes my gray sweatshirt. "What do I need to do?"

Something about this man renders me speechless. The setting sunlight washes over him makesing him look like a catalog model.

What would it be like to run my hand through those perfect curls?

Our eyes meet, and there's this look in his eye that makes me think he might kiss me.

But that's fantasy, Paige, because you don't actually know Connor. At all. Stupid daydreams.

"I..." The words get stuck. He crosses his arms. I clear my throat.

"I bang my elbow on that dent and push up on the latch really hard at the same time."

Connor shakes his head, then lines up his elbow. He brings it down, hard, and the trunk flies open. The bin of toiletries shifted during the drive, and the force of Connor's body hitting must have set off a kind of shockwave in the trunk, because just as the lid opens, a tampon hits him in the face.

8

CONNOR

When Ember called, I dropped everything to go to Paige's rescue. I left the other counselors moving their supplies into the cabins, and rushed away. I won't admit it, but it was more than just helping her get to camp. I will plead the fifth on my motives, but if I said I wasn't excited to see her again, I'd be lying. She was obviously crying when I arrived. Her tears make me glad I disobeyed the speed limits, and when I take in the state of her car, I can't say I blame Paige for the tears. I'd cry, too, if I had to drive this thing.

How has she been driving this thing? Does anyone look out for her? When was the last time she got this car serviced? Do they even service cars in this condition?

My thoughts are running a 5K as I open her trunk. The moment I make contact with the car, my thoughts change to something more colorful. If hitting your funny bone is painful, then this is doubly so, because it is doing that, but on purpose.

When I'm smacked in the face by a hard tube, I grunt. It might be a growl, but I'm trying not to show the pain. Whatever it was that hit me, it really stinking hurt.

Paige stands next to me, her eyes wide and her mouth agape. Her face starts to flush as red as her hair. "Oh my gosh!" She moans, then bends over and picks up a tampon.

I look in the trunk, noting a car jack and spare tire. "Is this everything?"

Paige keeps her eyes downcast as she nods, then reaches into the trunk to grab her bin. There is no way I'm letting her carry that. It's not that she *can't*. It's that I *want* to. She's had a hard day, and I wish I knew her well enough to hug her. Or so that me being hit in the face with a tampon was nothing to be embarrassed about. I'm surprised at how much I want to protect her.

"Hey." My voice comes out deeper than I intended. She turns her head to me as a question flits across her eyes. I indicate the bin. "Let me."

Paige frowns but stops. It's only after I grab the bin that I see why she maybe didn't want me to carry it. It's full of pads, two giant bottles of shampoo and conditioner, several jumbo tubs of trail mix, a jar of jelly beans, and a bear-shaped canister of small lollipops. I say nothing, but my eyebrows raise. I did not expect these items.

"For the camp," she says simply. "It's a hard thing for a lot of girls…" She trails off, but I catch her whisper. "I just want to be prepared for them."

"Admirable," I say, but my elbow and my face hurt, so my voice is rough. Though I meant it sincerely, the glare she throws my way tells me it didn't sound like I was being genuine.

"Thank you very much. It *is* practical to be prepared. That's all my stuff. If you don't mind, I'd like to get off the road." She flips her hair behind her shoulder.

I nod once, chastised by this woman with blue eyes and red hair and wishing I wasn't so bad at interacting with women after Kaleigh. I know I'll never be good enough for a woman, and it's best to just not try. Why try when you'll fail? Why try when you're clearly less than what *she* wants?

I carry the bin over to the hatchback of my green SUV. Paige stands a little to the side of my car, looking longingly at her own trash heap on wheels.

"You don't have to worry about someone stealing your car. I guarantee no one will take it."

"Yeah. Who'd want it?" She scoffs. "I'll need to call a tow though."

"Are you sure? You want to get it…"

"I can't just leave it!" The vehemence in her voice stops me. I thought we were in agreement that the car was undrivable. But she does have a pharmacy-worth of feminine hygiene products and has had a long day. I'm not helping.

"Of course. I'll see if Tom can help. He probably knows some-one who can tow it…"

I fire off a text. Tom responds immediately.

Tom

Sounds like a fun challenge. I'll fix it up with Archie. He needs practice before he opens his mechanic business.

I don't know who Archie is, but I show Paige the text. She gives a small smile, jams her hands in her jeans pockets before pulling them back out and turning to open the back door of my car.

"What are you doing?"

"Getting in your car—because you're giving me a ride to camp?"

My mouth twists. "Why would you sit in the back?"

Something incomprehensible flashes across her eyes. "I thought you might prefer it. I've been a little…frazzled today."

I absolutely would *not* prefer that. "You can sit back there if you want to, or you could sit in the front seat."

"Thanks," she mumbles, eyes on the ground.

"Here." I open the front passenger door and bow in a dramatic fashion. "Your seat, m'lady." I want to kick myself for reverting to jokes, but a ghost of a smile flits over her face as she climbs in.

I shut the door and take a deep breath. We ride in silence for a few miles before she says something that makes my blood run cold. "I'm sorry I'm already your troublesome employee."

That stupid word. Ember and Chet insisted on a strict no counselors dating each other policy. They reasoned that if counselors were into each other, and dating, it would take away from the kids' experience. I can't say I agree with it, but it's their camp and their rules.

This whole situation has me on edge because rolling into camp with Paige and all her stuff after the other counselors are settled in isn't a good look. Yes, I'd do it for anyone else if Ember called me, but I'm glad it was Paige. Six weeks of preparing the camp were not enough to squash down any attraction. If anything, seeing her again is like taking a match to dried kindling and expecting it not to catch fire—it's impossible.

"Don't worry about it," I say, my voice gruff as I grip the steering wheel tighter. I catch Paige weaving her fingers through her hair in my periphery. It's all I can do to focus on the road ahead and not stare at her.

We reach the winding drive that leads to the camp. I park outside the mess hall where the counselors are waiting for me. Everyone met briefly when they arrived, but now it's time for our first official meeting. I close my eyes as I mentally prepare to put on my 'boss Connor' hat. I'm late to the meeting I scheduled, and I don't want to draw suspicion to my feelings for Paige, so I don't wait for her as I hurry up the path.

Matt, Stephanie, Brooke, Jorge, and Lucas sit along the top step of the long porch, laughing and talking. I have several rocking chairs in boxes I need to assemble, but for now, the porch is devoid of furniture.

I've just reached the steps when a counselor lets out a low whistle. I turn, and of course, Paige is gorgeous as she comes up the walk. Her red hair is in a long braid over one shoulder, her light wash jeans are paired with a soft gray hoodie, and the glow of the setting sun frames her in golden light.

"Duuuuude," one of the boy's counselors says in a stage whisper. "I'd—"

"Don't you even finish that statement, Matt!" one of the girl's counselors snaps, and I hear a small oomph escape him.

Once Paige has seated herself next to Brooke and Stephanie, I forget my manners entirely. I don't introduce her, which would be the normal thing to do. Instead I say in my best I'm-the-authority-here voice, "At Camp CGO, there is a strict no-staff-dating policy." Boss Connor hat is on, and I'm rocking it.

I glare at the boys, lingering a beat on Matt since he's the one who said something about Paige. I don't know who whistled, but if I was a betting man, I'd place my money on him.

He meets my eyes with a challenge. "I read the rule book, and it said *no romantic activities among staff while campers are on the grounds.*"

Well, shoot.

9

PAIGE

I don't know what to make of Connor. He's attractive. Maddeningly so. But he's also unpredictable. I can't figure him out, and that unsettles me. I don't like *not* knowing where I stand with people. It's best to always know. And if you're unsure, make yourself smaller. It's easier that way.

A petite and slender woman whose high blonde ponytail has streaks of hot pink running through it says, "Hey, I'm Brooke. That's Stephanie, Jorge, Lucas, and Matt." She points to each one, and they wave in turn. "You must be Paige, right?"

I wave back. "Hi. Yeah, I'm Paige. I had car trouble on the way." I draw in a shaky breath. "But I'm here. I'll be the camp nurse and counselor."

Apparently I should not have said 'nurse' because Matt lets loose an "ow ow!" catcall. Connor's eyes could freeze molten lava from where he stands at the bottom of the steps. The way he crosses his arms makes him look like a stern parent.

"Not that kind of nurse." I waggle a finger at him like I would a child at Dr. Gartinen's office who demanded something ridiculous. It's the only way to deal with immature people—treat them like small children. "Bandaids, tick removal, general health…"

"Tampons," Connor supplies, his eyes narrowed as he locks eyes with Matt.

I bob my head, my cheeks burning after whatever *that* was on the roadside. "Yes, that sort of thing."

"Anyways," Connor says. "Let's get a few expectations ironed out for the counselors and also some dinner. Tom's making pizzas, so let's head inside. Please."

When we walk inside, Connor leads us to rough-hewn wood tables with long benches. The floor is the same honey color as the tables, while the walls and the cathedral ceiling are darker. Matt tries to slide into the seat next to me, but Stephanie hops onto the bench instead, and Brooke drops into the seat on the other side. Jorge does nothing to disguise his eye roll across the table as Matt joins him and Lucas on the other side.

An older man with a long gray beard and a ponytail wanders over to us, wearing a bright red apron and two matching red oven mitts. He has a long-handled pizza stone in his hand. "Outta the way. It's hot!" he commands.

We shift back as he sets the pizza stone down. It sizzles and hisses, the smell of burning wood accosting us immediately.

"Ah. You just burned a new table, Tom." Connor frowns.

"Needed more character anyway," Tom replies. "If you want these kids to be comfortable, you need to scuff up the new a little. Make this camp look used, lived in, loved." He lifts the pizza stone, and sure enough, there is a scorch mark. But the burn on the table makes a few shapes. It could be anything, really, but I see a little girl holding a balloon in the mark. Tom was right: the character is part of the charm.

Connor shakes his head, but a smile tugs at the corner of his lips. "Please don't burn the tables on purpose, Tom."

Tom gives a jaunty salute and saunters off back to the kitchen area. Connor is silent for a moment, then clears his throat. His eyes touch everyone around the table, but linger on me. He's still standing, his hands jammed into the front pockets of his dark blue jeans with his sleeves pushed up to his elbows.

"This is serious," he begins. "While I'm glad that Matt read the employee manual so closely, I need to remind everyone of some important things. This is a Christian camp. And we have a strict code of conduct. You read the code of conduct and signed off on it when you submitted your applications here. Breaching the code of conduct will result in immediate termination from Camp CGO.

"I am in charge of the day-to-day operations, but I want you to take the initiative to make this summer the best experience yet with the campers. We will have a group of campers for four weeks as they grow their leadership skills. We have a curriculum of activities planned. However, when the activities happen is flexible based on the needs of the campers and the weather."

Matt raises his hand.

Connor quirks a brow, but responds with a "Yes?"

"The code of conduct said we were not permitted to engage in romantic activities with other counselors *when* the children were present."

Connor's lips form a thin line. "Yes."

"And that we only have to abstain from alcohol when there are children on the premises, right?"

Connor's lips tip into a frown. "Yes. Is that a problem?"

"No, sir," Matt replies with an insolent fake salute. "So I could ask someone on a date here, and it would be fine, as long as the children aren't around?" Matt's eyes don't leave Connor's. The two of them are locked in a staring contest.

Connor's jaw tightens before he rolls his eyes heavenwards as if to say, *"Lord, give me strength."*

Tom mercifully breaks the tension as he comes out of the kitchen with plates and a pizza cutter. "Should have cooled enough to handle." He slices the pie into eight pieces and puts a slice on each plate.

"Look, you're all adults over the age of twenty-one," Connor says in a measured voice, but the way his fists have tightened shows that something about this is bothering him. "I have no problem with you having a 'get-to-know-you drink' while children are not here. And you're all adults. I can't stop you from forming romantic attachments with each other, but there will be *no* romantic activities between counselors while children are on the premises. We have four weeks to get to know Camp CGO and each other before the campers arrive. There are team-building activities planned, certifications for the different camp equipment, learning the trails, and studying the leadership curriculum." His eyes touch each counselor's before he claps and says, "I'll say a prayer, and then we can eat."

Connor bows his head and says a simple grace just as Tom appears with two more pizzas, one with pickle slices on it. After the prayer, Connor grabs a plate and sits. He stills and takes a moment before he begins to eat.

Tom sits down next to Connor and grabs a slice. Without looking, he deposits a pickle slice on Jorge's plate. Jorge looks confused, then interested. He takes a tentative bite, but then lets out a lengthy "*mmmmmm.*"

Matt and Lucas take one look at Jorge's pizza, then both grab their own pickle pieces. The five counselors begin talking together, teasing each other about their colleges. I feel oddly left out since I didn't go to a four-year college, and I'm at least two years older than the others.

Connor's eyes meet mine across the table. I give him a little smile.

He looks away quickly, like he's embarrassed to be caught looking directly at me. *Is there something in my teeth?*

Connor clears his throat. "Uh. One more thing." I find my eyes drifting over his muscular forearms, then up his lightly stubbled jaw. "Are any of you Catholic?"

Silence.

"Ok. It's just that we are a Christian camp and welcome campers of all Christian denominations, and I have a priest friend who can come out to offer Mass all four weekends, but there's a holy day in mid-August, so I need someone else with me to take the Catholic campers into town for Mass that day."

Brooke and Stephanie shake their heads.

"Sorry, I'm not Catholic, I'm Methodist," Brooke says.

"I'm non-denominational," Stephanie supplies.

Lucas, Jorge, and Matt all shake their heads.

"Sorry," Lucas says with a shrug. "My granny's Catholic, though."

I'm the only one who hasn't responded. The truth is, I am Catholic, or at least I was—until Mom left. Then Dad and I stopped going to church. I didn't even get confirmed. The air is being sucked out of the room by a giant vacuum somewhere. I've been keeping my eyes down and avoiding eye contact with everyone when the Christian-ness of the camp comes up. I haven't had a faith life since Mom disappeared, leaving only a heap of a car and gambling debts in the alcohol-scented refuse pile of her life.

Everyone's eyes are on me as they wait for my answer. I lift my chin to decline, but my gaze snags on Tom's bright blue eyes. He's pinned me in his gaze, and there's a perceptiveness about him. It makes me uncomfortable.

My mouth opens, and words I do not intend to say rumble out.

"I'll go. I'm Catholic."

10

CONNOR

I am relieved. I'm Catholic too. I haven't been a great Catholic in a long time, but I know I can do better. I have to do better when the campers are here. And it does help that I made friends with Tom's priest friend, Father Matthi, a few weeks ago when we drove into town for some supplies.

The Holy Day schedule issue came up, and I somewhat recklessly assured a concerned parent through email that we would be able to ensure Mass attendance on August 15th—which is a Tuesday. Campers who are taken off camp property are to be accompanied by at least two counselors. Paige being Catholic is… well, honestly, it's helpful.

"Great, thanks, Paige." I smile at her before I turn away. I'm afraid the smile was more of a grimace. Yes, she'll be a big help with the Catholic campers, but that also means I'm going to have to spend more time with her. She's gorgeous, and I can't lose focus. Besides, my last relationship crashed and burned, and I'm not ready for another round.

I'm trying to think about anything other than Paige and Kaleigh when the thought *I should probably go to confession* flies into my mind. It's been a while, but where did that come from?

I ponder my thoughts only to find my gaze lingering on Paige. She catches me and smiles. I'm totally unprepared for the little dimple that forms on her right cheek when her lips quirk up. I have to look away before I do something stupid, like resort to being comedic relief because I'm intimidated by my attraction and terrified of something real.

As I turn my head away from her, I catch sight of the three men we hired as counselors. Lucas and Jorge seem like a good fit, but Matt is already mouthy. He might be ok around the kids, but I'm concerned about him around the other female counselors—particularly one. I'm only a few years older than these guys in reality. Hopefully the fact that I've been out of college and working for three years gives my authority some weight.

Matt leans over the table and says something to the ladies. Stephanie laughs, her long black hair tossing with the motion. Brooke clutches her stomach as she giggles. Paige sits in the middle of the two, a dimpleless smile on her face. It looks fake and pained.

Matt doesn't notice. He raises a fist like he's holding an imaginary drink and shouts, "'Cheers.'"

Tom elbows me and I turn to him. He says no words, just quirks a brow in Paige's direction and nods.

"What does that mean?" I whisper.

"It means whatever *you* want it to mean," Tom replies.

"Well how am I supposed to know what I want you to mean?"

"I think you know."

"Tom. Cryptic statements are not helpful here."

Tom laughs, his peals joining the laughter around the table. Paige and I are the only ones who seem to have missed the joke.

When the pizza is gone, discomfort washes over me. Social situations have been hard for me since Kaleigh. I know that Chet deleted that video, but there's a fear of someone finding it and making fun of me for putting everything on the line for a woman. Tension builds inside me, despite conversation flowing easily around the table. Friendships are being formed—that's what this is for, right?

I push to stand, slapping my palms on my thighs. "That's all I needed from you tonight. We'll meet tomorrow at 0500. Go, get settled in. The ladies' bathhouse is ready. The men's bathhouse currently has no showerheads, so we have an outdoor camp shower for your use." I wait to see if anyone will take the bait.

"0500?" Lucas questions, a look of abject horror on his face. "That's like 5:00 a.m."

Jorge's eyes shoot skyward, and Matt's mouth drops open.

"Dude, this isn't a *prison* camp. It's a *summer* camp. You know, *summer*, like *FUN*." There goes Matt again with the snarky, helpful lines.

I frown, but inside I'm giddy. It's FUN like summer to egg him on. "Oh. I very clearly said 0800."

The look of relief on the counselors' faces tells me that I can't tease them yet. Not until they know me a little better. They begin walking toward the door. Matt angles himself next to Paige. She stiffens as he leans closer and whispers something in her ear. The other ladies laugh at something Lucas says, oblivious to her discomfort.

I take a few long strides around the table. "Paige!" I call.

The entire group stops, turns, and looks at me. Matt winks at me. I did not know a man would wink at another man, let alone their boss. This guy seriously needs a lesson in professionalism. Unfortunately, now is not the time for that. "I need to show you the nurse's station."

Paige's nose scrunches. "Right now?"

Come on, Paige, I'm trying to help you.

The other counselors watch on with interest.

"Yes, I need to order any last-minute supplies, so I need you to do an inventory."

"Oh, ok. I'll see you guys all later." Paige shrugs, then gives a little wave to the group as she detaches herself from it.

Tom walks by, sans apron. "You are not convincing anyone," he mutters under his breath.

I shush him.

Paige stops short of me, and I fight the impulse to pull her into my arms and hug her. *This is weird. I hardly know her.* "Where's the nurse's station? And what supplies do you have? Do you have a list of what you've ordered?"

"Uhhh." I run my hand through my hair. My fingers tangle in the curls resting on the nape of my neck. "I do need an inventory, but not right now."

Paige's eyes narrow and she cocks her head. "Then why'd you say that you need me to do one right now?"

"You seemed uncomfortable with Matt. Are you ok with him?"

She raises a brow. "Why wouldn't I be?"

I don't know how to answer that question. "You just seemed… stiff."

"How would you have noticed that?" Her tone sounds accusatory, as if I'm the one causing trouble, not Matt.

I scramble. "We were trained to watch for signals when I worked at the hotel in California. I'm sorry." It's a truthful statement —hotel staff were trained to watch for signals, but also to not interfere in certain situations. This is one where she looked uncomfortable, but she wasn't in danger. Maybe she doesn't like strangers much. I shouldn't have interfered. I overstepped. And I know the green-eyed monster caused it.

Paige bites her bottom lip. "I'm fine. Thanks. Can we do the inventory now? I'd like to see what we have to work with."

Tom drags a mop by. "And it would be more convincing."

Paige's brow furrows. "Convincing?"

Tom meets Paige's eyes with his typical unflappable demeanor. "You and Connor. Trying not to like each other. First he drives you here, then he spends all dinner making eyes at you, and now getting you alone."

Paige's eyes grow wide.

"It's not like that, Paige," I protest.

"No…I…" Paige starts, but I cut her off.

"You don't have to do anything that makes you uncomfortable here. I'm sorry I suggested the inventory. It's been a long day. We can do it tomorrow."

"Oh, thanks, I—"

"I mean it. Please go get settled in your cabin. Do you know which one you're in?"

She stares at me like I've grown a second head. "I'm not with the other girls?"

"Oh. Yeah. That would be…where…you…are going to sleep…"

She holds out her hand and I reach for it, wondering why she wants to shake my hand.

"Could I have your keys?" she asks, but I'm already grasping her palm in a firm grip and pumping.

Tom leans on the mop handle in the periphery, clearly bemused at my expense.

"Oh." I reach into my back jeans pocket. "Here."

I thrust the keys into her outstretched hand and back away, my hands up in the air like I've committed some sort of crime.

Paige slides the keyring around her finger and walks to the door.

"Hey, Connor," she says over her shoulder. "Thank you." She must catch sight of Tom because she says, "And you, too, Tom. Have a good night."

Then she disappears out the door and into the dusky twilight of a Northern Michigan summer.

11

PAIGE

Connor has an effect on me. So does Matt. The effects are op-posite. Matt is flirty, and I know he's harmless. He has no way of knowing my past, but it doesn't stop me from cring-ing every time he tries to flirt. He's just young and immature. Con-nor was weirdly flirty and then reserved. *Maybe he's uncomfortable?*

But I'm also the girl who was a vampire the first time we met. Not a great impression.

I click the unlock button on the keyfob, and the SUV gives a little chirp. I ease the door open and hoist one duffel to my shoulder.

Brooke appears at my side. The setting sun casts a halo of light around her face. "Can I take anything? It's not a long walk to the cabin, but it will be with lots of stuff."

I smile at her. "That would be fantastic."

"Great!" Brooke slides the other duffel out, then sees the other items. She lets out a shrill whistle that makes me drop the bag and cover my ears. "Sorry," she says sheepishly.

"What does Her Highness want this time?" Matt grumbles as he walks near her.

"Calm down, *brother*. Let's help Paige with her stuff." Brooke elbows Matt. I didn't know these two were brother and sister.

Stephanie arrives with Lucas and Jorge. "What's wrong? What happened…" Stephanie trails off. "Ohh. You need help moving your stuff to the girls' cabin?"

"Yep," Brooke answers before I can. "We can take it all right now if we all help. So, let's get helping."

Brooke might be a lithe, willowy person, but she has a commanding presence. Maybe she secretly spent time as an apprentice to a five-star general. Her confidence is admirable, if dizzying. Matt might grumble, but he still *does* what Brooke asks.

Jorge and Lucas gather up the heaviest of the bags, leaving Matt with the tub full of snacks and feminine care products. It doesn't weigh much, but it is cumbersome to carry down a gravel pathway for a quarter mile.

I'm left carrying my backpack and Larry Mr. Beary. When I pick him up, my mind flashes back to Connor holding him on the roadside.

Brooke cheerfully announces, "Forward, march!" and the others fall into a line. Matt waits for me to shut the doors, then directs a meaningful look at the mess hall.

"Guess *he* helped you enough today." I follow the jut of his chin over the top of the bin and see Connor leaning against the porch railing, his hands clasped loosely in front of the rail. His hat is on backward, and his eyes are narrowed as he watches us.

My heart sinks. Matt's right. He's watching, not helping. Surely a man who was interested would want to help. *Maybe he's one of those guys who's overprotective about his car.* The thought makes me cringe. If he's really the type of man who has to stare down whoever is near his car when we're all adults and I'm just getting my things…then he's not my type of man. Except, he *is* the type of man I've dreamed about for years.

"Guess not," I mutter. A thought hits me. "I need to give him back his keys."

Matt gestures to him. "Go ahead. I'll wait for you."

"Thanks."

"Anytime." He flashes a wide smile that somehow reminds me of a crocodile.

Great. Now "Never Smile at a Crocodile" *will be in my head for days.*

I inhale a fortifying breath of the cool Michigan air. I love the way it smells here. The scent of the Lake in the near distance, tantalizingly close by, mixes with the aspen and pine, giving off the uniquely woodsy scent of *north.*

I hold the keys out in my hand and march stiffly back to Connor, reminding myself I can't be attracted to him. He's my boss.

Connor's facial expressions morph as I approach. First, he smiles, then he clenches his hands at his sides, and finally, he frowns.

"Here." I thrust the keys at his chest in an attempt to run away from the way my eyes are drawn to his. He places a hand over the keys, trapping my hand. His heart beats wildly. I jerk my hand away like I've been burned. He's my *boss.*

"Paige?" he asks quietly.

I can't tell him I'm trying to squash feelings for him and currently imagining things that would make him less attractive. He's got to have terrible gas, or something gross. Maybe he never flosses, or worse, maybe he's one of those people who never uses mouthwash after eating garlic. None of these thoughts diminishes the attraction, though, so when he speaks, I can't help seeing the sincerity in his eyes.

"I could have helped. But I didn't want to interfere with the friendships you all are forming. You're the counselors here. I'm the operations manager. It's…complicated."

My stupid mouth blurts out a response: "You could be friends with us too."

Connor hangs his head. "You're right. But I think people will make assumptions…" He gulps. "About your character if I'm too helpful right away." He raises his brow, and I remember that Matt is watching this exchange and that Tom implied something was going on between us already.

I sigh. "I'm sorry. Thank you for picking me up earlier."

"Anytime," he replies, and his smile *does not* remind me of a crocodile. He pockets his keys and starts to whistle as he returns inside the mess hall.

I turn away from Connor and the confusing swoop my stomach continuously does around him.

Matt stares after Connor's retreating form. "What is going on with him? Are you two a thing?"

"No," I answer, because it's the truth. Even if I wished it wasn't. Every time I assume something about Connor, I'm proven wrong.

"So." Matt waggles his eyebrows. "You're single. And that means *we* can *mingle*."

I force out a fake laugh. "Nice try, Matt."

"I'm going to keep trying."

I blink. I don't want him to keep trying. I'm about to tell him as much when Brooke runs down the path. "Matt! Stop! It! She does *not* need you harassing her." She smacks his shoulder. He winces. "Sorry about *him*. He's a hopeless flirt with previously terrible taste in women."

"Hey!" Matt jerks his head around toward her. "I'll put up with the occasional twin sister abuse, but I won't let you slander my reputation."

Brooke rolls her eyes. "Mattttttttty." She huffs. "You dated nine women last year. And I did not like a single one."

"Fine. They weren't *your* style. But we got along *just* fine." He winks, and Brooke makes a gagging noise.

"Grossss. And I'm your twin sister. Who you date needs to be *my* style too. Don't trust a word he says, Paige." Then to Matt, she barks an order that sounds something like "Come on!" and "Hurry up!" meshed together.

What language was that?

12

CONNOR

Why does she have to be so attractive? I keep trying to guard my thoughts about her. She's my employee, sort of. Technically we're really both Ember and Chet's employees, but Chet and Ember are hours away. I'm in charge. Of the employees. So no, I can't be interested.

Would someone please tell that to my brain?

Paige's nursing station is ready, and the crew has managed to learn the safety systems in place for every possible scenario. The cabins are both set up and awaiting their campers.

We've got lifeguard certifications, easy because all of the counselors were already certified—rope climbing certifications for our rock wall and harnesses, basic wilderness field guides memorized, first aid kits, hiking trails memorized, and a curriculum that should inspire the preteens to grow their leadership skills. That's the hope, anyway.

I've watched from the sidelines with more than a little jealousy as the group of six grew closer over the past four weeks. They're friends. Matt's a hopeless flirt, but Brooke keeps him in line. Lucas is kind and a jokester. Lucas is the musician and sensitive for a guy. Both Lucas and Jorge have obvious crushes on Stephanie but are too shy to do anything about it. Stephanie thrives on order. Brooke might have the commanding presence, but Stephanie's the one who's checking things off behind the scenes and detailing the plans. And then there's Paige. She's a quiet, steady presence, calm, and drop-dead gorgeous.

The rule book says no romantic activities while campers are on the premises, but despite my heart continuing to want romance with Paige, I've kept my distance from the counselors. I've prayed a lot about my feelings for her, even begged God to take them away, but I haven't had any answers.

As if thinking of her summoned the real thing, there she is, jogging past the mess hall parking lot. She strides past her newly repaired car, her lean legs flying and her ponytail swinging. Her shoulders are bronzed and toned, and it's weird that my eyes are drawn to her shoulders, but the racerback tank top is cut in a way that begs 'show some appreciation here!' And just like that, I'm now a shoulders guy.

I shake my hair out of my eyes and try not to stare. She slows to a stop, and Stephanie comes running after her. Stephanie wears a similar outfit, but I don't notice anything special about her. It's that sobering realization that tells me just how much trouble I'm in.

Tom sidles over next to me. He leans one hip on the railing and yells out, "G'morning ladies!" to Paige and Stephanie. They wave, big smiles on their faces, but I feel like I've just been caught staring.

"Tom," I whisper-hiss. "Why did you call to them?"

He appraises me with one quirked, bushy, white eyebrow. "You do know that it's obvious to everyone, right?"

I swallow against the dryness that suddenly overtakes my throat. "What's obvious?"

"Connor." Tom shakes his head. "You have got to figure out how to act on your feelings."

"I can't."

"You can't, or you won't?"

"Both."

"Then you're letting her go. Because Connor, here's a hint about women: When the *mutual* feelings are there, if *you* don't act, they are liable to change."

I look off at the trees, focusing on how the green branches meet the blue sky as I digest Tom's words.

"Mutual attraction?" I ask. I could kick myself for the hope in my voice. I chance a glance at Tom. He grins wryly.

"Thought you might not have noticed. Paige is more subtle than you, but *she* watches you too. And it's so painfully obvious to each of us that you'd practically be doing us a favor if you'd ask her on a date."

"I don't want to mess around with the kids' safety and comfort though."

Tom props one hand on his hip. "Kids? Are there any *kids* on this campus right now? And are you saying that you think you're the type of man who would put his own pleasure ahead of the needs of children in your care? Because if you are, I think we have two different versions of Connor to work through."

I start to speak, but he holds out a hand in the universal *stop* gesture.

"No, Connor. You need to listen. You might think you're not worthy of love because of what happened with what's-her-name, but you are. I get the sense that Paige has her own weighty past. And, quite frankly, you are *not* the sort of man who sits by and lets a good thing go, *nor* are you the sort of man who would jeopardize the safety of a camper in pursuit of your own interests. I've been working with you for months now. I know you well. You owe it to Paige, and to yourself, to be honest. So. Ask. Her. On. A. Date."

"But…but…Matt," I splutter.

"Matt is a flirt, and Brooke wouldn't let *that* happen unless Paige wanted it to. She sees her brother and her friend for who they are, and recognizes that they're incompatible. She's smart. And have you ever considered that maybe Matt is trying to get a rise out of you?"

"But…I don't…want to date and then stop and cause awkwardness."

"What if you date and don't stop?"

"The…the rules, Tom. I can't."

"Or, you could tell your brother and sister-in-law that two adults have entered into a relationship where propriety is observed, and where you show the campers what healthy romantic feelings look like in a Christian context."

"Oh." I breathe out the word. I like how Tom phrased it. I like the hope he just offered me. Hope that Paige and I might be a *thing*.

"Have you been praying?"

I nod, because I can't say 'yes' if I still don't have any answer other than to watch and wait.

Tom raises his eyebrows. "Any answers to your prayers?"

I shake my head, this time a 'no.'

"So go talk to her, Connor. It's good to move on and let Kaleigh go. Your story doesn't end with the wrong woman, and that's what *she* was. Maybe Paige will be the *right* woman. Don't give up on love because you tried once with the wrong person."

The hope I've squashed down for the past month takes flight. I push myself off the porch railing and jog toward Paige and Stephanie. "Thanks, Tom!" I yell over my shoulder.

He raises a mug of steaming hot coffee in a 'cheers' gesture as he settles into one of the rocking chairs on the porch.

If I was paying the man, I'd give him a raise.

13

PAIGE

A morning run always soothes me. Every day since Mom left, I've woken up and enjoyed the glorious few seconds where I don't worry about being enough. I don't worry about being left. I just marvel at the fact that I am awake and at peace. And every morning, those few moments of perfect peace are shattered, and the truth of what happened slices into me like the shards of a broken bottle.

The physicality of running became a way to ease that pain. Not easy or always practical in a Northern Michigan winter, and yet, running became my coping mechanism. Sometimes I worry that I'm addicted to running, and if my mom was an addict, then I am too. But my therapist assured me that running was a healthy response to processing the emotional neglect and grief.

I didn't like Dr. Hubert much, but I appreciated those words.

I grab clean clothes, my shower caddy, a towel, and slip on flip-flops. Connor assured us that the showers were new in the ladies' locker room, but I do not want any fungal infections. I am *antifungal*. Community showers equal footwear.

"

Thinking of Connor causes my heart to beat just a bit faster. My watch shows "recovery heartbeat" after a run, and the little spike in the graph is obvious. I roll my eyes at myself, because *really*, he's just a guy, and he's been very standoffish from the counselors this past month. He's a competent boss, and he's had us working hard, but he's definitely been reserved.

I grab my phone so I can play music while I shower and notice a few text messages. They're from an unknown number. My stomach drops.

Unknown number

Need money

Will pay u back

Help me

Send it, u know u should love ur mom more

The last text trails off. I frown. Mom texted and demanded money occasionally throughout my teen years. I blocked her number after years of crying about it and being unsure what to do. How could I send her money? All I did was babysit for Blaze. I wanted to help, but it wasn't until I finally told my dad and Dr. Hubert about these texts that I understood what she was doing. Emotional manipulation.

Dr. Hubert told me to change my number, but I couldn't do it. I'd already lost my mom, but maybe she'd come back. Maybe one day the text wouldn't be about me giving her things. Maybe one day she'd text to say she was sorry.

The self-loathing that always accompanies contact from Mom brings tears to my eyes.

"Paige," Stephanie calls from the doorway. "Are you ok? You were smiling and then you…went all pale."

"Oh. Yeah." I bite my lip. I don't want to tell anyone about my mommy issues. "I just… yeah." I walk past her, keeping my head down so she won't see my tears. I shuffle as fast as my flip-flops will let me to the shower. I'm vaguely aware of someone calling my name, but I can't talk to anyone. I block the number as my stomach cramps and my hands shake.

It's a relief when I step into the warm water and can let the tears fall. I turn the water as hot as I can, letting the pellets sting my skin in a near burn. I know what I have to do and loathe myself for it. But each time, it only becomes more and more necessary. I have to fix this once and for all.

I take a deep breath and turn the water temperature down. I scrub every inch of my skin, hoping maybe I can wash the stain of my family away. No matter how much I understand that I need to cut Mom out of my life entirely, I always feel a disgusting coat of slime on my body after any interaction with her.

I think about my attraction to Connor and bite back a self-deprecating laugh. I thought maybe, the way he was watching me from the porch today…maybe he was interested. This is just another reminder that I'm not lovable. That I'm broken, that I come from brokenness, and that romance isn't an option for me. A *family* isn't an option for me.

I shut off the shower and towel off.

When I'm dressed, I know what I need to do. I hope that Stephanie or Brooke will go with me into the city tomorrow and not ask questions. Maybe I can sneak it in as a supply we need for the infirmary. We could use more milk of magnesia. Constipation is brutal for kids when they're away from home.

I'm glad I let all the tears fall in the shower, because if I hadn't, I'd be crying now. I'm severing ties with my mom once and for all, and blocking her isn't enough.

Now, I have to get into a town and change my phone number.

14

CONNOR

"**P**aige!" I call as she strides out of the cabin and toward the ladies' showers. She keeps her head down and doesn't acknowledge me. I fight against the hurt in my chest at the slight. It's possible she didn't hear me. It's also possible I haven't been friendly and she has no feelings for me.

Stephanie walks out of the cabin. "Hey, Connor." Her eyes follow mine and land on Paige's retreating form. "She was really upset by something just now."

I can't help being concerned. Concern is a reasonable response. I'd be concerned if any of the staff here was called "really upset" by another staffer. "Did she say anything? What happened?"

"No," Stephanie says. "She was looking at her phone and she went all pale."

"Oh," I breathe, unsure how to respond. "Do you think I should go talk to her…"

Stephanie blinks several times. "Connor, she's in the shower."

"Oh, right…" I swallow my embarrassment. "I meant, after…"

"Connor?"

"Hmm?" I hum in response, looking anywhere but at Stephanie's face and willing the flush creeping up my cheeks to go away.

"You should give her a little space right now. But we're having a bonfire by the lake tonight and you should come."

"Right, but that's kind of awkward since I'm sort of your boss…"

"Connor, we're adults. You can be friendly with us and still be our boss. Actually, you can even be romantically interested in one of us"—she jerks her head over her shoulder to indicate where Paige disappeared—"and *still* be our boss. Come down around eight. It will be fun. Tell Tom to come too."

"Ok." I shove my hands in my pockets. "Maybe."

I walk away, but the tiniest tremor of excitement zaps through my muscles at the idea of finally talking to Paige. I wonder if I can help her with whatever the problem is. *I want to help.*

A breeze blows off Lake Superior this evening. The sun is setting below the mountains to the west, but it won't be fully dark for an hour. Tom politely declines my invitation to the bonfire. "I got something to do," he says, and then gets into his beat-up truck and drives away.

As soon as Tom leaves, I call Chet. Surprisingly, he answers right away.

"Hey, Con," he says, "what's up? Everything ok at camp?"

"Yeah." I draw in a quick breath. "I didn't expect you to actually answer so fast."

"You caught me at a good time. Emb and Blaze are both busy, and I'm just waiting for Blaze to call so I can pick him up from practice."

"Oh…okay." I'm not sure what to say. It's still weird to hear

Chet talk about his life so…*domesticatedly*. "Uh. That man who's been helping me here. Tom…"

"Yeah?"

"I think we need to pay him."

I swear I hear Chet's scowl through the phone. "Listen." Chet sighs heavily. "Funds are tight right now. If we can get another grant, we can absolutely discuss taking him on as staff. But if he's comfortable volunteering, that's what's best for the camp."

"I hear you—"

"No, Connor, that's actually a good point. Does he have the volunteer paperwork filled out? The background checks completed? The campers are coming in…what, two days?"

"Yeah, two days…"

"And the background stuff?"

"Yes. He filled it out weeks ago, and it's all come back clean. He's great. And I think he might be the most important person on staff."

"Woah. Connor, Tom is *not* on staff until we get more grant money. And even then, does he *want* to be on staff?"

"I'm treating him like he's on staff."

Chet blows out a frustrated breath, and I scrub my hand down my face, catching the edge of my five o'clock shadow with my palm.

"Ok. Tom is an honorary volunteer staff member for now. Anything *else*?"

I don't want to tell him about being interested in Paige, but I also know I have to. I'm going to talk to her tonight, and Chet should be aware.

"Uh. Yeah, so please don't tell Ember."

"Connor." Chet's voice is sharp. "I don't keep secrets from my wife."

"It's not a secret, it's just that…"

"What?"

"I've kept my distance from the counselors, but"—I mumble this next part—" I like one of them, and I think she likes me too."

"Come again?"

"I like one of them. And I think she likes me too."

"Ok… but there's a no-dating policy among counselors."

"Technically, the employee manual says when kids are on the premises, and technically, neither of us is just a counselor."

Chet sputters. "You and…PAIGE?" I can't tell if it's good or bad, but his voice drops lower. "Dude, Emb is gonna flip."

"You aren't going to tell Ember," I hiss. "I'm trying to be a responsible adult and make you aware that we might have feelings for each other, but that it will not get in the way of my duties here."

"Right…ok. And you don't know if she likes you? So, this is a preemptive conversation?"

"Yes." I huff, annoyed that Chet does not understand.

"And I can't tell Ember."

"Could you please just let this go where it goes without meddling?" I think carefully about how I'll phrase this next part. "Ember is great, but she'd…meddle with this."

"Fair enough. She loves Paige…and with the baby, we don't need to give her anything else to stress over."

"Ok?"

"Well, neither of you is technically a counselor, and you're older than the college staff. So, if you can fill out a relationship disclosure form for liabilities sake, and make sure the children are your first priority, and agree to a code of conduct regarding PDA when campers are on the grounds, then yeah. It has to be ok, I guess."

"Good."

"Hey, Con?" Chet says. "I'll send the paperwork over once I hear from our HR rep, but you do know you'll have to talk to her first, right?"

"Bye, Chet." I roll my eyes and hang up.

I grab a black zip-up hoodie from the hook by my office door, stick a flashlight in my back jeans pocket, and walk outside, whistling all the way to the lake.

15

PAIGE

I'm always awestruck by how *big* Lake Superior is. I grew up on it, but the view at Camp CGO is something to behold. A small rounded bay gives shelter from the biggest of the waves and currents, making it a safe place for swimming. There are cliffs on either side, and a hiking trail leads up to the cliffs on the west edge. The bay is plenty deep, and though Tom assured us it's safe for jumping, we don't want the campers to get any ideas. The hiking trail to the cliffs will be closed off once campers arrive.

I'm the first of the girls to arrive at the beach where Matt, Jorge, and Lucas play keep away with a football. It's awkward just standing here, but it will be just as awkward if I sit alone.

A hint of a whistle-stop song meets my ears just as I decide to walk over and join in with the boys and the football.

I stop short and spin around, searching for the sound. I'm not sure *why* I hear the song for the opening credits of the cartoon *Robin Hood*, but I definitely do.

Just as my eyes find Connor whistling down the path—baseball cap on and a black short sleeve shirt stretching across his chest, a black zip-up jacket in his hands, and white sneakers—Matt runs backward toward me. He reaches over behind his head and snags the football from just above my head.

Matt's elbow smashes into my face and I go sprawling on the warm sand.

"Yeah!" Matt shouts while I spit out a mouthful of grit.

Matt must turn around and see me because suddenly Matt is way too close to my face. "Paige?" He gets closer and I don't like it. I try to scramble away backward, but unbeknownst to me, Lucas and Jorge are behind me. I end up crashing into them, and Lucas falls on my hand.

"Are you ok?" Matt asks.

"I'm fine…just…need…some space…" I grind out.

"You shouldn't be in the middle of a game, Paige," Lucas chastises.

I bite back a retort about not watching where you're going when playing a game.

"Hey, is everyone ok?" Connor's voice cuts through.

"Yeah. Paige wasn't paying attention and I crashed into her. We're good, though, right?"

I clench my teeth. We are *not* good. Careless sports are dangerous, and I'm still in pain. "Fine," I lie. "We're fine. Lucas, please get off my hand."

"Oh." Lucas gets up and extends a hand, but Connor's hand is there too. "Sorry, Paige," Lucas says sheepishly.

I can't decide what to do. It would look weird to only grab Connor's hand, and Lucas sounds truly apologetic. The best option in this case is the most awkward one. I put one hand in Connor's and one hand in Lucas's. They help me to my feet.

"Thanks," I say, brushing sand off my shorts and arms. "I think you should be more careful though."

"Noted, Nurse Paige." Lucas salutes, then turns away to Jorge and Matt, who have moved to throwing the ball in the ankle-deep water. At least now I won't get hit.

"Great Lakes, Great Wrecks?" Connor asks, his eyes twinkling in the setting sun.

It takes me a full minute to understand that he's talking about my shirt.

"Oh." I sound like an idiot. "Oh yeah. I like shipwrecks."

I'm a meme. I'm the *I LIKE TURTLES* meme. Send help.

"Shipwrecks." He cocks a brow.

"Yeah. The Great Lakes have a ton of shipwrecks, and because they aren't in saltwater, many are really well preserved." Ok, now I sound like a brochure at the Shipwreck Museum.

"Do you have a favorite?" Connor asks.

I stare blankly.

"A favorite shipwreck?" he supplies.

"Oh. Yeah. The Edmund Fitzgerald. I just…everytime I'm in the water, I think about them."

"That's the one with the song, right?"

"Yeah. November 10th is the anniversary. I always try to do something to remember them that day."

Connor nods in response. The boys throw the football in the water, and he watches them. But then he grins at me, puts one finger to his lips, and points at something running up behind Matt.

I shield my eyes against the glare of the setting sun and watch as Brooke sneaks up behind her brother. Lucas and Jorge see her as she gestures to throw the ball to her instead of Matt. Lucas spirals the ball her way, and Matt jumps up to grab it. As he does, Brooke elbows him in the ribs, causing him to miss the ball as he brings his arms down to protect his sides.

Matt splashes onto his knees in the water, and Brooke snakes out an arm and grabs the football gracefully.

"Matty," Brooke says, laughing as she launches a perfect spiral pass to Jorge. "You should really —"

But Matt is back up and grabs his twin sister, hauling her out of the water like a suitcase, where he dumps her in the sand and then *sits* on her stomach.

"I should what, Brookie Cookie?" Matt hollers.

Brooke shoves him off and he plops onto the sand. "Don't call me that, *Matty*."

Stephanie appears from under the pine trees, where she watched the entire exchange. It's clear she was in on the prank. "Ok, you two. Time to separate and make up."

"Nope." Brooke folds her arms. "Not gonna happen."

Stephanie snorts. "Sure thing. You won't forgive your twin brother." She arches an eyebrow.

"Fine." Brooke swings her pink-streaked blonde ponytail over her shoulder. "Matty, I forgive you for being a brute."

Matt laughs. "And I forgive you for being a turd."

Brooke shoves him and says something in gibberish again. He wraps an arm around her. "Ok, General," he says, then lets her go.

Brooke and Stephanie catch sight of me and Connor. Stephanie waggles her eyebrows, but Brooke bounds over like a dog ready to sniff out a new toy.

"What's going on, guys?" she asks, a wide smile on her face.

"Just watching the sibling wrestling match." Connor laughs at the mischievous expression on Brooke's face. "You won, by the way."

Brooke lights up. "I did. But you know, Matt's not so bad. You should go make friends with the guys, Connor. Throw the ball around with them a little. It's fun. Literally, harmless fun."

Connor opens his mouth to say something, then snaps it shut. I'm the *I LIKE TURTLES* meme, but Connor is *a turtle*. A brief frown clouds his features, but then he shakes his head, rolls his shoulders back, and smiles. "Yeah, that would be fun." He turns and jogs over to the guys, motioning to Lucas to toss him the ball, which he catches with a graceful jump.

Brooke and Stephanie follow my gaze, and Brooke lets out a low 'woah.'

Brooke clears her throat. "I've got drinks in the cooler. Let's get that fire started. We can watch these fine men, and ugggh, my brother play their silly game."

Stephanie smirks at me. "Or we could play too."

I frown.

"Come on, it will be fun." Brooke does a little shimmy while she nods her head toward the guys.

"Ok," I mutter.

"Excellent." Brooke and Stephanie cackle in unison. Then the two of them run to the water and start shouting directions to the guys.

I walk along with trepidation, but if everyone's going to play, I'm not missing out. No matter how *bad* at football I am.

16

CONNOR

Brooke and Stephanie come splashing into the water. "We're playing too! Guys versus girls!"

"You're *on*," Jorge shouts.

Matt frowns at Brooke but doesn't say anything. Lucas grins while Paige makes her way to the water.

"Girls!" Brooke commands, and Paige picks up the pace, running to meet them. They form a huddle.

"Strategy time, gents!" Matt yells, drawing my eyes away from Paige. "Circle up, fellas. Here's the deal. Brooke needs to be double-teamed at all times. She will *beat* us single-handedly if we give her any chance."

"Wait," I say. "What game are we playing exactly?"

"Keep away." Matt looks at me like I'm an idiot for asking, but it has *not* been clarified. "Have you played before?"

"Yeah, but I'd like to know the rules you have in mind for *this* game."

"Girls throw ball, we take ball away. We throw ball, we do not let girls get ball," Matt says. "Sound good?" When the guys nod, he says, "I'll guard Brooke with Jorge. Lucas, you guard Stephanie. Connor, you guard Paige."

"Sure," I say. "But I think we should play on the beach and not in the water. It's going to be cold here soon with the sun going down."

"Brooke!" Matt yells. "We're playing in the sand, not the water. You good with that?"

"Does a bear…." Brooke shouts back, but Stephanie clamps a hand over Brooke's mouth to stop her from the rest of that statement.

"Sand's good!" Stephanie calls back, removing her hand from Brooke's mouth.

"What! I was going to say the PG-version."

Paige shakes her head, a small, bemused smile on her face. The three ladies stalk over to us, and Brooke grabs the football from its resting place on the sand.

Pleasant surprise rushes over me when Paige chooses to stand by me. It's possible the counselors are trying to get us together. It's also possible everyone sees us as the least threatening. The competitive nature I usually keep locked down rears its head before nervousness about talking to her takes over.

Would she be interested in a date? Or something? What if I'm reading everything wrong? I read everything wrong with Kaleigh.

I'm too busy thinking to process the football coming straight at Paige. I could move around her and catch it, but instead, I stay planted just behind her feet, thinking about asking her on a date.

The ball lands in Paige's arms without her having to move at all. Brooke has an impressive arm. Paige gives a wry smile over her shoulder at me, and I'm done. I'd do anything to see that playful look directed at me again.

"C'mon, MAN!" Lucas yells. "You're supposed to STOP her. You're at least a FOOT taller than her. Put those gadget arms to use!"

"Sorry…" I sputter. "I didn't realize we'd started…"

The next time a ball comes Paige's way, I reach over the top of her head and snatch it from the air.

She turns with a scowl. "That was mine, you know."

Now it's my turn to grin playfully back at her and watch the blush bloom on her cheeks.

The sun sinks lower, and soon it's too dark to really see. Our game ends with absolutely no way of knowing who won, but despite being highly competitive, I don't care. I got to stand closer to Paige than would normally be considered appropriate, and she looked at me like I'm more than her boss. I'm a sap. It's fine.

We all migrate to the firepit, where Paige lights the kindling. Matt grabs a cooler and pops the top off a beer.

Paige sinks down into a camp chair circling the firepit, and Matt flops into the chair next to her. Lucas pulls out a guitar and begins strumming.

Soon, everyone is singing.

Everyone but Paige.

"Do 'Landslide'!" Stephanie calls to Lucas as she giggles behind her hand. Clearly she knows how complicated that song will be for Brooke to sing.

Lucas breaks into the first verse, with Brooke surprisingly on key. Paige stands up with a little jerk and walks away from the fire, heading to the trees.

No one else seems to notice she leaves, and this might be the perfect time to talk to her, so I follow.

Paige leans against the thin trunk of a sapling aspen tree, taking deep breaths. She faces away from me, and I make certain not to scare her.

"Paige?" I call softly.

She stiffens and stands, but before she turns around, she brushes her hands across her face.

"Y-yeah?" she says, still facing away from me.

"Are you ok?"

"Yep," she responds too quickly.

I walk until I'm standing right next to her in the darkness. "I don't buy it."

She turns her blue eyes to me. I can make out the pinpricks of stars reflected in her pupils behind the sheen of tears she tried, but failed, to wipe away. I have the completely irrational desire to lean in and kiss her.

"Fine," Paige whispers. "I'm fine."

"Then why'd you walk away?"

"That song."

I wait for more, but she leaves it at that. "It is pretty sad."

"No, it's not that. It's just..." She bites her bottom lip. "I had something happen today."

"Oh?" I ask, considering how much to press, but still, Paige is opening up a little. "Stephanie said you were upset after your run."

"Yeah." Paige's shoulders slump and she closes her eyes. "I heard from...someone...I'd rather not...today."

Internal alarm bells blare. "Paige, are you in danger?"

"What?" Her eyes fly open. "No! Of course not!"

"Okay, but that sounds like someone is bothering you. Is it a boyfriend or something?" It's a cheap shot at information, but I need to know.

"No." She sighs. "I don't know how much Ember told you about me..." She trails off.

"Ember hasn't told me much about you."

"Oh." She worries her lip again. "I—" She draws a deep breath. "I don't know if I want to talk about it."

"Ok." I look up at the underbranches of the pine trees and catch a glimpse of the starry sky. "Want to walk?"

She studies me for a moment, but nods. I extend a hand to her and she grasps it, the coolness of her palm soothing against mine. It takes everything in me not to bring her hand to my lips and kiss it, so I squeeze it instead.

17

PAIGE

Connor just asked me to walk. Which isn't a weird thing to do, but also *is* weird because he's been so aloof from the counselors this whole time. What also *is* weird is the way he squeezed my hand. And also, *why* did I find that so attractive? Maybe he is interested, like Stephanie said.

The glimmer of hope that flares as I think *that* thought is quickly squashed when I remind myself that I'm unloveable and utterly leaveable.

Connor starts off toward the cliff hiking trail, our hands loosely clasped together. No matter how great the contact feels, I can't let myself get hurt, so I shake my hand loose and shove it in my pocket while we walk. Connor doesn't do anything with his hand. He leaves it swinging, taunting me, as if to say, *I'm right here, you could take me back.*

"So," Connor says. "You were dressed like a vampire the first time we met."

A flush creeps up my neck and ears. "Yeah…about that."

"Hey, Paige," Connor responds, angling his body toward me as we're walking. "I thought it was clever."

"You did?" I blurt out, surprised. "You seemed to think I was a lunatic."

"Well after Ember explained to me what you did for a living, and the fact that your boss doesn't understand the difference between Halloween and April Fools, *then* I thought it was really great."

"Oh… well…that's something."

"Yes," he breathes. "You're something."

I bite down on my tongue to stop from saying anything else. Connor makes me believe I could tell him anything. I can't though. I can't get attached. I can't have *feelings* for someone. Especially not someone who's just going to leave me.

I grimace, and Connor notices. "What's wrong?"

Instead of saying, "I bit my tongue," or some other reasonable response, I blurt out, "I can't date you."

Connor stops and blinks several times. His hand twitches at his side. "Why not?" he challenges.

That is NOT the reaction I was expecting.

"Uh." I flounder. "I…" I stare down at my feet, wishing I could melt into a puddle and then be carried away by the Lake tides.

"Hey, Paige." Connor places his warm palm on my upper arm. The sudden heat from his touch makes me shiver. "It's ok." He smiles. "Are you cold?"

Before I can respond, he holds out his black zip-up hoodie and slips it over my shoulders. It's comforting and warm, and he's such a darn gentleman. A niggling thought worms its way into the back of my brain that he deserves answers. And that I *would* really like to date this man.

"Uh. Thanks." I close my eyes for a moment. "I…my mom left when I was little." I sneak a glance at Connor's face to find it stony.

"I'm sorry," he says, and then waits.

"Yeah, and I have a lot of…things to work through with that."

He studies me for a minute. "Sometimes it's good to talk about things like that. Especially with friends."

"Yeah, but no one knows what it's like to be twelve years old and to have your mother leave to go spend all her and your dad's money on cards and booze and drugs, and then have her *call* you periodically demanding you send her more money because her latest boyfriend stopped supporting her bad habits." I stop, stunned at how much I just revealed. "It's not exactly a fun thing to discuss, and no one wants a whiner."

We reach the top of the cliff trail.

"Let's sit," Connor says. He leads me from the copse of trees and out onto the flat rocky outcrop of the cliff top. He sits down and leans back on his hands. I sit next to him.

He hasn't said anything else after my outburst, but he tips his face up to the sky, the inky darkness twinkling with the lights of stars and the waves of Lake Superior beating against the cliff below.

I mimic his posture and take a deep breath, catching a scent that's not lake and not forest from his sweatshirt. I hate how much I like it. And I really hate how much I want to be brave and see if maybe I am lovable.

"You know," Connor says from his place next to me, "I like to think about what's out there."

"What do you mean?"

"I mean that I like to think about what's bigger than *us*, people here on Earth sometimes."

"What, like aliens?" I scoff.

"No." He turns to me, serious. "You said you had a faith—Catholic?"

"Oh. Yeah, well, I was, or am, or I don't know. Everything fell apart after Mom left. And, I haven't…I still believe in God, but I don't know why. He hasn't answered my prayer for..." I stop, ashamed of my weakness.

"Paige," Connor says into the darkness. "That was a horrible thing you went through."

I hold my breath, scared to break whatever words he's saying into words that will crush my soul anew.

"You shouldn't have had to experience that. But, Paige, maybe you haven't been praying for the right thing."

I frown at that. "I don't understand."

"I don't really know what to tell you, but I do know that I stopped feeling awful about my past and started to feel like I could move on when I started praying for peace."

"It's that easy?" I retort. "I pray for peace, and suddenly I feel great because my mom left me and my dad, but she still asks me for money?"

Connor shifts so he's facing me instead of the Lake. "Is that what upset you today?"

I can't find words because stupid tears are falling, and I *know* he can see them. I bob my head.

"Oh, Paige." He leans over and wraps an arm around me in a half hug.

"I know I need to change my number, but I never wanted to because what if she calls and says she's sorry?"

Connor digests this for a moment, and I think he doesn't have an answer, but then he does. "Are you blocking her and she's still contacting you with unknown numbers?"

I nod and his arm tightens around me.

"Paige, people like that…don't change without help. She's not getting help. If she wants to tell you she's sorry, she'll find a way that doesn't involve impacting your daily life."

It's too much, and I feel too raw, too broken, so I scoot my body away from Connor's just enough to make his arm drop. Immediately, I miss the comfort and strength.

"Paige, if you don't want to be romantically involved with me, that's fine. But I would like to help you, as a friend."

I find his eyes searching mine in the starlight. His gaze lingers on my lips for half a beat. He leans forward, and I think he's going to kiss me, but he doesn't. I really regret that. He brushes a piece of hair off my forehead with his thumb and forefinger. "I need to go to Marquette tomorrow. Can I take you into town so you can get a new number?"

"Yeah," I breathe, afraid to break the magic of his touch.

And then words so soft they might as well be the whispers of the pine and aspen just behind us, I swear I hear him say, "I can wait."

18

CONNOR

Paige's words pulverize my heart. I can see the brokenness she tries to hide, and even more than that, I can see that she doesn't like talking about it. It does not stop me from wanting to hold her, to comfort her, to take away all that pain. *If only I could.*

The protectiveness in me surges, but I know I have to fight it back down. She said no, and I respect that. I'll be her friend, even if all I am to her is a ride into Marquette tomorrow. Somehow with the way she's looking at me, I don't think that's all I am to her. But she needs time to understand she's worthy. I wish she would let me show her.

Paige stands up and places inches that feel like miles of distance between us as she looks up at the night sky. "We should get back to the fire."

"Yep." I jam my hands into my pockets to keep them from doing something stupid like holding hers.

She zips the jacket up a little higher, and I bite back a laugh at how my old jacket hangs on her. She looks good in it, but I can't say anything about it, not now.

"You coming, or what?" she asks.

I smile. "I think I'll be down in a few minutes. I like to look at the constellations. They remind me of when I used to look at the night sky with my grandpa."

"Oh." She shifts a little uncomfortably.

"That one," I say, pointing to the sky, " is Orion's belt."

"I've never really studied constellations before." There's a tiny longing in her voice, and I am willing to take it as a win.

"You know, the old maritime sailors used to navigate with the constellations."

She gives a small smile, her teeth flashing white in the dark of the night. "I did know that. I just never…took the time to look at them and learn them, you know?"

I shake my head in agreement. "Yeah. I probably never would have if it wasn't for Gramps." My throat tightens and I look away, staring off into the vast distance of Lake Superior.

"I'm sorry for your loss," Paige breathes.

"Thanks," I say, which is the worst response I could come up with, but there's literally nothing else.

"I'll leave you to it, then." She walks away. I listen for her footsteps until they fade down the trail.

I close my eyes and pray for peace with whatever happens between me and Paige. When I'm done begging God for peace and to tell me what to do, I open my eyes and watch the waves roll. It's incredibly surprising when, out of nowhere, the thought *pursue her* flashes like a lightning strike through my mind. I've never been so sure of God answering my prayer as I am at this moment.

After a few minutes of staring out at the Lake by myself and digesting the response to my prayer, I decide to join the group by the fire.

Paige should be far enough down the trail that I won't look creepy if I follow now. I push myself off the rock and dust off the back of my pants. There's a chill in the air that makes me rub my arms. I touch the spot where the tattoo of a northern aspen tree and a big wave curls around my upper arm. I got it after Gramps passed, because it reminded me of both *him* and *here*. I've always been careful to keep it covered up, and even chose a spot higher on my arm than most people would for ink. As long as I wear a short-sleeved shirt, it's hidden. It's not a tattoo for anyone else's eyes but mine.

The question of whether Paige likes tattoos runs through my mind, but I stop it. I need to slow down that line of thinking. *Pursue her.*

I take off down the path at a light jog. It's dim and dark, but my eyes are adjusted, and I don't want to be alone on a cliff anymore.

I'm about halfway to the bottom of the trail when I hear voices. I slow and listen.

"Paige-ay, bay-bay."

I think it's Matt.

A soft murmur that must be Paige.

"We're gonna get baptized in the lake. Jump in, be baptized like that song." He starts singing something, and it sounds like a combination of "Wade in the Water" and "Going to the Chapel."

Another murmur.

"We've gotta good thing going, you and I...a really good. Good. Things everywhere here."

Matt's words are slurred, and it does not take long to figure out that he's drunk. After what Paige just revealed to me, and after her mom contacted her today... The protective instinct that I fought down wastes no time in taking over.

I rush down the path where I find Matt, an arm looped over Paige's shoulders, leaning unsteadily on her. Her legs begin to buckle under his added weight, but she keeps herself upright.

"Nope. We're not going to jump off the cliffs right now, Matt," Paige says, her voice stern. "We're going to go get you some water, and then you're going to get some food to eat."

"Can we have ice cream and chicken nuggets?" Matt asks like a little kid.

"No, but I have some chips," Paige replies.

I run to Paige. "Are you alright?" I mouth.

Paige tips her head toward Matt. "He's drunk," she says under her breath.

I nod, because I already knew that. "Do you want me to take care of him?"

"Noooooo!" Matt yells before wagging his finger. "Only Paige-ay. No you."

I hook my arm under Matt's right arm so he's leaning on me and Paige now.

"We're gonna go swimming, right, Paige-ay?"

"Not right now. Remember, snacks," she says.

I marvel at how calm she is. How in control she is. How... *This isn't the first time she's had to care for someone like this.*

Anger at Paige's situation bubbles up into my throat. Then the anger turns to ire. Matt put her back in this position. He made irresponsible choices, and while I don't want him to do something stupid and get hurt, he already betrayed my trust by drinking too much tonight. I'm going to have to be a boss and discipline him tomorrow.

Paige and I steer Matt back to the fire, where he plops down into a chair. Paige heads to the cooler and opens it.

"You want a drink, Paige?" Brooke says from where she's sitting close to Lucas while he strums the guitar, and I notice Stephanie has slid closer to Lucas than mutual friends would sit.

Paige stiffens, her entire body tense in the fire's glow. "No, thank you. I'm getting some water for Matt."

Brooke directs her gaze at Matt for a moment. Her jaw drops and her eyes widen.

"I'm sorry, I…" she sputters. "We didn't…uh. I didn't watch him, because…"

"Brooke," I cut in. "He's an adult. He doesn't need *watching*. This is on him, not you."

"Please don't fire him," she pleads quietly.

"I'm not firing him." I huff. "He's going to have to be on probation. I can't fire him two days before the campers come. But no more drinking on the grounds."

Brooke shakes her head, moisture gathering in her eyes and a bead of a tear falling down her face.

I'm moved by her care for her brother, but then Matt is back to being a menace. "Paige-ay bay-bay. We can be Mage-ay. That will be *our* name."

I catch Paige's eye roll. "No."

"But…so…good. That name." Matt slurs the words together.

"No," Paige says again, giving him the water bottle and watching as he gulps it down. "C'mon, Matt. Let's get you to your cabin."

"We…can….cuddle."

"Nope," Paige responds. "No cuddling."

Paige waves me over. "Help me, please."

I grimace as I help her pull Matt out of the chair. He's not very steady on his feet, and he wobbles toward Paige. She starts to crumple under his dead weight, but I heave him over to me.

"To his cabin?" I ask.

"Yeah," she grunts. "I'll bring some chips and water over." She pants. "And tell Lucas and Jorge to keep an eye on him tonight."

"I'll stay with him until they get back."

It's a long trudge up the path to the cabins.

And with every step, all I can think of is Paige as a young girl, having to do this for her mom. An adult that was supposed to love and care for her unconditionally, but didn't.

19

PAIGE

Connor helps me haul Matt to the boys' cabin. I'm raw. Every step I take reminds me of Mom. Every move Matt makes chafes my heart. From the slurred words to the lack of control and zero inhibitions. It's enough to hurt, and it does. But I am a master at masking it.

I stop just outside the cabin door. One look at Connor tells me he knows exactly what I'm feeling. I swallow down the emotional pain while my breath hitches. "I…" I start, but don't know what to say. I can't go in that cabin. I can't put Matt to bed. I can't watch him to make sure he doesn't asphyxiate on his own vomit. *I can't.*

Connor shifts Matt so he's leaning more solidly against him. "I'll stay with him."

I huff out a relieved "Ok."

"Uh. What do I need to do, exactly, do you think?" Connor asks.

I'm sure that he's dealt with intoxicated people since he managed a hotel before, but the fact that he's asking me validates everything I've been through. It's also too much.

"I...I'll get Lucas and Jorge. Just keep him on his side."

"Ok." Connor nods and I escape.

When I arrive back at the fire, Brooke stands up. "I'm so sorry, Paige."

I hold up my hand to stop her. I can't hear it right now. "Lucas, Jorge. One of you needs to be with Matt. I'm not staying there overnight to babysit him."

Lucas flashes Brooke a smile and stands, looping the guitar strap case over his shoulder. "Sure. I'm an RA at school, I've dealt with lots of people under the influence. I know when to call for help and when to let it go."

The way it doesn't seem to faze him shocks me. But the relief that courses through me is also shocking. "Great. Connor's with him right now."

Lucas gives a salute and saunters off toward the cabins, but that leaves me in the awkward position of either turning and trailing him or sitting by the fire.

Stephanie walks over to me and puts a hand on my arm. "Hey," she says quietly, concern in her voice. "Are you ok?"

I smile as best I can, but I can't answer her question. "I'm going to head to the cabin."

Jorge stands up. "I'll handle the fire, it should be out in a few minutes."

I nod, then turn on my heel to head back to the cabin, alone.

Brooke and Stephanie murmur something, but I don't stay to hear what they say because tears are threatening and I've been through theme parks' worth of emotional rollercoasters today.

The sound of footsteps behind me is just enough of a cue to wipe the tears from my eyes with the corners of Connor's sleeve cuffs.

Connor's sleeves. Why do I like that so much? And why am I so unlovable?

Brooke walks up next to me. "My brother is a lot better than you've seen."

I frown while her words float away.

"He's immature, Paige. I know that, but if you're interested..." She trails off.

Stephanie pipes in. "She's not."

I wonder for a moment how she could know that.

"She's interested in Connor," Stephanie says, as if it's obvious. "And Matt isn't right for her anyway."

The matter-of-fact manner that Stephanie has makes me want to ask her *how* she knew my thoughts and voiced them so concisely. I didn't even know how to say that.

"Are you?" Brooke asks.

I swallow. "Uh. Um," I stutter. "I'm. Nothing's happening."

Stephanie grabs my hand and gives it a friendly squeeze. "Whatever's going on, it's going to be ok. Connor's a good guy. I think you'd be good together. He's interested in you, Paige. But you don't have to be in a relationship with anyone if you don't want to be."

We reach the ladies' cabin, and the motion sensor light flips on. Brooke looks me in the eye, her pink-streaked hair hanging down past her shoulders. "I'll tell Matt to leave you alone."

"Thanks," I mutter. "I...I'm not..." I don't know what to say because I want to be honest, but I also don't want to say I like Connor. Even if they know I do. I settle on, "I'm not interested in Matt."

Brooke looks crestfallen for a moment, but she and Matt have a weird twin bond thing going on.

"I think he's a good guy, but he's not for me," I add.

"I get it," Brooke says with a nod. "I will talk to him."

We ready our things, and when I finally slide into my bed, my limbs relax. It's only the soft sinking of my body into the mattress that tells me how tense I was this entire day.

Stephanie breaks the silence of the darkness. "So, Paige, what are you doing tomorrow?"

I grin in the dark when I think about it. "Connor's taking me to Marquette to change my phone number."

I can just make out the glimmer of teeth as Stephanie grins back at me from across the bunk room.

20

CONNOR

I dress in nicer clothes than usual for our trip to Marquette. It's about an hour away, and while there are small towns closer, Marquette is the closest biggest city complete with phone service providers. In the middle of the nightI decided to trust God with the *pursue her* directive.

I meet Paige at eight a.m. by my SUV. She's already waiting for me when I come out of the mess hall after showering in my personal room. After last night with Matt, I am glad to have my own private suite.

Paige stands, blinking in the morning sun. Her red hair is down, falling below her shoulder blades, and she's wearing a loose green t-shirt and dark jean capris. My eyes scan her, noting how beautiful she is, but they snag on her hands. She holds my black zip-up jacket at her side.

I don't want her to give it back.

"Hey," she says as I approach.

"Hey." I keep my voice as even as I can.

"I brought your sweatshirt back." She thrusts it toward me, holding it awkwardly away from her body.

I frown, but try to stop it. Her eyes lock on mine and she steps backward slightly.

"Unless, oh my gosh, I'm so sorry," she says. "I wasn't thinking. You want me to wash it?"

"No."

She blinks, still holding the sweatshirt out. My heart hammers.

"I don't want that back."

She looks at the ground. "Oh."

"Paige." She turns her eyes up. "I liked you wearing it."

She looks away again, but I see the blush climbing her cheeks and obscuring the freckles that have popped across her cheeks the past few weeks from being in the sun.

"Paige." I say it again, unsure of where this confidence is coming from, but running with it. "I know you said you can't date me, but I would very much like to. When you're ready. If you're ever ready."

I step forward to take the sweatshirt before she drops it in the dirt, but she pulls the sweatshirt back and then reaches out her other hand to touch my arm. Her eyes bore into mine, and a flicker of fear passes through her. She looks away before she looks back at me.

"Ok," she says. "When I'm ready. I don't know when I will be, but I…I like you too."

"Really?" I ask, heartened by her response. "Can I hug you?"

She nods and I step forward, folding her into my arms. She is warm and soft and solid all at the same time. I bring my nose down and catch the smell of her hair.

"I've wanted to do that for a long time," I whisper to her.

"Me too."

I swallow down my regret over not talking to her sooner and keeping my distance from all the counselors.

She steps out of the hug far too soon for my liking, but I remember my manners enough to open the passenger door for her. She climbs in and gives a shy smile as I shut the door.

When I sit in the driver's seat and start the ignition, I catch Paige's wide eyes on my shirt sleeve.

"You have a tattoo," she blurts.

"Yeah. I don't usually show it. It's for me. This shirt has shorter sleeves than most."

"Oh, sorry." She looks away.

"Hey." I catch her gaze before beginning to drive down the drive and off Camp CGO property. "You don't need to apologize. I'm glad you saw it."

She smiles, then asks, "What is it?"

I push up my sleeve with my left hand, keeping my right on the wheel.

I hear a hiss of breath and worry that maybe Paige doesn't like tattoos. Her finger lightly traces the outline. "It's beautiful."

"Thanks." I huff against the emotion building in my throat. The woman is making it really hard to focus on driving. "I got it to remind me of here actually."

She hums, and it's silent for a minute. "Thanks for taking me into the city today."

I shake my head, acknowledging that I heard her, but it doesn't seem right to answer that with a typical 'you're welcome,' so I stay silent.

Paige sits quietly, and the silence is awkward, so I flip on the radio. The strains of something familiar hit my ears, but I can't tell what it is until the lyrics begin.

I catch a glimpse of Paige out of the corner of my eye smiling broadly. I don't think I've ever seen her smile like this. And I can't imagine why the haunting ballad "The Wreck of the Edmund Fitzgerald" makes her smile.

"Paige?" I ask. "Why are you smiling?"

The silence that follows tells me that she's been *humming*.

"I love this song."

I blink. That's kind of a weird thing to love.

I raise a brow. "You love Gordon Lightfoot's 'The Wreck of the Edmund Fitzgerald'?"

"Yeah," she responds. "Don't you? It's my favorite song." And then in a move I do not see coming, she flips the volume up louder and begins *singing along* with Gordon Lightfoot. It takes a moment for me to process this. Paige, singing along loudly and happily to the saddest song I know, *in my car*.

I'm glad there's no one else on these backroads because my eyes are constantly drawn to her. I've been reserved, but so has she. I did not anticipate shipwrecks being the topic that drew her out of her shell, but I'll run with it. There's only one thing to do, and that's to join in.

Our voices join together in the cabin of the car, remembering the twenty-nine men in the shipwreck.

When the song ends, Paige flips the volume dial back to its regular setting, and the *tick* song comes on. I itch to change the channel, but Paige doesn't seem to mind. For all I know, this could be her second favorite song. *I really hope it isn't her second favorite song.*

Paige's sigh draws me out of my thoughts about this stupid song. "I've always wanted to go and see the memorial service. To hear the bells ring."

"Where's that at?" I ask, my mind immediately conjuring up ways of making that desire a reality.

"Mariner's Cathedral? It's in Detroit."

"Oh." I shove my dreams down. Detroit is far from here, like hours and hours.

"Yeah. I've never been over the Bridge, or even out of the Upper Peninsula. One day." She turns to look out the window at the scenery flying past.

I'm shocked. "You've never been? Anywhere but *here*?" I regret the words the moment they fly from my mouth. I try to soften my tone. "Why?"

Her shoulders slump. "Money. Time. Things aren't easy when you have a parent with…like mine."

I frown. Paige's teen years must have been so difficult. It explains the piece-of-junk car at least.

"Hey," she says. "Have you been to the museum?"

"The museum?" I ask. I'm going to need more clarification.

"The Shipwreck Museum."

"Oh. No, I haven't."

"We should go. When camp's over."

I smile. "It's a date."

21

PAIGE

I think I asked Connor on a date to the Shipwreck Museum. Could I possibly be any more awkward? But also, internally, I'm giddy because he said yes.

I'm not sure what I'm doing with Connor, but at least I know that he likes me and wants to date me. I don't know when I'll be ready for that, but one day, I think I will be.

The closer we get to Marquette, the more I wish I had a turtle shell to hide in. I'm grateful Connor's taking me into the city today, but the more I think about it, the worse I feel. Connor's *not* my boyfriend, and it's not his job to help me out. I know he volunteered to drive me, but I wonder what's in it for him.

"I hope it's ok that you're taking me today," I say.

Connor scratches the shell of his ear. "I offered to, didn't I?" He doesn't sound offended.

"Yeah, but I hope you're getting something out of this too."

His eyes drift off the road to my face for a moment before turning back to the road. "Paige—"

"I mean, I hope you can use this trip because you have things to do in Marquette too."

I catch the frown on his face and the tensing of his jaw. "Yeah," he says gruffly. "I have stuff I can take care of. Which phone store do you need?"

I pull up the GPS map on his car's touch screen and discover he's already programmed the right one. "This one's good."

"Ok." He says nothing else, and I am uncomfortable with the amount of vulnerability I've shown around Connor the past few days. I don't tell people things about me for a reason. Panic about him knowing too much sets in. I have to look away from him. The soft strains of the country music are soothing, and I lean my forehead against the cool glass of the window, making sure I'm angled away from Connor's gaze. The pressure builds in my eyes and I blink back tears, finding it easier to just keep my eyes shut.

A gentle tap on my shoulder wakes me. I'm disoriented and confused. I blink open my eyes and see a parking lot.

"Paige, wake up. You can wake up now."

Why is a man telling me to wake up? Why am I in a car?

I give my head a shake and turn bleary eyes toward my left.

Frozen banana icicles.

Connor leans over the center console, his hand gently resting on my shoulder while he softly rubs it. I meet his eyes with my own mortified ones.

"Morning, sunshine." He smiles. "You must have needed that."

"Uh…yeah. Sorry," I say, hoping against hope that I don't have post-nap breath. *Is that a thing?*

"So, I'm going to run into the store to get a few things for CGO while you're dealing with your phone number. I can meet you back here, or if you're done before me, I guess we could meet up later?"

I struggle to think through what he's saying, because his blue eyes are captivating, and I think they've held my thoughts hostage. "Ok," is all I can manage at first. Then I think a little harder. "How long do you want to stay before we head back to camp?"

"I need to confirm something with Father Matthi, and then he has Mass at four, so at least until then."

"Oh." I wasn't expecting to spend five hours in the city, but I guess I will. "Yeah, I'll explore when I'm done. And meet you at the church at four?"

He swallows, and I watch as his Adam's apple bobs. "Yeah, ok."

I grab my bag and phone and open the door to begin taking care of something I really should have dealt with a long time ago. Unfortunately, I'm still buckled in.

I jerk back because the seat belt is doing its job admirably at restraining me from careening into an abyss. I mutter under my breath and twist to unbuckle it, but the belt is locked, and I can't reach the button to release it.

Connor's low rumble of laughter hits my ears, and my face flames. He leans further over the console and grabs my hand, then guides it to the release button. He lets go as soon as I've clicked it and am freed from my overly restraining seatbelt.

My face flames. "Thank you."

Amusement dances in his eyes. "I've never seen anyone so frustrated by a seatbelt before."

"Then you haven't seen the clips of angry people when the seatbelt law got passed," I quip back.

Connor sobers for a moment. "I'll see you at four at the church. Text me with your new number if you want to meet up before." He hops out of the car, whistling something that sounds an awful lot like

"The Wreck of the Edmund Fitzgerald."

At this moment, I hate my heart. I hate that it's calloused and bruised, because I know *he's* good. And I know he doesn't deserve to be stuck with someone like me.

I hate that I am a burden.

22

CONNOR

I force myself not to stall by the front of the store and watch for Paige. The plaza has multiple stores, and the large home improvement store does have things I need for the camp. A conversation with Chet a few days ago reminded me that I should have an extra weather radio, spare batteries, and since Lucas has volunteered to take care of the flower beds because he's studying botany, I pick up a hose and special nozzle just for him.

All these items are not placed in any logical order around the store, so I find myself running back and forth as I search for them. Hopefully by this time next year, I'll know where everything is.

When I finally leave the store and place my purchases in the car, I pop into the phone store to see if Paige is still there. The bell above the door rings.

"Hey, man. Welcome. Can I help you with your phone today?"

I blink, my eyes adjusting from the bright sunshine outside to the dim light of the store. *Why are phone stores always so dark?*

"What?" I ask, surprised by the man standing so close to the door and, by default, me.

"What can I help you with?" he says. This time, I get a good look at him. He's average height, has bleach-blond hair, and is wearing khaki pants and flip-flops, along with the vertical-striped phone store polo. The ensemble is ridiculous and I'd laugh, but I have enough training in hospitality to *not* do that.

"Oh, nothing. I was wondering if my friend was still here."

"*That* girl is your friend?" the man asks incredulously.

I find his nametag. His name is Marvin. *Marvin.*

I fix him with a look, because what is that supposed to mean?

"Sorry, man, it's just that girl is *definitely* outta your league."

I shrug. "Did she leave?"

"Yeah. We got her all set up with her new stuff, and she left, like, fifteen minutes ago."

"Thanks," I say, turning to leave.

"Dude…I kept her number and I'll be getting after that," Marvin says to my retreating back. Except he doesn't say 'getting after.'

My blood rushes to my ears and all I can hear is a roaring sound. I take a step forward and grip Marvin's polo in my fist. "Marvin," I snarl. "Do *not* contact her."

Marvin's hands fly up in the 'I surrender' pose as he tries to back away. "Dude, sorry, didn't know she was yours."

"Marv." I deliberately shorten his name and keep my voice low and deep. "Don't even think about her again."

"Uhh. Yeah. Ok." Marv gulps.

I drop his shirt from my fist and wipe my sweaty palms on my jeans. I'm startled when Marvin thrusts a phone in my face and takes a picture.

"You can leave now, sir," Marvin says. "You will not be welcome back at this store after threatening me."

I roll my eyes. I don't know what the law is, but something

about him keeping her number and planning on contacting her is *wrong*. I will *not* be returning to this store. Also I don't even use this service provider.

I push the door a little harder than intended after that encounter, making the bell clang instead of cheerfully jingle. My whole body tenses. I want to know that Paige is ok after interacting with that slimy man, but I also don't have her number anymore.

I climb into my car and let my forehead hit the steering wheel as I take several deep breaths. Marquette is walkable, but I have no idea where Paige went. All I know is that she will call or text me if she wants to, and she'll meet me at the church this afternoon.

A glance at the clock tells me I have hours to kill before meeting Father Matthi.

A few more deep breaths, and my body calms. Now that I'm not shaking with anger, I can think clearly. The campers arrive tomorrow, and I suspect I won't have much free time after that. I smile wryly. A sub sandwich from a shop in town and a trip to Presque Isle Park with a book sounds like a great way to spend the afternoon.

My phone alarm jolts me from the pages of my book. *Reach* is hard to put down, but I'll have to in order to make my appointment with Father Matthi. I push off the sand and brush my hands down my legs to clear the soft grains from my jeans before I climb into my car and drive to the church.

There's a little bit of nervousness rolling around in my stomach about meeting with Father Matthi. He's more Tom's friend than mine, but he wanted to discuss how things would go when he helps us at camp.

I shift into park and step out of the car, stretching my hands over my head before I walk into the church office.

"Hi," an older woman with gray curly hair and hot pink cat-eye glasses perched on her nose calls. "How can I help you?"

My voice crackles as I speak. Darn nerves. "Hi." I clear my throat. "I'm here to see Father Matthi."

"Oh, are you Connor?"

I nod.

"Great. Father said you can meet with him in the back garden. Do you know where that is?"

"No, sorry."

"Oh. I see. You're not from around here. I can tell from your accent. I'm Theadora, but everyone calls me Teddy."

I blink at her, but she keeps talking, completely unperturbed by my confusion.

"Yeah, you don't say 'eh' or 'sorry' the same as most Yoopers."

"Oh. Sorry?" I respond, putting emphasis on the 'or.' She smiles, then sticks a foot out from the side of her desk. It's clad in a walking boot covered with vinyl stickers that range from an Upper Peninsula cutout to a pirate ship to an Appalachian Trail symbol to a pink pony with balloons.

"I'd take you back there myself, but I'm not supposed to do much walking. It's not hard to find though. Go straight down the path between the church and this building, and then turn right at the statue."

"Ok," I say, smiling at the woman because she's eccentric, but she also reminds me a bit of my mom. Then, because this woman's stickers are as eclectic as they come, I say, "I like your stickers."

"Oh." She laughs. "My grandchildren insisted." She points to the other side of the boot. There's an astronaut, more ponies, a race car, and a sticker that says 'pot head,' but the words are centered over a stick figure whose head has been replaced by a coffee pot. I burst into laughter.

"Yeah. They know Meemaw loves coffee, so my five-year-old granddaughter insisted on this one."

I give Teddy a wave as I start off down the path, still chortling. It doesn't take long before I find Father Matthi. He kneels in the dirt where he's weeding in a pair of hot pink garden gloves. "Hey, Father Matthi."

Father Matthi gets up and tosses a weed into the orange bucket by his side. He claps his hands to shake off the dirt, then removes the pink garden gloves. "Hi, Connor." He extends a clean hand for me to shake. I do. He looks down at the pink garden gloves and shrugs. "I always lose them if I buy a more neutral color. The pink sticks out from wherever I've left them."

"Solid reasoning. More men should consider the benefits of neon pink." We don't know each other that well, but it's well enough that I can give a bit of a quip.

Father Matthi grins, the corners of his eyes crinkling and his tan skin stretching wide as he smiles. His brown eyes have a way of looking at you as if he knows everything. It's unnerving, but also comforting. "So, what do you need? How can I help? Let's sit here." He points to two cafe-style chairs around a small metal table.

I pull my chair out and sit, but my frame is quite a bit bigger than Father Matthi's. He is probably close to Paige's height. *Why am I always comparing everything to Paige?* I grimace.

"Connor? Is everything alright?"

I shake my head and blink. "Yeah, yes. Everything's fine. I needed to make sure we're good for the Saturday evening vigil Masses for the Catholic children we're hosting at camp."

"Yes. But you know that," he says gently. "What's really bothering you?"

I wrack my brain for what to say, because nothing's really bothering me except for Paige, and then hoping everything goes well at camp, and all the things with Kaleigh, and...a lot of things that he can't possibly know about.

"Tom told me that there's a woman."

Tom's a gossip, apparently. I scratch my neck to buy some time, because I don't know how much I want to say.

"I thought gossiping was a sin," I mumble.

Father Matthi smiles. "Yes, it is. But Tom wasn't gossiping, Connor. He cares about you and the young lady. Sometimes, it's good to talk about it."

I sigh. His words sound a lot like the words I said to Paige last night. "I'm confident in the team, but nervous that I'll come up short with the campers and their parents, and disappoint my brother. But mostly, I just don't know how to act around Paige."

Father Matthi quirks a brow. "And why's that?"

"I…" I scrub the light stubble on my jaw. "I had a long relationship with someone in California." I choose my words carefully, because even though I know Father Matthi is a good man and a good priest, I'm still raw, and I'm afraid he'll challenge me to dig deeper than I want to go.

He nods in understanding and waits for me to continue.

"She was… I really thought she was the one, and I proposed." I opt to leave out the *Twilight* theme. "She said no. Repeatedly. It was embarrassing, so I packed up my life and fled California to come back here and run this camp for my brother and his wife."

"Why was it so embarrassing? You asked and she said no."

I grimace. "I staged something elaborate. To make her happy and fulfill a fantasy of hers, I guess. We'd been together for years, so I wanted to show her I was something special. Something worth hanging onto. She said no, and the videographers I hired recorded it. Chet destroyed the copy they sent to me, but I know Kaleigh was given a copy too."

"Oh." Father Matthi frowns. "So you did something grand—a grand gesture if you will—for a woman you loved, to show her your love and propose marriage, but she rejected you, and it's on video somewhere?"

"Yeah, that about sums it up."

"Are you worried that this woman will do something with that video?"

"Not really. I moved across the country to let her keep our friends, her job, and her life as normal as possible after we broke up. Or, after she broke up with me."

"So really, you are concerned you won't be good enough for the campers or the other woman Tom mentioned because…"

"If I was with Kaleigh for so long, and she knew everything about me, and she *did* after so many years together, but I still wasn't enough for her, how could I possibly be enough for *anyone*?"

"Have you ever considered"—he pauses for a moment—"that she's still holding you back?"

The truth of his words hits me hard. Nausea churns in my stomach. He's right. Kaleigh still has a hold on my life. I haven't let go.

"How do you let go?" I whisper.

"I think the answer to that is different for each person. But faith and trust. Prayer and asking. Being humble enough to ask God for what we need, knowing He knows our requests before we do but desires our cooperation with Him and His plan for us." Father Matthi stands up. "I have Mass at four. Stay for it."

I nod.

He leaves to prepare, but I sit in the chair for a bit longer thinking about letting Kaleigh go and pursuing Paige.

23

PAIGE

Church is familiar and terrifying. I told Connor I'd meet him here, but I'd rather be *anywhere* else. After dealing with creepy Marvin at the phone store, I didn't want to talk to anyone for a while. I wandered around Marquette, had lunch at a cafe, and spent most of the day at a beach where I watched families play in the Lake and tried to calm my body by focusing on the gentle cadence of the waves.

No matter how hard I tried to keep an eye on each wave, every so often, a larger wave would break on the rocks, spraying me with droplets. Unpredictable, beautiful, calm, and violent all at once. A lot like life, I guess.

Connor's car is in the parking lot by the office, but he isn't with it. He never said if he'd be at Mass or if he'd just be waiting for me at four. Since he's not there, he must have gone to Mass.

I slip into the very back pew of the church, trying to make myself as small as I can. I don't belong here. I'm too broken, too angry, too full of shame. It washes over me, thick, hot, and suffocating. I don't make eye contact with anyone even though the church is full of happy Mass-goers. I know my shame must be present for all to see. Despite the very real temptation to look for Connor or to scream and run out of here, I keep my eyes down the entire time. But I listen, and something pierces me in the heart.

I stay in the pew the entire time, even when people go to receive communion. I know I'm not ready, and not in a state of grace. But the idea of confession feels like a boulder tied to my ankles as I stand on the edge of a Lake Superior cliff. In short, not good.

The final notes of "Amazing Grace" float through the building, and I wait for the shuffle of people's feet to leave before I grab my phone to text Connor that I'm here.

A tear leaks out of the corner of my eye, and I swipe it away in frustration. I scowl at my now-wet palm as movement crosses my periphery.

"May I?" a man asks. I see his black pants but don't look at his face.

"Sure." I scoot down the pew a little further to leave us some space.

"Do you need any help?"

"No, no, thank you. Just meeting a friend here."

"Well, you look like you could use something."

The instinct to look up and see who I'm talking to wins out. *Of course*, I mumble internally. It's the priest. "Uh. No, I just need to text my friend. He's my ride back to camp."

"Ahhh. Is your friend Connor?"

"Yes," I say, looking into Father's brown eyes. I couldn't lie to him even if I wanted to.

"Connor was here for Mass. Did you not see him?"

"No. Maybe he didn't see me when he left."

"Sitting with your head down and trying to be invisible does make it possible for someone to miss you in a crowd, I believe."

I start to smile, but can't seem to get my face to cooperate, because *how did I end up here? Talking to a priest, of all people?*

"Do you want to talk about it? I've been told I'm a good listener. And sometimes it helps."

I shake my head no and then look at my feet, because I don't want to talk about it, and I don't have words.

"When you're ready, then. Do you have a faith?"

I glance up at him. "I did…I guess. It's complicated."

"It always is," he says. "I'm Father Matthi. I'll be at the camp every Saturday for the next few weeks. If you want to talk, I'll be ready." He pats the pew twice before getting up and walking away.

I unlock my phone and find Connor's contact information. As much as this day has beaten me raw, he is my ride to camp. I don't know what to do with the feelings coursing through my body, but I do know that I need to be back and ready for the campers tomorrow. It is my job and livelihood.

I start to type out a text to Connor. I hear low voices in the back of the church, but I ignore them. I delete what I type at least three times. Finally, I settle on:

Paige

Sorry. Needed some time to myself today. This is my new number. Let me know where to meet you. I'm at the church.

I hit send and let out a breath, long and slow.

A buzz sounds to my left, and my traitorous eyes look over to see what made the noise.

Connor slides into the pew next to me. "Hey," he says, his voice quiet, low, and serious. "Are you alright, Paige?"

The way he says my name is a gentle caress, and I wish I could hear him say it over and over again until I believed I was worthy of someone speaking to me in that soft tone.

"Yeah," I say, but my voice breaks. Before I can stop it, tears erupt out of my eyes and flow down my cheeks, and there is no way to stop the dam from breaking. I shake and wrap my arms around my torso, just like I did as a little girl when Mom was drunk, or shouting at Dad, or shouting at me, or slamming things, breaking things, breaking me.

Something warm and solid lands on my shoulders, and then suddenly I'm pulled into Connor's embrace, my cheek resting just on his shoulder.

I can't stop it any more than I could stop a fully loaded freight train, and Connor feels warm and right and he's *here*.

I'm not sure how long we sit together, his arms around me, sheltering me from everything that hurts, but I know I'm safe with him. Eventually, my sobs subside, and I still. I break the embrace and don't look at him.

"Sorry." I wipe my nose with the back of my sleeve. I know it's not classy, but it's the best I've got right now.

"Hey," he says. And when I don't look up, he tips my chin to meet his eyes. "It was a big day."

"Sorry," I say again.

Connor chuckles softly, and even though his arms aren't around me, the rumbles vibrate through the pew. "Today, I met the most interesting woman. She told me she knew I wasn't from here because I don't say 'sorry' like everyone else."

The absurdity of that statement gives rise to my own bubble of laughter, which quickly turns into a hiccup. I *hate* hiccups.

"I think I'm ready to go home," I say between hiccups.

A grin spreads over Connor's face as he extends a hand to me and stands, helping me up from the pew. He lets go of my hand as he genuflects toward the tabernacle but takes it again once he's standing —and I let him. We walk hand in hand to the car, and I think that maybe I do deserve someone who sees me in my brokenness and still wants me.

24

CONNOR

There are very few things that could have filled my wounded pride the way holding Paige did.

Truthfully, Paige isn't the only one who had a hard day. Between Marvin's disgusting creepiness, not being able to contact Paige, then talking with Father Matthi and realizing I've hung onto Kaleigh for far too long, I'm emotionally shredded.

I can only imagine how Paige feels. Cutting your mom out of your life completely like that *is* a big—and painful—deal.

I don't let go of her hand as we reach the car. Instead, I bring her hand to my lips and kiss her knuckles. Her bright red hair frames her face, and I want more than anything to kiss the lips that have formed a perfect O. I stop myself by opening the door for her before I drop her hand.

I know what I need to do. I spent time sitting in that uncomfortable chair realizing that I could let Kaleigh go. I didn't have to hang onto a relationship that wasn't endgame. When I stood up and felt the weight of everything Kaleigh roll off, I understood what Paige needed from me. And while I understand that she needs time, I also understand in a way I haven't before today that she needs someone to *stay*. I will not leave her.

The readings at Mass, the prayers, the familiarity, the peace—it was something I've been longing for, and with every moment I spent in prayer, it became more and more clear to me that Paige is special. That I want a future with her, and that it's my job to show her that she can trust me.

I begin the drive back to Camp CGO, but a sudden inspiration strikes. I turn onto a side street lined with houses and pull over. "Can I take you to dinner, Paige?"

Paige looks up from her phone. Her eyes are bloodshot and her lashes damp, but I think she looks beautiful. Her lip trembles. "I…I don't know. Maybe it's not a good idea right now. I'm a mess."

"I've heard food usually helps with that. But if you would really rather eat at camp, we can go back and have the cook's special."

"Who's cooking today?" Paige asks while a small smile plays across her lips. Each counselor has been assigned cooking duties for the camp. Most of the dinner menus are easy, but a few items have been more challenging for some. Matt's first time making pancakes resulted in acrid smoke and charred flapjacks.

"Pretty sure it's Matt on the rotation. He's making pancakes again."

Paige swallows. "Then it's probably for the best if we let him burn our portions. It's an act of service to *not* go back and eat."

"My thoughts exactly."

Paige gives a brief smile before turning her attention back to her phone, typing away methodically. "But it needs to be some-place casual."

"Yes, ma'am," I say. "I know a place."

I head around the block, turning back toward downtown. I maneuver out of the busy downtown to the waterfront and park in one of the designated lots for The North Ore Restaurant. Paige is still typing on her phone.

"Paige?"

She jerks her eyes up to meet mine. "Sorry," she says. "I was trying to send a message to everyone about my new phone number.
And...my dad texted back."

"Oh?" I really hope he was encouraging about this, but Paige
hasn't mentioned much about her dad to me. I know he raised her
after her mom left, but I don't think they're particularly close.

"Yeah. He..." Paige looks down at her lap and her slender neck
cords. "He said he was proud of me." She brushes her hand over her
face, and I see the sheen of a tear she wiped away.

"Are you ready?" I ask, tipping my head toward the restaurant.

"Yeah." As if on cue, her stomach growls. "Yeah, I am."

I hop out of the car and circle to her side, only to find that she's
already exited. She slides her phone into the back pocket of her jeans
and swings her bag over her shoulder. "Which one are we going to?"
She scans the rows of buildings.

I take her hand again. "North Ore."

Her eyes widen. "Isn't that kind of fancy? I'm not really prepared
for that. I mean, I look like *this*."

The invitation to look her over is too tempting to resist, so I do.
My eyes catch her toned legs and smaller frame figure but are drawn
back to her face in moments. I'm not even embarrassed about checking her out as I look into her eyes and inform her of the truth. "You
look beautiful."

A flush creeps over her face and she looks away from me, gazing
out at the water. "It is beautiful here," she whispers. "I love the Lake."

"Me too," I murmur before we stroll across the lot to the restaurant. I know it's not exactly a date, but it feels like one, and I grin to
myself because I can feel that this is the first of many.

25

PAIGE

For being last minute, this certainly feels like a date. It's everything I ever imagined for a first date, and I only wish I'd been less cowardly this morning when Connor asked if we could date. The North Ore is rustic, with Edison bulb lights strung overhead, round wooden tables surrounded by heavy metal chairs, and the neutral tones of hardwood everywhere with decor that nods to the iron ore industry and Great Lakes shipping.

The hostess asks Connor if he'd prefer indoor or outdoor seating. I don't miss the way she subtly appraises him before turning on the charm. She leans over the hostess stand, giving a view of her impressive cleavage, and smiles up at Connor. She bats her eyes and twirls her blonde locks around her finger while she waits for his response.

My body tenses, and the familiar fear of someone else being chosen rolls over my skin like a wave. Apparently Connor doesn't miss it either because he pulls me close to his side, wraps his arm around my waist, and leans down to ask me in a whisper intimate enough to make a point, "What would you prefer?"

"Out—" I stutter as I catch the flecks of gray in his blue eyes. *Get a grip, Paige.* "Outside."

"Perfect." The hostess snags two menus off the stack and adjusts the deep v-cut of her t-shirt higher with a haughty snort. "Follow me," she says, her voice clipped. She leads us through the busy restaurant and to the outside patio. She stops at a two-seater table in the back corner. We have a perfect view of the Lake over the half wall separating the patio from the sidewalk and street. In the distance, colorful sailboats bob on the gently cresting waves.

"Bern'll be your server today. Enjoy." The hostess tosses the menus onto the table and gives me a look that says she would enjoy her job a lot more if I wasn't here.

I worry my bottom lip between my teeth. I despise confrontation.

Connor pulls my chair out and pushes it back in when I'm seated. I'm surprised by the gesture. No one has ever pulled out a chair for me. No one has ever *chosen* me when faced with another option.

Tears begin welling up again.

This has to be a record for the most times a person can cry in front of the guy they like that they aren't even dating.

I tense my jaw and grit my teeth to stop the tears from falling.

Connor sits in the chair across from me and stretches his long legs out before opening the menu.

"Do you know what you want?" he asks after a moment of perusal.

A quick glance at the prices has my eyes widening. "Just a salad."

Connor's eyes narrow. "You can get a salad if you want, Paige, but I'm buying this meal, and I insist you have an actual entree."

"I can't let you do that. This is…"

"You made a huge step forward today. It doesn't seem like it, but it's something to celebrate. That's what *friends* do." The emphasis on friends hurts slightly, because I want to be more, but it's my own fault we aren't.

"Yeah, but it's too much and I…I'm not—"

"Don't you dare say you're not worth it, Paige." He leans closer to me over the table, his eyes boring into mine as his hand finds mine and flips my palm up. His fingers trail circles on my palm and my wrist. "You are worth it. You are worth *everything*."

I am frozen. I can't move. Connor has bewitched me, body and soul, and I understand exactly what Mr. Darcy meant when he said that to Elizabeth. This is a gender-flipped situation, but still.

"I'm going to order an appetizer and an entree, and you are going to do the same because I know you work hard, and I know you had a hard day, and it's ok to let a friend treat you."

"It just feels wrong, letting you pay for it, when…" I stop myself.

He knows exactly what I mean because he gives me a half smirk when he responds, "We could change that, you know." He still draws circles with his thumb on my palm.

"I…" I've been brave today. I've been brave more than once. I stared down something that I've avoided for years, and then I faced an entire church building. I've shed enough tears to fill half of Lake Superior in front of him today, and still Connor chose me over the hussy hostess.

I swallow the nerves down. "I'd like that," I mumble.

Connor stops tracing my palm and squeezes his much larger hand around mine. I meet his eyes for a fraction of a second, half afraid of what I will see and half afraid of missing his reaction. His blue eyes glitter and his lips curve into a genuine smile. "You have no idea how happy that makes me."

"Awwww. Alright, how sweet to have big brother taking little sister out for her birthday dinner. Congratulations on turning twenty-one, honey. You get a drink on the house today," the waitress, an older woman with gray hair and heavily laden with jewelry, interrupts.

Connor jerks back at her voice, clearly surprised. "I…uh… what?" he asks.

"Willa said you're taking your sister out for her twenty-first birth-day. Congratulations, sweetie. It's nice to see a brother being brotherly for once."

I blink in horror. The implication that we're brother and sister makes my body burn with embarrassment.

Connor is a little faster this time. "We're not brother and sister. And it's not her twenty-first birthday. Actually, this is a date." He waggles his eyebrows at the waitress in a suggestive manner, but it's also so overdone that it's funny.

Bern's eyes widen, then narrow as they land on me. "So I take it you're not twenty-one today?"

"No."

"The things people do to get a free drink around here," she mutters.

I hate the way that sounds. It sounds like she's talking about me trying to game the system, or steal, or something.

Connor faces Bern, his mouth drawn into a thin line. "Paige has never once asked for a free anything. And since Willa lied to you, I suggest you take it out on *her*, not on your patrons."

Heat floods my body for a whole different reason. Connor just stood up for me, and it's...really, really attractive.

Bern shakes her head and steps back. "Oh my. I'm sorry, sir. Miss Willa's been going through some tough times, but she shouldn't have done what she did. I'll straighten her out. And I didn't mean any disrespect, miss. I have people trying to get free things every day, and I'm a bit soured on the twenty-one-year-old birthday drink policy around here. That drink comes from someone's pay, and I'll bet you can tell whose."

"I don't drink," I blurt.

An awkward silence follows.

Connor smiles gently at me before he says, "I think we'll each have water tonight. And Paige, do you know what you'd like to order?"

Emboldened by Connor's attention and care, I glance at the menu and order the thing that I really want. "I'll have the salmon risotto with a cup of the whitefish chowder to start."

It's only after Bern leaves that I realize I ordered the most expensive thing on the menu.

26

CONNOR

Hospitality is more a degree in dealing with difficult people than anything else. Entitled people, jealous people, ambitious people—I've seen and dealt with them all. But the hostess at this restaurant, with her manipulative attempt to ruin my date with Paige, takes the cake for the most vindictive person I've dealt with.

Never mind the fact that I don't even know her. She saw something she liked—me, presumably— and decided that I had to be hers. I'm no stranger to having women indicate their interest. It *does* come with the territory of being somewhat attractive and behind the front desk of a hotel. But I am a person, not an object. I always hated these types of interactions in California. This is the first time it's happened since moving to Northern Michigan, and I forgot how itchy they make me.

I release the fist I curled into a ball at my side. "So," I say, trying to relax after *that.*

Paige looks up at me from across the table. "Does that sort of thing happen often when you're on a date?"

"Are you jealous?" I won't lie, I kind of like seeing Paige jealous. But also, I don't want her to worry.

She looks away from my face and gazes out at the Lake.

"You have nothing to worry about with me."

She glances at me. I see the flicker of hope in her eyes and hope that I can prove this. "I guess…" She scrunches her eyes shut. "I guess we need to talk about a few things. About how this works."

"I'm pretty clear on how it works actually." I smirk at her and watch her blush.

"No—that's not…Connor!" Her skin reddens, and the fluster that accompanies it is adorable.

"I'm teasing, Paige. We can go as slowly as you want with this. I'm just happy you're giving me a chance."

Her eyes lift to the heavens. "I meant about the campers and the counselors, and how *this* will all work with them."

"Oh." I don't really want to think about that right now, but she has a point. "I…uh…we have some paperwork we can do and a thing we need to sign for Chet and Ember."

Paige crinkles her brow. "Why would there be paperwork? I thought that there's a no-staff-dating policy…so how would Chet and Ember know?"

I scratch the back of my neck. "I talked to Chet and told him."

Paige's nose scrunches in confusion. "When? We just…like…a minute ago…agreed…to. Are we… I don't know what to say. Wait? What even is this? "

"A DTR, apparently."

Bern arrives with cups of the whitefish chowder and soft, warm rolls in a basket. "Here you two are. That Willa's got nothing on you, sweetheart," she says to Paige as she sets the cup in front of her. "She's got jealousy issues, that one. It's hard to never be chosen, but she's going about it in all the wrong ways."

Paige's shoulders droop and she shrinks back as Bern, oblivious to the impact of her words, turns away.

Paige stares at her soup.

"Paige." *How many times can I say her name in a day?* "I'm serious. I only ever date one woman at a time. I have no interest in hurting you. I'd love it if you were my girlfriend, but I don't know if that's what you want. We can go slow and figure this out together."

"That's what I thought you meant, but then I realized I didn't know. And I know you're not supposed to ask…"

"Who said you aren't supposed to ask?"

"Uh. Every magazine ever written for teen girls."

"Sounds like some solid advice. When in doubt, don't ask."

She picks up her soup spoon and takes a bite. "I can see now how silly that advice is. I just meant, I'm really new at this. I've never had a boyfriend before."

My mind latches onto the word 'boyfriend,' and I have to tell her the truth. "I talked to Chet about how I was going to talk to you. About how I was going to see if you'd like to be with me, romantically. And he sent over paperwork for us. There's a code of conduct too. We can sign and scan everything tonight after we get back."

"Oh," she says around another mouthful of soup. "That's helpful."

"And Paige." She meets my gaze with one of her own intensity. This woman is fathoms deep, and I want to know everything. "We can go as slow with all of this as you're comfortable. But I'm not someone who's going to leave you."

Bern reappears with our risottos. I watch Paige dive into her food and can't believe she didn't think I would spend the price of a full entree for her.

We finish eating, Bern clears the plates, and I slide my card into the black book after giving the receipt a cursory glance. When I close the book, it makes a slapping sound and Paige twitches in her chair.

"What's wrong?" I ask.

"Sorry," she says. "Loud, unexpected noises…are hard for me."

"Why?"

"Uh. I think that might be too much for our first date, Connor," she whispers.

I lean over the table so that I'm as close as I can be to her face while I meet her eyes. "I want to know everything you want to tell me, Paige."

She turns her head back to the Lake. "When I'm ready, I will."

That's good enough for me.

21

PAIGE

Connor is quiet on the ride home, but I am too. Truthfully, I am exhausted. The radio plays soft country music, and the sunset's all golden and orange to the west. Connor's thumb brushes over the back of my hand as he drives until the roads begin winding sharply. When he removes his hand, I immediately miss his touch.

I wrack my brain for some indication that this is normal. *It's normal to be so attracted to a man when you've only had one date, right? A date you didn't even know was coming? And it's normal to cry on him before said first date? And it's definitely normal to admit you've never had a boyfriend on that first date? It's totally normal to envision a future with him, even if you'll never, ever, tell him that, right?*

Ok. No. None of these things sound normal. But really, all I have to go off of is cheesy romantic comedies I watched with Ember and the conversations at the occasional high school girls' sleepover. My research isn't viable.

I stretch my legs out and shift in my seat. Connor clears his throat. "Are you comfortable?"

"Yeah," I murmur as I lean back, letting my head fall against the headrest so that I can see his side profile. It's really not fair that he's so handsome. But I am determined to take advantage of the fact that he's driving and can't see me staring.

"Paige?" Connor asks after a few minutes.

"Hmm?"

"Why are you staring at me?"

I'm busted. "I was just…thinking…about…the campers."

He sighs. "It's going to be great, right? How hard can it be to have forty preteens learning leadership skills on our campus?" His tone is teasing, but I hear the disguised worry under his humor.

"They will all come away from their weeks at CGO changed in some way," I reply. I have to keep it positive. It's a curse. I'm always looking for a way to make things better for people. Usually it's me being smaller, or adding words of wisdom that are never attributed to me. I have the role of supporting friend down, and it's easy to say the right thing here.

"I hope so."

Connor pulls into the gravel parking lot in front of the mess hall, where he parks next to my car. Tom and a man named Archie repaired it. For free.

"Well, there isn't smoke pouring from the building, so that's good." He smiles at me. "I still think we had a much better meal."

"Definitely." I grin. We won't be eating a meal like that for at least four weeks.

He smiles back, and if my legs spontaneously melt and I'm found in a puddle on the ground, I blame the dimples he's flashing at me. He tenses. "Uhh. I know this is awkward, but I think we need to do that paperwork tonight since the campers are arriving tomorrow."

This has to be one of the most awkward ways to end a first date in the history of first dates, but I can see that it is necessary.

"Sure." I try to keep my voice light and breezy, but truthfully, my stomach is churning. I have no idea what the code of conduct will say, but I hope it doesn't permit *too* much. And I also really hope it permits *some* things.

Connor's office is part of a suite of rooms attached to the mess hall. He leads me through the dark and clean mess hall room, down a hallway, and opens a door marked "PRIVATE." He flips on a light as he steps through, and I can see the other rooms attached to the office are a bedroom and a bathroom.

As counselors, we knew where Connor's office was and knew he had his own apartment somewhere around here, but I've never seen it.

He closes the door to the bedroom as he walks by it, but not before I've taken in the navy and gray plaid comforter neatly covering the double bed and the soft glow of evening light coming through the window. His office has a desk and chair, computer, printer, and filing cabinet along one wall. Along the other, a small, old couch with a blanket tossed over the arm and a TV mounted on the wall across from the couch. The floor is polished hardwood, and the honeyed wood continues up the walls. It's rustic, but charming. Everything has a place, and everything is organized. A big window looks out over the greenspace with a giant bell in the center of it. We call it '*the meeting place*'. The few times Connor's mentioned working in hospitality make perfect sense when I see the order and general cleanliness of his space.

He clears his throat. I've been looking around his private space and gawking. I snap my eyes to his, and he holds out a piece of paper. "This is the HR form," he says. "And this is the code of conduct. We have to initial each item and then send it back to HR, and she'll send it to Chet."

At the mention of Chet, my stomach sinks. "Chet knows?"

Connor's eyes crinkle. "He is kind of our boss. And I did tell him I was—"

"No, it's not that. It's that if Chet knows, then so does Ember, and I don't know. I don't like how big of a deal she'll make this. It's too much pressure too soon."

Connor frowns and steps closer. "I asked Chet not to tell Ember until you or I could tell her ourselves." He lowers his voice. "We both agreed that it isn't keeping secrets, it's not giving her anything else to worry about this close to the baby. And also, Paige, you should know no one is pressuring you. I will *never* pressure you, but I will pursue you."

The intensity of his gaze makes me want to do unhinged things. Like jump into his arms and kiss him, or run away because he's saying too much with far too much perfection. It should be illegal. Those two conflicting reactions must have a near-net-zero effect because I lean forward but rock back on my heels, shaking my head.

I glance at the form in my hand. It's pretty simple. It's a legal document saying that I agree I'm in a voluntary relationship with Connor, that my relationship with him will not impact my duties as a camp counselor, and that I agree to the code of conduct when campers are present on the premises.

I brush past Connor as I move to the desk. I lean down and move the first form out of the way. The code of conduct glares back at me.

Half afraid to look and terrified not to know, I read it.

At the last line item, I let out a laugh. Chet wrote this, and it's obvious.

Connor stands beside me, and his hand lands on the small of my back as he leans down to read the paper too.

When he gets to item 16 —*No making out unless you're married, and then it's completely fine because your babysitter who catches you is awesome and never says a word to you about it. But really, keep it G-RATED. The campers should not even know you're dating.*—Connor snorts. "Do you really ignore that?"

I flush. "I…I think it's sweet how much he loves Ember."

"Yeah, well, I lived there for a few weeks, and let me tell you it is *not* sweet to see your big brother gnawing your sister-in-law's face off every day."

I choke back the laugh bubbling up. "He does have a unique kissing technique." The words hang there before I realize what I implied.

Connor's eyes widen and his mouth hangs open before it snaps shut.

"Are you an expert on kissing, Paige?" His tone is teasing, but his eyes are serious.

"What?" I shake my head, trying to clear the intensity of his gaze from my face while shaking off the embarrassment. "No, no…I meant like what I've seen in movies. And…I just. Ok, next time I catch him and Ember, I will absolutely say something because I don't want to talk about this anymore."

I hide my face in my palms because I am embarrassed beyond belief. Warmth surrounds me and Connor's body brushes against mine in a hug.

The other rules are really strict, and I'm both relieved because this new thing between Connor and I has to go slowly and disappointed because I'm finding I like when Connor touches me. The one positive is that these are rules for when the campers are *on site*.

Since I can't hold his hand, hug him for longer than 2.5 seconds (yes, the code of conduct stipulates that I'm allowed to count *1 Mississippi, 2 Mississippi, Missis*), be alone in a room with him with closed doors, conduct myself in any way that could cause people to think a scandal had occurred, or kiss him for the next four weeks while campers are here at CGO, I have a decision to make.

I lower my palms and find Connor's eyes locked on mine. His gaze is heated, and I want to lean in, but something stops me. He frowns and then leans in so his lips are by my ear. I shudder.

"I don't kiss like Chet," he whispers against my ear. I can't help it, I giggle and Connor begins laughing too. He pulls me closer and my arms snake around his torso, warm, solid, and strong.

"It looks like we have four weeks of going really slow with our relationship," I murmur against his chest.

"Is that good?" Connor asks.

"Yeah," I say. "Yeah, I think it's good. I've never had a boyfriend before, so I think this is…good for me."

"I'm glad for you." Connor starts to release me from the hug but then brushes his lips softly over my hair, leaving a fuzzy sensation. He tightens his arms against me again, and he whispers quietly, "But I will be counting down the days until the campers leave and I get to kiss you properly." He steps back from me and smiles. I did not expect those words, or that kiss—I especially did not expect that kiss to still be lingering warm and soft comfort. "We should get some sleep before tomorrow."

I nod and walk out the door, feeling the heat of his gaze on my back as I leave. My heart is pounding, and all I can think is:

How is it possible to be this far gone for a man at the end of your first date?

28

CONNOR

I call Chet once Paige leaves. Just when I think it's going to voice-mail, he answers. "Hey, bro."

I grimace at his slang. Cringey is not even close enough to the right word to describe it. "Hey."

"Why are you calling me?"

"You really made an impression with that code of conduct."

He sighs. "I don't know what you want me to say about that, Connor. You two are adults, but you have a job to do. And your behavior directly impacts Ember's and my livelihood."

"Did you have to be so puritan?

"Uhh. Connor. Yeah, I did."

"But the kids shouldn't even know we're dating?"

"Obviously not. If you were engaged, they could know, but that's…they can't know. The parents are very protective, and need I remind you that we are hosting children to learn leadership in the form of *Christian* values."

I grumble. I know he's right, but at the same time *doesn't he know me?* Can't he trust his brother?

"Listen, Connor. I understand that this isn't what you wanted to hear me say, but going slow with Paige is a *good* idea. You *proposed* to the last girl you dated—the *only* girl you've dated—and from what Ember told me, Paige has never had a boyfriend. Don't be too serious until it's time to be serious."

I flop onto the bed in frustration. "That's rich coming from you."

"Hey!" Chet gets defensive.

"I'm just saying," I mutter. "You don't exactly have the best history with romance either."

"That's enough." His anger almost radiates through the phone. I know better than to poke the bear about his past mistakes, but sometimes, I have to. "I'm your brother, Connor, but don't throw that in my face again."

"Fine. Whatever. The kids won't know we're dating. Thanks for having my back, *bro*."

"Connor." Chet says my name in a fatherly tone. "You know I really *do* have your back. That's why I talked to HR and sent you the forms and code of conduct. It's to protect you. I don't want you to make my mistakes."

I scoff. "There is a fat chance of that happening. Especially with your *rules*."

"Exactly. Look, Ember's not feeling great and she's calling me, so I have to go."

Chet's mention of Ember makes me soften a little. I do love my sister-in-law, even if I have no idea why she loves my ridiculous brother. Love makes no sense sometimes. "No baby yet?"

"No, not yet."

"Well, tell her I hope she feels better."

"Will do."

Chet hangs up, and I'm left staring at the wooden ceiling as the overhead fan spins.

I know Paige wants to go slow, but even molasses in January would be faster than the rules Chet provided. I'm frustrated because I know what I want. For the first time in over a year, I have clarity on a relationship, and now I'm supposed to act like I don't have any interest.

But I already did that. I tried to ignore the feelings I had for Paige when she showed up at Ember and Chet's house and spat her vampire teeth on the floor. I tried. And I failed to squash them, and just now when I've decided to embrace them…forty preteens are going to be watching my every move.

My phone buzzes and I scowl at it before turning it over to read the text. I'm sure it's Chet instating some new restriction.

It's not. It's Paige.

Paige

I had a really good time today. Thank you for the date. See you tomorrow.

Suddenly my irritation with Chet fades. Paige is a genius, and I could kiss her. Actually, I am definitely going to kiss her as soon as I can—which is still *least* four weeks and one day out, but still. Chet didn't mention anything about texting in his absurdly strict code of conduct.

I start to type out a response, but second-guess my first words. Finally, I settle on:

Connor

I had a great time with you today too. And you're welcome. I can't wait to take you on another one. See you in the morning.

Everything with Paige feels so new and also so old at the same time. It's exciting and fresh, but also solid. Maybe it's because she's been a fixture in Chet and Ember's lives for so long. Maybe it's because she's opened up to me instead of others about her past and her hurts. Or maybe it's because I got so close to the edge with the wrong person that thinking of the future doesn't scare me. Not when Paige is in it.

A knock sounds at my door before I can hit send.

"Coming," I call as I grab a fresh gray tee from my dresser. I change quickly, shoving it over my head and making sure I look presentable before opening the door. Hospitality habits die hard. Even when I'm in a tee shirt and athletic shorts, I still have to check my reflection in the mirror before I open the door and interact with 'customers'. I know no one at camp right now is a customer, but these habits will not stop.

I open the door and find Matt and Brooke standing outside.

"Hi," I say, questioning why these two are staring at me.

"Hi," Brooke says, then elbows Matt hard in the ribs. He winces.

"Hey, Connor. I…ummm. Could we talk privately?" Matt says.

"Uh, sure." I scratch the back of my neck as I open the door wider to let him in.

Brooke shoves him across the threshold and then leaves.

I raise a brow. "Sisterly intervention?"

Matt rolls his eyes. "Something like that."

"So?" I prompt.

"I know I need to apologize for last night. I realize my conduct was irresponsible, and I broke your trust. It won't happen again. And I won't be drinking on the premises again."

I nod at his words. With everything that happened today, I forgot about Matt and last night. If that doesn't tell me how far gone I am for Paige, nothing will. "Thanks for coming here and apologizing. I know we all make mistakes, but getting that far gone puts stress on the other employees here." I think about Paige and her reaction to Matt's drunken behavior. I don't want to tell him her secrets, so I settle for something close to the truth. "We're a team. Team behavior is expected every moment from now until the campers leave. We have to be in this together. The reason we allowed alcohol for the counselors when children are not on the premises is because my grandpa loved sitting around a fire and sharing a drink with friends. It's a way to honor his memory, not a way to lose control."

Matt shakes his head and his Adam's apple bobs. "Thanks for not firing me, boss."

I grin. "You're welcome. Brooke dumped all the rest of the alcohol out last night. She was *mad*. I think she was probably harder on you than I was. No need to beat you down twice."

Matt laughs. "Yeah, that's Brookie alright."

"You know," I say, "I'm kind of scared of her."

If Matt was laughing previously, now he full-on guffaws. "She is terrifying. I'm so glad it's not just me."

He extends his hand and I shake it.

"Just so we're clear, though, Matt," I say, pumping his hand, "this is your first and only warning. You are officially on probation. You exhibit behavior that is negligent again, and you will be out of here, no matter what Brooke says. She's not scary enough to make me risk the lives of the campers."

Matt sobers. "Yes, sir. See you tomorrow."

"Yeah. See you then."

I shut the door softly behind Matt even though I would love to slam it just for the catharsis after an emotionally tumultuous day. I am a master at closing doors quietly after years of working in a hotel—yet another habit that I can't shake.

I shrug and finally head to the shower. I should be thinking of all the things I need to do to prepare for the campers, but all I can think about is the way Paige's eyes softened when I placed a kiss on her head. It was as PG as a kiss could be, but it meant something to her and she was clearly affected.

I can't help the big grin that spreads over my face, and I'm thankful no one can see me now. If she was so affected by a brush of my lips to the crown of her head, I can't wait to see how she reacts when I kiss her for real.

Four weeks, one day.

I can do this.

29

PAIGE

I bite my lip as I toss my phone away. I shouldn't have texted Connor.

Brooke looks up from where she's sitting cross-legged on the bed with a ball of yarn and a crochet hook.

Stephanie raises her eyebrow at me while she brushes her hair. "Want to tell us about it?" she asks with a sly grin.

Heat floods my cheeks. "Uh."

"C'mon, Paige. You know we're not idiots," Brooke supplies while she furiously works her hook.

I grimace. I could trust these two young women. I like them. They'll just leave, too, though. It's why I only really have Ember as a friend, and she's been more of a big sister to me than anything else. The two of us, being left by people, have a certain bond. Her story has a happy ending, but mine… I've been brave today, and I wonder if maybe I can be brave again.

"Did you and Connor go on a date?" Stephanie asks.

I gulp. I don't want to hide my fledgling relationship with Connor from my friends. And make no mistake, after the hours of time we've

138

spent together working on things for Camp CGO, we *are* friends. "Yeah. We did go on a date."

"I *told* you!" Steph points at Brooke. "I told you there was no way he wasn't going to take her out to dinner on a date."

"Hey!" I say, throwing my hands up. "He would not have taken me to dinner if I wasn't ok with it."

Brooke's eyes are fixed on mine as she works the hook down the row. "He's a good person. I like him for you. I'm just sorry my idiot other half messed things up."

I shrug. I accept that Brooke and Stephanie are my friends, but I'm not ready to reveal everything about my mom to them.

"So where'd you go to eat? Did you kiss? Details, *please*," Stephanie says as she slides across the wooden floor in her socks and sits on my bed.

I focus on the campers' empty bunks, knowing they'll be filled tomorrow afternoon. I'm not great at talking with friends, but this is my last opportunity to tell someone before everything has to be hush-hush.

"North Ore for dinner."

Brooke sighs. "That's a really nice place."

"Yeah." I chuckle. "I thought so too. Listen, I…ummm…I've never had a boyfriend before, so I don't really know what I'm doing, but Connor and I are…together…but we can't tell the campers. Like the campers can't know. And there's a really strict code of conduct, I think it's because Chet—" I stop abruptly when I turn my gaze back to Stephanie's face and her jaw is hanging open.

"I don't think I've ever heard you say that many words at the same time." Brooke puts down her crocheting and joins Stephanie and me on my twin bed.

"Sorry," I say, and they both laugh.

"So you've really never had a boyfriend before?" Stephanie asks, sobering and staring at me with her chocolate eyes.

"Uhh. No. My home life was…not conducive to that."

Brooke frowns. "But you said there's a code of conduct? And the campers can't know you're dating? So, like, what can you *do*? Can you *kiss* your boyfriend?"

"Not when in the company of campers or when on the premises while campers are here," I respond.

"Harsh," Stephanie says, then brightens. "And you say that Chet has a story? As in, the Chet who owns this camp with his wife Ember?"

"Yeah," I say. "But it's not my story to tell. Ember's like a sister to me, and I…it's up to her how much of her personal life I share."

Stephanie pouts for a moment, but then shrugs. "Fair. But I sense a really interesting romance story there."

I laugh, then glance around the room. The counselor beds are not bunked. We each have a twin bed in a strategic location around the cabin to help campers who might need something in the middle of the night. Under each of the counselor beds is a pull-out drawer for our own personal comfort items. Stephanie's is full of romance novels. She is the epitome of a romantic soul.

Brooke's drawer is full of candy and, surprisingly, yarn and crafting books. My drawer holds a sketch pad and pencils, but not much else. I used to spend hours sketching Lake Superior when I was a teen. Sketching was the one thing that made me feel normal after Mom left. I could get lost in the lines and perspective. Life got busier and I haven't sketched in ages, but I'm hopeful that maybe I'll have some time to do it this summer. I have my stash of candy in the infirmary, which is attached to the mess hall on the other side of Connor's suite. Thinking of Connor makes my face flush.

"Awww. She's thinking of *him*," Brooke teases, but it's not unkind.

Just then, my phone vibrates. Brooke and Stephanie stare at it as if they can't make any sudden moves or else it will explode.

"Wait. A. Minute," Steph says, over-enunciating every word. "Did you *text* him after your date?" She's incredulous.

I grimace. "Yeah…"

"You do not kiss and then TEXT him, Paige. He texts *first*." Stephanie's eyes bore into mine.

"Hey," Brooke says, setting a hand on Stephanie's arm. "She's never had a boyfriend, and I don't think she's a romance expert quite like you. And maybe what works for their relationship isn't what would work for yours."

"But Paige!" Stephanie gestures wildly. "He's supposed to *pursue you*."

I grimace. "I guess I messed up then—but he texted back."

"Well, what did he say?" Stephanie scoots closer to me.

I read it silently and relax. I know Brooke and Stephanie will never let me off the hook, so I read it to them. "He says, 'I had a great time with you today too. And you're welcome. I can't wait to take you on another date. See you in the morning.' So maybe it wasn't a mistake to text him."

"Fine," Stephanie concedes with a huff. "You're shipped. I love it. Now tell me more about this code of conduct. And if you can't kiss him starting tomorrow, please tell me you kissed him tonight."

"Uhh." I stumble. "No, I didn't kiss him. But he kind of kissed me."

They squeal so loudly, I wouldn't be surprised if people heard them halfway across the peninsula. I shrink back and grab my pillow, hugging it to my chest while I count down from ten. When I still feel anxious about the loud sudden noise, I try twenty. By the time I get from twenty to zero, I'm calmer.

Stephanie and Brooke are staring at me.

"Paige?" Brooke asks. "Are you alright?"

"S-s-sorry," I stutter. "I don't… I have…a loud noise thing…it's not great…"

"I'm so sorry." Stephanie gently squeezes my hand. "I get too excited about *love* sometimes. I'll rein it in a little."

"Circling back to the topic at hand," Brooke cuts in. "Connor kissed you?"

"Yeah," I say, "but it was…"

They wait, staring at me with puppy eyes like they're puppies and I have an entire jar of peanut butter at my disposal.

I settle on describing it as, "It was very sweet. Like it might have been nothing."

"Uhh. Did he kiss you on the lips? Or was it like a nose kiss?"

I blush again. "My hair."

Brooke and Stephanie look at each other and burst into giggles. "Yes, because a kiss from the man who's been standoffish and then decides not to be and takes you on a date less than twenty-four hours after he decides not to be clearly means *nothing*."

"Fine," I concede. "It was something. And I think he is going to pursue me."

"How would you know that?" Stephanie's all heart eyes.

I grin as I recall his words about pursuing me earlier. Not only will he pursue me, but he promised he wasn't someone who would leave.

I let the butterflies in my stomach take flight as I answer Stephanie. "He said he would."

Brooke's hand flies to her mouth and Stephanie clutches her heart. "How *swoony*. Please tell me you understand how swoony that is. And he's so hot too. If he wasn't so clearly interested in you, I'd be jealous, but I'm happy for you."

Brooke butts in. "I'm happy for you too. But now you have to pretend to not be dating for a month. How are you going to do that?"

I shrug. "I want to take things slow, so I'm good with it."

Brooke and Stephanie shrug. "But you guys are so bad at hiding it."

"Bad at hiding what?"

"That you like each other," Brooke says, while Stephanie bursts out with, "That you're destined for each other."

"It will be tough," I say, "but the campers can't know. I don't want Connor to get in any trouble with Chet and Ember, and I don't want a bunch of preteens up in my business about my love life."

Brooke cackles. "They will definitely be up in your business about who you're dating, especially once they see Connor make googly eyes at you."

I chew the inside of my lip. "I'm just going to have to be good at not answering questions, I guess."

Stephanie picks up my phone and turns it over in her palm. "You know…" she says in a quiet voice. "The code of conduct said the kids couldn't know that you and Connor were together, but you can still get to know each other while they're here."

Brooke and I stare at Stephanie. She holds out the phone.

"You'll have to do a sort of letter writing thing, but through texts. Calls will be too obvious, but you can still grow together. It will be so romantic, like a historical romance. Like when soldiers went off to war."

"Pretty sure that was letters, not texts," Brooke retorts. She catches my hope-filled face and softens. "But still, texts could be romantic. Just. Nothing…you know…risque."

Horror floods my face as I think about doing anything even close to related to *that* through a *text*. "Oh my gosh. No. Way. Absolutely not. I would *never*."

Brooke laughs. "I didn't think you would, but I just had to make sure."

Stephanie pulls a licorice package out from her kangaroo hoodie pocket and peels the rope off. She passes one to me, then one to Brooke. "To new things! New friends, new semi-secret relationships, and tomorrow, a whole new Camp CGO experience!" She raises her strand in a 'cheers'. Brooke and I do the same, and suddenly my heart feels lighter than it has for half my life.

30

CONNOR

The first thing I do when my alarm goes off in the morning is groan. The next thing I do is remember that Paige agreed to be in a relationship with me, and I got to take her on a date. Then the sudden realization that the campers arrive *today* tamps down the joy flooding my body. And in order to follow my idiot brother's code of conduct, I have to hide my very real, very front-and-center feelings for Paige from forty eleven- and twelve-year-olds.

Seriously, Chet? Why are you punishing me for your own past? But I also know why. Chet's worked hard to make amends with Ember and Blaze, and he has. He's working hard to make this camp a success in honor of Gramps. He's a good person, even if he was misguided and stupid as a young adult.

I throw my legs out from the bed and stretch while I peek out the window. The sun is shining, but there's a bank of clouds over the Lake. Late afternoon storms aren't uncommon, but I do hope it holds off when the campers start arriving at one.

All the counselors except for Paige were given instructions to prepare the cabins for the campers. Paige was told to be in the infirmary, making sure everything was perfect and preparing to do a lice check for each camper that arrives. I shudder. Parasitic bugs are the worst. I have a healthy fear of lice, bedbugs, and mosquitos. They give me the creeps.

I squash the thoughts of bugs and find myself grinning because Paige will be here in the infirmary while the counselors will be dealing with the cabins. I have the very sudden need to lay eyes on her, like I need to see her in order to breathe. I know that's ridiculous, but I don't care.

I dress in official clothing for the day, a forest-green polo with the CGO logo embroidered on the chest paired with black golf shorts. I slide into my white trusty training shoes. The memory foam cushioning in these is unbelievable, and I would know after working a job that required me to be on my feet for up to fourteen hours a day.

I throw open the door to the rest of the mess hall and whistle as I think about where I'm going, and *who* I'll be seeing.

There was one small flaw in the plan: Tom.

Tom is in the mess hall, sweeping the floor, wiping down tables, and making sure that the already spotless dining area is up to operating room–cleanliness apparently.

"G'morning." He leans against the broom handle and grins. "So you finally told her?"

I scowl. I don't really want to talk about it with him, especially when he's so amused. "Finally told who, what?" I ask, feigning innocence.

Tom rolls his eyes. "Go get your girl. She's in the infirmary."

I start to walk over to the infirmary, crossing the dining space to the hallway on the other side, when I stop in the middle of the room. "Tom," I say slowly.

He looks up, grinning, but his face falls when he sees mine.

"Chet sent us over a really strict code of conduct. In order to follow it, the campers can't know. So please don't say anything in front of them."

Tom frowns. "Why would he do that?"

I shrug. "My brother's fixed up his life now, but he had a tough past with his wife before they got married."

Tom nods in understanding. Then he mimes zipping his lips, which is somehow both in and out of character for him. In character because I've known him and worked with him for months, but also out of character because this man with the long gray beard and ponytail tucked through a beat-up ball cap pretending to zip his lips like a third grader might will always look funny.

"Thanks, Tom." I let my feet take me to the infirmary.

The mess hall is set up to have the dining area just off the front porch. The kitchen is in the back of the dining area, with the food service stations separating the actual cooking appliances from the dining tables. While the dining room and the kitchen fill the round space of the building, there are two hallways that jut off the sides of the space. The one hall on the left leads to my office and rooms, as well as a bathroom. The hall on the left leads to the infirmary, a pantry, a room with our deep freezers, and another bathroom.

I find the door to the infirmary cracked open, which means Paige is already inside. I knock once, and then push it open.

Paige sits on the ground in a patch of morning sunlight streaming through the window. Her eyes are closed, and her face is framed by wavy red hair that is so vibrant I want to run my fingers through it and see if it's real. At the sound of my footsteps, she opens her eyes and meets me with a hungry gaze. I sense her drinking me in, and I puff up just a little. Because the woman staring at me is gorgeous, and she likes what she sees in me.

"Good morning, beautiful." The words are out before I can stop them.

Her eyes widen. "Hiya, handsome?" she tries and then bursts into a sweet laugh. "We can't do that in…" She checks her watch. "Four hours, so it's probably not a good habit to get into."

I cross the room and sit beside her on the floor, bringing my arm around her waist and pulling her closer to me. "There are a lot of things we won't be able to do in four hours."

She tenses.

Ok. I won't be kissing her properly *yet.*

I squeeze her waist with my arm.

"Like hugs. Or holding hands, or even calling each other cute names when we see each other for the first time each day. Or telling people that we're together," I say.

She relaxes, and I know I read her body language right.

"I…" She meets my eyes briefly, then looks away. "I was thinking…that we can't say things in front of other people, but we could still get to know each other a little more over the next four weeks."

I think I know where she's going with this, but I stay silent.

"We could, you know, like, text conversations?" She blushes. "Not like…*that* though. Just like talking, but with texts?"

I smile at her and release my hand from her waist. I take her left hand in my right and bring it to my lips, planting a kiss on her skin. "It would be an absolute honor to be your text-only boyfriend for the next month." I say it with enough dignity to befit royalty.

She stifles a laugh, and I know I could spend the rest of my life listening to that sound.

My phone buzzes with the alarm I'd set about checking in on the other counselors and making sure everything is good to go for when the campers arrive.

I push to standing, but first I brush a kiss to the side of Paige's head, because I can't resist showing her affection and I'm about to have to restrain myself for a month.

"Duty calls," I say, gesturing to my phone. "Is everything all good in here? Do you have everything you need?"

"Yeah," she says, standing up. "Just enjoying the calm before the storm, you know?"

I nod, because I do know.

The clouds hang low over the Lake, but they're still a ways off, and for that I'm grateful. Minivans and SUVs have overtaken the gravel lot and meeting area of Camp CGO. Forty preteens converging upon the camp is chaos, but thanks to my plan and the counselors' help, there's organization amid the insanity.

I sit outside the mess hall at a folding table with a clipboard, highlighter, and pen. I have a list of every camper we're expecting, and spaces next to their names for emergency contact information for their parents or guardians to confirm. After the adults confirm, they head into the infirmary with their kids, where Paige does a lice check. Thankfully, thus far, she hasn't found any.

When the children and parents are done, they are given directions to the cabins. A female counselor and a male counselor are in each cabin to help the children get settled in. Another counselor is outside behind each cabin with a ball, hula hoops, and a bunch of ice-breaker games. Goodbyes happen in the cabin, because once the children's things are settled, they head to play games while the parents leave.

I check my list. We're waiting on three more campers, but everyone else has been checked in. The SUVs and the minivans are pulling away, slowly but surely. It's been at least thirty minutes since I sent a child and their parents back to see Paige.

As if thinking of her summoned her, Paige pulls the chair next to me out and sinks into it. "Hey," she says, a smile on her face as she takes me in. I don't miss the way she takes advantage of the *lack* of people to look me over.

"Hey, you," I respond, then cringe internally. I never said I was witty.

"So, how's it been going out here?"

I shrug. "Pretty well actually. It's a lot like hotel check-ins."

"Sometimes I forget about the hotel. Was it glamorous? In California? Were there celebrities who came to your hotel?"

I shake my head. "Woah there. It wasn't *my* hotel. I just managed it. I had an internship in college and did everything from room cleaning to check-ins. When the owner needed a new manager right after I graduated college, she asked me to fill that position."

Paige's face falls a little, then brightens into something wide-eyed and playful. "But still, *handsome* celebrities?"

I laugh at her expression because she is teasing me, and I love it. "A few. Most were B-list actors who thought they were the next big thing. I did have a famous stunt double once though. It made—"

I stop myself. I have never once mentioned Kaleigh to Paige, and I really don't want to. It's not that she's a secret, but she's a part of my past I'd rather forget. I have no desire to bring up my biggest humiliation. I'm sure it will come up at some point, but today is *not* the day.

Paige tilts her head to the left a little and squints. It's like she's trying to see my thoughts. I swallow. "It made someone I knew, who was obsessed with *Twilight*, very jealous."

Paige's eyes widen. "*Twilight*? Like the books? About vampires?"
"Uhh. Yeah."

"Never read those. And the movies were…popular among certain people in high school, but not with my circle of friends."

I nod along, not once mentioning that I read the books multiple times to try to understand what Kaleigh wanted from me, and I also watched the movies with her. A lot. I know more *Twilight* lore than anyone who actually *wasn't*, or *isn't*, obsessed with the series should.

A car rumbles into the gravel lot, but this isn't just a car. It is a behemoth. It is a gigantic van, akin to an airport shuttle. The horn toots with cheery blares to the rhythm of the song "The Entertainer" as it rolls to a stop.

The door to the van slides open, and I watch in shock as three identical triplets climb out, followed by two surly teen boys.

The triplets are girls, with blonde hair hanging down their backs in twin braids. The thing that's most shocking, however, is the headwear. And I don't mean orthodontia. That wouldn't faze me. I have seen some bizarre things in the hospitality business, but I have never seen three identical preteen girls wearing matching outfits, except for the *things on their heads*.

I can't even call the *things* on their heads hats, because hats, they are not.

I hear Paige give a small gasp as she sees the three girls link arms and approach the table.

I can't decide if I should laugh at the girls, but also *why? Why* show up to camp wearing *those?*

The girl on the right's head is topped by a giant turkey hat where the turkey is also holding a drumstick and its beak is open as if to consume its own cooked leg. The turkey's feathers are all bright colors in a fan along the back, but over its torso is an apron with the words 'Good Eatin' Year Round' painted in garish red. The entire effect of the turkey hat is gruesome. And odd.

The girl in the middle wears one of those cheese hats from football games but with a twist. The cheese hat has a hole where an animatronic mouse periodically pops out, shouting in a tiny voice, "FEAR THE CHEESE!"

The girl on the left, her hat seems comparatively normal—until I get a closer look. Her hat isn't just a tie-dye stocking hat. It's a tie-dye giant squid, complete with one eye that opens and closes slowly. The back of the eye, when it's closed at least, blends into the rest of the pattern.

A brunette woman in a yellow dress with a baby in her arms and inexplicably no shoes on her feet and a man with tiny braids in both his long red hair and chest-length beard approach the check-in table. The two teen boys stand by the van, their arms crossed and their faces set in nearly identical scowls.

"Hi." The man extends a hand to me.

I stand. It's polite. "Hello. Welcome to Camp CGO. I take it you are the…Lightagers?"

The woman snorts. "Lightagers? Girls. That's a fantastic one!"

I feel like I'm a step behind as the teen boys and the parents begin hooting and hollering with laughter while the hat triplets look cautiously at each other.

The turkey hat girl senses my discomfort. "Guys," she says loudly, while her sisters look on. "I don't think he understands."

The rest of the group continues laughing.

I turn to her, keeping my face as blank as possible. "Could you clue me in?"

"Yeah." The turkey bobs along with her head. "We're kind of… different. And my sisters and I are triplets."

"I can see that," I drawl. It's not professional, but I am at a complete loss here.

Paige puts her hand on my arm gently. "Connor," she warns. It's enough to snap my demeanor back to professional hotel manager Connor, not frustrated, confused Connor.

"Yeah, well…" The girl starts twirling the end of her braids with her hands. "We…uhhh…we signed up for the camp without telling our parents, thinking it would be a good joke."

My eyes bug out. I don't need a mirror to know that I look like a cartoon character. "Ok…so…all the forms are…"

"Uhhh…a joke…"

"But you're still here?"

The woman steps forward, having recovered from her laughing fit. Strangely serious now, she fixes the three girls with a glare. "Yes. When we found out what they did, we decided the only way to make them see the error of their ways was to bring them here and publicly face the consequences."

"But...but..." I sputter.

Paige intervenes after briefly checking my clipboard. "And will the three girls be staying? We do have room for them. And they did put down the required deposit."

The man and woman look at each other. "Yes. They will be staying."

"Ok." I blow out a breath. "Could an adult please revise the forms for the three children? It may take a while..."

The three girls shift uncomfortably. It's fairly obvious they didn't think they'd be staying here for four weeks, let alone coming at all. It's a joke gone wrong. By a *lot*.

Paige swoops in. "Hi, girls. I'm Paige. I'm the camp nurse, and also a counselor. Before we can check you in, I need to check your heads for lice."

The girls brighten. "If we have lice, do we have to stay?"

Paige frowns. "If you have lice, you have to be treated and then can return once I've given you the all-clear."

The girls grin.

"Maybe we have lice!" squid hat girl whispers gleefully. "That will show them!"

Paige shakes her head. "Come on, girls, follow me."

The girls follow her, three hats trailing her that look just as strange from the back as they do from the front.

The man stands tall, having spent the past few minutes doubled over in a laughing fit. If any word describes this family, it's *odd*. He's suddenly serious and snakes an arm around the woman's waist, whom I assume is his wife. "We are *not* the Lightagers. We are the Buttons, and those three girls are Avila, Aleigha, and Allison."

I nod in understanding, because I have a feeling I'm not going to know what comes next with this family.

He jerks his thumb toward himself. "I'm Jesse, and this is my wife, Jessie."

"Nice to meet you," I say through the sudden tension headache that began beating on my brow when I heard the three *Al* names. Now I hear Jesse and Jessie are married.

Ok, Connor. You're a professional. You can do this.

"You as well." Jesse is suddenly professional compared to his previous demeanor. "Could we get those forms? And will we need to fill out three sets, or just one?"

At least this is a normal thing to ask. "Just one for the family. I'll need an emergency information card for each child though."

"Sure thing," Mom Jessie supplies and somehow procures a pen with a dandelion wrapped around it from her pocket.

"I…need to print the forms for you, but it will just be a minute. But you can start on the emergency information cards." Thankfully, I've had a stack of cards at the check-in table this entire time. Mom Jessie passes off the baby to Dad Jesse and begins filling out forms. The man promptly begins making silly faces at the baby, and the baby responds with giggles.

I'm inside Green Eggs and Ham.

I duck inside, print the forms and continue back out, but pause in the dining area when Paige's voice filters down from the infirmary. "So you filled it out as a joke and didn't know you were coming until today?"

"Yeah," one of the girls says.

"They are really mad," another one says, or maybe not. Maybe they all have the same voice and it's the same child talking. I have *no* idea.

"Mom spent all morning getting everything on the packing list ready for us, but we didn't know until we got here."

"They just said, who's ready to go out for a joke! It's a long car ride, but be ready."

"Is that why you were wearing those...uh...hats?"

"Yeah. We didn't know until we got here that they were making us...face...our choices. We thought if they *thought* we were leaving, we'd get more attention. The baby is ok, but he's needed a lot of doctor stuff. And then the LARPing takes up the weekends, and I just wish Mom and Dad would notice us sometime."

I scrub my hand down my jaw. Because LARPing just *fits* the people I've met. Not in a bad way, but in a *yes, I could really see you enjoying LARPing, have you tried it yet?* type of way. Also, what on earth? Who has the type of money to not notice when their preteen daughters pay not one, but *three* deposits on a four-week camp? The girls paid the deposits and sent in the fake forms months ago. Suddenly I feel for the girls because it sounds like maybe the parents have been preoccupied with the baby.

I grit my teeth to continue the oddest interaction I've ever had in a hospitality space and return to the Jesse Buttons, forms in hand.

31

PAIGE

The three girls, Avila, Aleigha, and Allison, are subdued during their lice check.

"Good news, girls!" I say cheerfully. "You're free and clear."

They sigh in unison.

"Great." Avila quips. She's the turkey hat wearer and seems to be the spokesperson for the group.

"Come on now, Camp CGO is going to be super fun. I mean, you girls get four whole weeks here to learn leadership skills and make new friends!"

Aleigha's lips twitch in a frown. "We don't need new friends. We have each other. The three Buttons."

I tilt my head to the side. I have a lot of experience talking children into something they deem unpleasant (because yes, drawing a child's blood is *not* pleasant). Sometimes I think children are wiser than adults. At least they have superior gut instincts about sharp, pokey things.

"Well. You still get to have each other. All the girls are in the same cabin, and you'll be able to choose activities you'd like to do either together or apart."

The girls look at me with horrified faces.

"We're gonna be split up when we do stuff here?"

I shake my head and hold my hands up in a 'hold your horses' gesture. "Woah. No, I meant that if you chose to do something on your own, that would be ok, but if you all choose to do the same activities when there is a choice, that's ok too."

Avila pops the turkey hat back on her head, and Aleigha and Allison do the same with their hats.

"So… What's the story with the hats?" I ask.

The girls launch into the story about how they didn't know they were coming to camp for real, how the new baby has been sick with lots of digestive issues and allergies, how they can't eat Cheetos anymore because their mom won't let them because even though they were a sometimes-food, now they are a never-food because of the ingredients, how they hoped that maybe they would get some attention if their parents thought they were leaving. They didn't count on actually being taken to Camp CGO when they piled into the car. Apparently random adventures are how the family tends to roll.

A few tears well up in the corner of Allison's eyes. She wears the squid hat, which is honestly the only way I can tell them apart right now.

"Mom and Dad are…being kind of mean." Allison sniffles.

I bite my lip because I don't know if it's *mean*, but it does seem harsh to have loaded them in the car for a long drive and force them to face their ill-advised behavior like this. It's definitely *odd*.

I take a moment to look each girl in the eye despite their strange hats. "I'm glad you're here, Avila, Aleigha, and Allison."

The girls move as one and launch themselves into my arms. It's a total dogpile, and I am at the mercy of the six arms encompassing me while they blubber. I can't tell who is blubbering, or who is laughing, or if it's a strange combination of both.

Avila breaks away first, and her sisters follow immediately after. "Paige, you're the *best*. Will you be with us for everything?"

"Not everything, but I'll be with you for a lot of it."

"We've never been away from home without our parents, but I think it's going to be fun now that I know you're here."

I offer a tight-lipped smile because some sort of attachment just transferred to me, and I'm not sure what to make of it.

"I think we should head back outside," I say to the girls. They nod and then trail behind me through the dining area like ducklings. It's actually not that far off of a comparison.

The girls stand beside me as I sink into the chair next to Connor. He gives me a look that is *so* flat, not giving anything away, that I know something is wrong but he can't tell me what.

I reach deep inside and pull out a fake smile and direct it at the parents. The woman is filling out a form with a pen topped with a dandelion. "The girls are all set to stay," I say with enthusiasm.

"Excellent," she responds with narrowed eyes. "You girls will have learned your lesson by the time you're done here." She mutters under her breath, "Attention mongers."

Connor's back is ramrod straight, but I see the tiniest tick of his forearm muscles tightening.

"There!" the woman says, handing the form back to Connor. Connor hardly even glances at it while she puts the dandelion pen back into her dress.

"Great," he says in a lifeless voice. "We can show you to the cabins now. Then, you'll leave from there, but the girls will join in with the other campers and activities. Goodbyes happen at the cabin so the kids don't watch as their parents drive off."

The man, now holding the baby, and the teenage boys wander over from where they've been standing a little bit off to the side. "Jesse, they're ready for us to take the girls to their cabins."

She puts an inflection on the word *cabins*. It's like Mother Gothel in *Tangled*. I cringe. Connor shakes his head ever so slightly at me, and I hope no one else noticed it. The two teen boys haven't said a single word to anyone this entire time.

Connor points at the man, who I learn is *also* named Jesse, to the dirt lane that will let the Buttons park nearer to the cabins. Earlier, it was so crowded that the families carried their supplies, but now I get the sense that Connor wants these people out of here as quickly as possible.

Tom passes Dad Jesse and gives him a smile. I hear him call out, "Nice beard. I should try the braids too."

Jesse beams. "Thanks. My wife does them for me on weekends. I can't dress like this at my day job as a CPA. The kids thought we were going on our usual weekend LARP, so I needed to make sure I looked the part."

I meet Connor's eyes for a moment, and he squeezes them shut. Presumably because my face is comical after *that* news. It's not so much that they LARP, but that he's a CPA that has me internally confused and ready to laugh, but also horrified.

Tom stops, takes in the man and the family, and extends his hand. "I'm Tom. Nice to meet you..."

Jesse the *man* smiles as he pumps Tom's hand up and down with vigor. "Jesse. This is my wife, Jessie; our sons, Allan and Alvin; our daughters, Avila, Aleigha, and Allison; and our newest little guy, Rupert."

Tom takes this all in stride while I try not to gasp, or make any sudden movements because this situation keeps getting stranger and stranger. "So what's the LARP been recently?" Tom asks like this is a perfectly normal question to ask a complete stranger. Maybe it is. I've never met anyone who was into LARPing.

"Lately, Vikings."

"Solid choice," Tom supplies. "Nice to—"

"We're going to be doing vampires next, right, Jesse?" Jessie the *woman* says.

"Yes. The Buttons will become the Cullens, right, my beautiful Jessie-Swan?"

Jessie blushes and looks at her feet. Connor, who has already been as stiff as if a two-by-four was attached to his spine, stiffens further. Rigor mortis appears to be setting in.

"*Twilight*," Tom says. "What an interesting choice for LARPing."

"Well don't worry, we use organic cherry juice for…" Jessie lowers her voice. "The bloody stuff."

"Ahhh, yes." Tom nods. "Organic cherry juice makes sense."

Connor seems frozen. Tom shoots Connor a glance and sighs. Something about it makes me worry, but this whole interaction has been nothing short of bizarre.

A quick glance at my watch tells me that Tom needs to start dinner prep, and the girls are already missing out on activities because of their late arrival.

I snap into action. "Right!" I call. "Girls, would you like to walk with me to the cabins? We can meet your family there."

The girls gather around me, and I point in the direction we'll be going. I challenge them to a race, and they take off at a sprint. Before I kick it into gear and run after them, I see Tom pass by Connor and place a hand on his shoulder while Connor shakes his head and looks at the ground.

I briefly wonder what that's all about, but girls call, "PAIGE! WE'RE WINNING!"

Duty calls—and I have a race to win.

32

CONNOR

The Buttons need to leave. A sour taste fills my mouth as I keep my face neutral. I've always had a soft spot for kids, and these three girls, pranksters though they may be, are being humiliated on purpose. It's wrong. And I have learned that whenever you're interacting with children and a sense of *wrongness* settles in your gut, you don't ignore it.

Paige has rescued the triplets from their family's laughter and taken off racing down the dirt track that is really designed for walking only. I want to get the Buttons out of here as quickly as possible, so instead of asking them to walk and haul their three children's things to the cabin a quarter mile down the track, I tell them to drive. I don't want to hover, and I haven't been to the cabins for any of the other check-ins. I'll wait for the Buttons to drive back and send them on their way.

Scrubbing my hand over my jaw, I feel the slight scruff of my five o'clock shadow that's grown in since this morning. It's been a *long* day. Actually, today has been fine. It's just been a *long* half hour.

I trudge up the steps to the mess hall and head toward my rooms. I'm going to splash water on my face and then check in on Tom. He's definitely got everything covered, because he's amazing like that, but still. A good manager checks in, even when they know their staff is competent.

Tom sees me walking across the dining area and calls out, "Connor!"

I look over and discover that he has the kitchen onion goggles on. I've been in enough industrial kitchens to not laugh. But the sight of him wearing worn-out blue jeans under an apron, his long hair tucked into a hairnet with a backward cap on his head, and the onion goggles on is enough to make me stop and stare for a moment.

"Yeah, Tom? Everything going ok in here with dinner prep?"

Tom gestures with the santoku knife to the mounds of neatly diced onions. "Right as rain in here. But I was going to ask you the same question."

"Oh." The word comes out in a whoosh. "Yeah. Fine. That's not actually the weirdest…" I stop myself. I can only think of one other interaction that was even more bizarre, and that one involved a gorgeous redhead in a vampire costume so I'm not bringing it up.

"Something about it bugged you."

"The kids," I say slowly. "They made a mistake, and it wasn't justified, but their hearts…"

"Those three will be a handful. But they will make camp fun for everyone, including you. And yeah, shaming kids publicly never sits right with me either."

I shake my head in agreement as my shoulders slump. "It seemed so over the top."

Tom gives me a 'chin up' gesture with his own chin. "Maybe that's just how they are. They were definitely the march-to-their-own-drum type of people." He must catch my look because he amends, "Doesn't make it right. But those girls are here, and they can learn how to advocate for themselves. This leadership camp might be the best thing that's ever happened to them."

I brighten at his words because, per usual, Tom is right. "Thanks, Tom."

An hour later and the Buttons have left the camp premises, their airport shuttle van leaving with the cheery sounds of "Thunderstruck" by AC/DC blaring through the speakers. The song was so loud that, despite them being out of sight, I could hear the music down the long drive to the main road. When that song ended, "Clair de lune" trickled over the breeze.

When the music faded, complete and utter relief washed over me.

It was short-lived because yes, the Buttons are gone, but in their wake, I remember I have forty preteens in my care. Thankfully, the counselors have been with the children, but in mere moments, they will converge on the mess hall like a swarm of hungry locusts.

The smell of beef and beans, onions, peppers, and salsa fills the air. Tacos for the first night's dinner is sure to be a crowd-pleaser. They're also easy to adapt to any dietary needs, which was a big part of planning our meals for the next four weeks.

After the Buttons drove off, I changed into more casual clothes and went to the front porch of the mess hall. Now I lean against the railing as a herd of hungry children thundered down the dirt lane toward me. I don't get nervous that easily, but this is a lot of children.

I slide my palms down the soft fabric of my athletic shorts and wipe off my sweaty palms.

When the children are close enough to the porch steps, I stand in the middle with my arms out wide, blocking their path past me. The counselors must have reminded the children not to go up until given the all-clear, because they obediently stop at the bottom of the steps and stare at me with wide eyes.

I take in the group of twenty boys, twenty girls, and the counselors. Matt has a smile on his face. Lucas carries a football. Jorge has hula hoops slung across his torso like a sash. Brooke stands in the front of the pack while Stephanie stands off to the side. She's got her game whistle on, the red plastic standing out against the green of her official counselor t-shirt. Paige is the last counselor to arrive. She's walking with the triplets. They've lost the crazy hats and the girls wear easy smiles on their faces.

I take a breath and begin my speech. "Hey, guys. Welcome to Camp CGO. This is a really special place. Does anyone know why?"

Several preteens raise their hands.

"It's where you can go dirt biking!"

"It's got paintball!"

"It's got new friends!"

"It's got…"

"Those are great ideas," I say. "But actually, this camp belonged to my grandpa. It was his dream to have it become a Christian leadership camp, so that's what we did. I'm glad you're here. My gramps. ..well, it's his name that we decided to make the name of the camp. His favorite things were nature, good friends, good food, and helping people reach their full potential. That's what this camp is all about. Every Friday after dinner, we're going to have a camp circle where the counselors can honor the campers who showed the core values best in their activities." I pause and hold up a bag full of bracelets. "Each camper who is honored will receive one of these. The camper with the most bracelets at the end of the summer will receive a special opportunity." I toss an exaggerated wink at the kids. "Trust me, you won't want to miss out on this opportunity. So remember to show others respect, integrity, perseverance, and curiosity!" I pump my fist in the air, and the kids all follow suit. Matt is the loudest, but it's his cheer that starts the kids whooping and hollering.

I smile and stand off to the side to give fist bumps and say 'hi' to the kids that pass me as Brooke leads the charge into the mess hall.

Paige is the last to come up the steps. Her eyes lock with mine and she smiles the smallest of smiles, and I'd move mountains to see her smile at me every day. "That was quite a speech, Connor."

My mouth goes dry. "Th—" I cough. "Thanks."

"Yep," she says, and her voice takes on a teasing tone. "Wish I knew what the special opportunity was though."

"It's...uhh. It's a chance to choose the last meal at camp and..."

Paige laughs lightly. "That's a prize."

I shrug, a little embarrassed because it's not really a prize but a chance for the kids to practice and implement their leadership skills. They'll have a list of acceptable options based on what we have with our supplies, but they'll need to think about everyone. And I came up with the idea.

Paige starts to pass by me, but I can't stand it. I reach out and touch her back to stop her. She turns and fixes me with a look I can't quite decipher. She takes a step backward. "Wait. How was it with the..." I swallow and drop my voice in case the triplets are within hearing distance. "The last drop off."

"Oh," Paige breathes. "Yes. It was good. It was..." She looks around, scanning for the triplets. Apparently I am not the only one who suspects the triplets might be lurkers. "It was a continuation of what happened here. But thankfully Brooke got their things all set out on their beds and then sent the parents off. It didn't take too long. Mostly because I texted Brooke that we had *difficulties*, and she was prepared."

I chuckle. "You're something else, Paige."

"Thanks?" she questions as her stomach rumbles. She presses a hand to her middle and her eyes widen.

"It's a good thing." I incline my head to the door. "You should go get some food."

She nods once and strides through the door.

I'm left on the porch alone, thinking about how stolen conversations about camp goings-on aren't going to be enough for me, but will have to suffice.

I whip out my phone and compose a text to Paige. Before I can overthink it, I hit send and walk through the door with the confidence of a man who is delusional enough to think nothing will go wrong with forty preteens here for the next four weeks.

33

PAIGE

Counselors are required to keep their phones on their person at all times, as well as emergency long-range walkie-talkies. Each counselor has an over-the-shoulder fanny pack bag, which the preteens call a 'belt bag.' I'll give them that, 'belt bag' sounds cooler.

My phone vibrates against my back as I'm about to go through the food line for my dinner. Tom is helping the kids in front of me, so I fish out my device while I wait. A quick tap of the screen shows that it's Connor.

My stomach should not swoop when I see his name on my phone screen, but it does. For all I know, he's texting me and telling me I need to make sure we have enough mosquito repellant.

I open the text and bite my lip to keep from smiling as I read it.

Connor

You're beautiful today. Thank you for all
you did to help with that last check-in.

My eyes are drawn to the door where Connor stands surveying the dining area. When his gaze finds me, it lingers. I meet his eyes for a moment and smile, but remind myself we can't let the campers know we're romantically involved, so I tear my gaze away.

When tacos with fresh pico de gallo and guacamole are on my tray, I make my way to a dining table. Counselors will usually sit together at meals and supervise from a bit of a distance, but Connor requested that we intermingle with the campers tonight.

Avila, Aleigha, and Allison wave me over. They're sitting at a table with a few other girls. The boys and girls weren't told to stay separated, but a natural line has formed, and there are no boys sitting with the girls.

I walk to their table. "How's it going, ladies?" I ask.

"Good!" Avila answers. "We made new friends!"

I set my tray on the table and loop my legs over the bench. "That's awesome! That's the best part of camp." I don't mention that seeing the girls make friends easily is both heartwarming and bittersweet at the same time.

"Hi, girls," I say to the four other girls sitting at the round table. "I know I met you all at check-in, but in case you forgot, I'm Paige."

"Jill," a brunette with her hair in a very long braid down her back says around a mouthful of her taco.

"Beth," an African American girl with round glasses says.

"Annette, from Canada," a blonde girl with braces responds.

"I'm Edith," another blonde girl, but this one with no braces, says.

"So, Annette's from Canada." I take in the group. "Where are the rest of you from?"

The girls answer in turn. The triplets are from Wisconsin, Jill and Beth are friends from near Detroit, and Edith's from Duluth. It's a great group, and I'm thrilled to see that they wouldn't have known each other without this camp.

I ask the girls questions about their schools and homes and families and they answer, devolving into giggles when the triplets share about their favorite prank to play on their older brothers. It's not Avila who tells the story of the time the triplets made fake mice and spiders out of pipe cleaner and pompoms and shoved them in their brothers' shoes. It's Allison. She tells the story with perfect comedic timing, and I'm choking on my own laughter as she describes her oldest brother's reaction to the fuzzy creations.

I snort just as Connor walks by. "Everything going ok here?" he asks in that smooth, deep voice that does something to my heart every time I hear it.

Tears form in my eyes from holding back laughter. The rest of the girls at the table are doubled over, holding their sides as they cry from laughing so hard.

I look up, locking eyes with Connor.

"Yes," I say, gasping. "Yes. We're all good here."

"Hey!" Beth interjects. "We should plan some pranks for *here*."

My eyes go wide, and I start to think about how to shut it down, but before I do, Connor surprises me. He hops over the bench and sits next to me, leaning forward and grinning at the girls impishly. "I *love* pranks. What are you thinking?"

His thigh presses into mine under the table, and I can't tell if it's on purpose or on accident, but my mouth goes dry. The girls launch into a string of potential pranks, each one more elaborate and unlikely than the last.

Connor's eyes are fixed on the girls as they talk, but I feel him shifting near me. "What about the one where the campers tie their favorite counselor's running shoes together and put them at the top of the flagpole?"

The girls giggle. "That's not original enough, Connor!"

He puts his hands up. "Hey, you asked for ideas!"

The girls look at each other and then burst into even more laughter. "No, we didn't!"

"Oh. My mistake then." His knee knocks against mine. I take a sip of water from my bottle. "Ladies," he says in parting as he stands. He leaves the bench, but bends toward the table again behind me. "Pranks where no one gets hurt or embarrassed are a great, fun part of camp. But make sure no one will get hurt, and no one will be embarrassed by your actions. A leader knows how to have fun, and how to make fun, but it's never at someone else's expense." I feel the lightest of touches on my back before Connor leaves to visit with other tables.

All the girls, except Aleigha, are talking about their prank ideas. Aleigha leans closer to me. "Is he your boyfriend or something?"

I internally snarl at my fair coloring because I'm sure my skin is blushing. I wait a moment before answering. I'm not sure how to say no without lying. How do you *not* say, *He is, but we're on hold right now because you can't know we like each other and signed a form saying we're not going to tell you that?* Here's how: you don't.

I settle on a truth that doesn't admit or deny anything. "He's the camp manager."

"But you want him to be your boyfriend?"

"Uhh…" I'm not sure how to answer that. "He's a friend. But he's also in charge here." I take another sip of my water and deflect. "I thought his flagpole prank idea was genius. But clearly he's never seen *The Parent Trap* because those girls had some amazing pranks."

At the mention of *The Parent Trap,* the girls all look my way. The girls sound like a chorus as they all exclaim something to the tune of, "No way! Paige, you love that movie? I love that movie!"

I make a mental note to select *The Parent Trap* as a Friday movie night option.

It rained overnight, and surprisingly each of the girls in the cabin slept well. The rhythmic pitter-patter of the rain on the roof probably acted as white noise. I wake earlier than the children and slip into my running shoes. I cleared my morning runs with Brooke and Stephanie. If I'm up before the campers, they have no issues with me sneaking in a quick run. The first few days, we won't have many breaks from the campers as we help them adjust to Camp CGO, but we've been intentional about saying what one thing we need to do solo for the next few days.

Brooke is on dinner duty tonight with Tom, and she's going to take her crochet to the mess hall half an hour early so she can have a few minutes of quiet. Stephanie is supervising a morning rock wall climbing group with Brooke, but asked if she could sneak out for a walk after lunch.

I ease out the cabin door and begin my run, feeling thankful that Brooke and Stephanie are already the closest friends I've had as an adult. I think they're the closest friends I've had since I was ten and my best friend Vera moved away to Texas. Thinking of Vera always brings a pang to my heart, but today the twinge is short-lived, because in the fresh, dewy morning, just in front of me down the path, is Connor.

Connor's running. He's heading down the path away from me, and I can see the earbuds in his ears. He can't hear me. The children are all under supervision, and all this talk of pranking has me thinking that now is the perfect time to make my move.

34

CONNOR

The rain kept me up last night. Were the cabins leaking? Was everyone ok? What would happen in the morning? Would the kids be happy to be here? What if it never stopped raining? *What if…what if… what if…* By the time five-thirty rolled around, I knew that I needed to simply start the day instead of fearing it.

At six a.m., I'm out the door and striding down the trails. I would run by the cabins to check in on things, but I don't want to disturb the sleeping campers. And the counselors would have sent me a message if anything was wrong. *No news is good news.*

I take a deep breath of the sweet summer air and decide to run to the main road. If I take a trail there, it will be a three-mile out and back. The perfect running workout before a long day.

Jamming earbuds into my ears and queuing the music I downloaded when we were in civilization, I take off down the trail, relishing the feel of my feet pounding on the earth.

I've gone maybe a half mile and am on the part of the trail where thick stands of trees line each side. I slow, sensing something behind me. There are animals in Northern Michigan that I'd prefer not to run into. Our game cameras haven't shown anything, but it's good to be alert.

I glance behind me to see what's there.

My eyes make contact with Paige, who's chasing me down the trail with a smile on her face. I can tell she is gaining on me, so I try to pick up my speed. I'm still moving forward, despite looking over my shoulder, and don't see the root splicing across the packed trail.

I hit the ground hard, hip first. The impact forces the air from my body and I lie there, stunned.

"Connor?" Paige's face swims into view. "Connor? Are you alright?"

I close my eyes against the vision that is Paige's face framed by the morning sunlight. "Yeah." I push off my elbow and start to stand. "Just knocked the wind out of me."

"Is anything hurting? I'm so sorry. I was hoping to just startle you and then run with you for a while if you wanted. I'm so sorry."

I'm fine. And I wish she'd stop apologizing. I pull up the corner of my shirt to show her where I made impact with the ground. "Just right here."

Paige's eyes widen, then contract. "You're going to have a bruise."

I shrug. "I've had worse." I start to stand, but Paige offers me a hand. It's entirely too tempting to pay her back. Grasping her hand in mine, I pretend like I'm going to stand, but tug her down to the ground instead.

She was clearly not expecting it because she topples forward and lands on my lap.

I couldn't have planned this better.

"Sorry!" she squeaks as she presses her splayed palms against my chest and looks into my eyes. Her blue eyes are an even deeper hue than I'd realized until they were framed by the pines around us. Her lips are a soft pink, and her cheeks are flushed from running, and heat emanates from her body. Her eyelids lower as her lashes flutter. It's instinct. I lean toward her just as she hops up and apologizes again.

"Sorry!"

I grumble a curse word under my breath. "Paige." I groan. "Would you please stop apologizing."

"Sor—"

"You're doing it again."

Her lips purse as she sighs. "Yeah. I over-apologize."

I stand, dusting off my shorts as I go. "What were you trying to do exactly?"

She bites her lip, but there's a twinkle of mischief in her eyes. "I was hoping to surprise you… To run past you and then maybe race."

I blink. "Did you just challenge me to a race?"

She grins and sprints down the trail ahead of me. All I can do is laugh at myself and take off after her, the bruise on my hip forgotten.

Paige wins the race. It's not because I'm slower. I really enjoy watching her run, and I can't watch her run if I'm in front of her. When she bursts onto the gravel parking lot near the mess hall, she turns and pumps her fist in the air. "I won!" she calls out, her voice breathy and her red hair flying behind her. I'm only steps behind her as she relishes this victory.

"Fine," I huff. "You won this time." I take a moment to catch my breath, then open my arms for a hug.

Paige steps toward me, but her eyes widen and she shakes her head *no*. She holds her hand up for a high-five instead.

Have I mentioned how much I despise my brother sometimes?

I give her the high-five and step back, just in time to see Brooke and Matt walking toward the mess hall with six of the girl campers and four of the boys. Avila is wearing the turkey hat again today. "Paigeeee!" she calls and runs out of the group, crashing into Paige in a hug. It's insane, but I'm jealous.

"Oof." Paige winces at the impact. "Hey, Avila." She surveys the rest of the group. "Hey, Brooke. Matt. What are you all doing up?"

Brooke rolls her eyes at Paige's obvious attempt to direct the attention off of me and her. "*We* were all up early and decided to go play some games at the meeting place on the green until breakfast." Her eyes sparkle.

Matt chooses this moment to narrow his eyes in suspicion. "What were you *two* doing?"

"Running," Paige says at the same time I say, "Nothing!" which, of course, only serves to make us sound guilty of *something*. Even if the only thing we're guilty of right now is flirting.

"Mmkayyy." Brooke says with a knowing glance at Paige. "Who's making breakfast today?"

I check my watch. "It's me. I'll get it started as soon as I'm showered up." The kids' eyes bounce back and forth between Paige and me. When in doubt, deflect suspicious preteens with conversations about food. "It's French toast!"

The kids cheer. I start to say something to Paige, like, "I can't wait to race you again," but my phone rings, the screen filling with Chet's picture.

I wipe the sweat off my brow with the back of my hand. "See you soon, then," I call to the group as I walk away from the curious eyes.

Paige gives a half-hearted little wave and says something to Brooke.

Chet's voice is at inhuman volumes. "Connor! I'm a dad!"

"You've been a dad, like, since before you even knew it, you doofus."

"Yeah, I know, but Ember had the baby!"

I grin. "That's great. Everything's good?"

"Everything is amazing!" He's practically yelling, and I can tell he is too worked up to give details unless I ask him the questions.

"So is the baby a boy or a girl?"

"It's a GIRL. Connor, I have a daughter!" He sounds thrilled, and also like he's had straight caffeine for hours on end.

"That's great. What's my niece's name?"

"Samwise!"

I pause for a moment. "Like the hobbit?"

I hear Chet swallow. "No…uhh…her name is…Samantha Elizabeth."

"Sure it is." I snort. "I do hear that babies are a lot like hobbits, you know. I believe they love multiple breakfasts, lunches, teas, and suppers."

Chet groans. "You're never letting that go, are you?"

"Nope."

"Well, *Sam* is perfect. And Ember's doing great. Blaze is coming to meet her later today after Jayden's mom can get him here. And now I'm going to call the rest of the family, who will *not* be told that I accidentally called her a hobbit name. And also, in my defense, having a baby takes forever, but I couldn't eat anything because the smell bothered Emb, and I didn't want to leave her, and *The Lord of the Rings* was on the hospital movie channel, and all I've had the past twelve hours is coffee because I needed to stay awake. But I wanted to let you know everything is great here."

I smile at Chet's verbal barrage. "Glad all is well with Samwise O'Malley. Send me a picture once everyone is decent!"

I hang up on Chet before he can respond. I wanted to talk to him about the ridiculous relationship stipulations while at camp, but now isn't the time.

I can't help the chuckle that escapes me as I duck into the shower after my run. *Samwise, indeed.*

35

PAIGE

The next week of leadership camp flies by. Our campers have developed a routine, and the boys and girls have started forging friendships not only with their cabinmates, but with the opposite gender.

Father Matthi comes by Saturday afternoon for Mass, and the triplets, another girl, and four boys attend. I'm surprised when Connor appears with Tom and sits on the log bench nearest the altar in the small wooden chapel. He passes where I sit at the very back of the chapel while I keep an eye on the children, and gives me a gentle squeeze on the shoulder. The touch makes me want to melt. Connor has been visible to the campers, helping lead excursions around the grounds, supervising swimming, and helping in the kitchen. I haven't had kitchen duty this week, so I haven't had any alone time with him since I ambushed him on his run.

Embarrassment about how I ended up on his lap for a moment, and how I would have definitely broken the code of conduct if I wasn't worried about him being hurt, courses through me. I'm distracted for all of Mass by the lingering weight of Connor's touch.

The Saturday dinner of chicken sandwiches with mashed potatoes, creamed corn, and Brussels sprouts is followed by brownie sundaes. I'm stuffed as I head to the Saturday bonfire with Avila and Beth. All the other girls are already at the campfire site, but these two insisted they needed to go back to the cabin first.

"I feel like you might need to roll me there, girls," I say, a hand on my belly. "I'm so stuffed."

Beth giggles, then pushes her glasses back up her nose.

Avila grins. "Like a cannonball or like a log?"

I consider for a moment. "Definitely a log. What was your favorite activity today?"

The girls were in groups different from mine earlier. I think they went swimming and hiking while I manned the fifty-foot climbing wall with Lucas and a group of all boys. It was a lot of fun as the boys raced up the wall and threw challenges at Lucas and me. At the end, Lucas gave the boys his stopwatch and they timed him. When he came back down, the boys insisted I try to beat his time. Laughingly, I tried. And also failed. The boys were sweet and encouraging the whole time though. Watching their fledgling leadership abilities grow has been healing something inside me.

"I liked swimming because Connor was there," Avila says with narrowed eyes and fake innocence.

"Ohhh. Yeah, he's super cute," Beth responds.

"Girls," I cut in. "That's not appropriate." Even though my brain is laughing. *Yeah, he is, and ladies, he's with me.* Also, even as I tell them it's not appropriate to harbor a crush on a camp counselor, my brain supplies, *Doesn't every twelve-year-old have a crush on a camp counselor at some point?*

"Yeah…" Avila twirls a strand of hair around her finger while she looks off. "He's too old for us."

"Like a grandpa," Beth supplies.

"Hey, now!" I say. "If he's old like a grandpa, that makes me really old too. I'm almost his age."

I regret the words as soon as they are out of my mouth. Avila and Beth stop and look at each other while some sort of nonverbal communication passes between them.

"Ooooooh," they say in unison.

"Paige and Connor are about the same age…" Avila starts.

"And Paige thinks he's *cute*," Beth adds.

"Woah!" I hold up a hand. "Wait. Girls, I didn't say that…"

"You didn't have to. It's written on your face every time you see him." Avila sings her replies now. She sounds like that scene in *Miss Congeniality* where Sandra Bullock's character sing-songs all her responses.

"What…No…I…" I'm flustered and even more confused when Avila looks behind me with wide eyes and a gigantic cat-got-the-cream grin. She tugs Beth's hand and yells, "Byeeee!" as she runs down the path to the campfire, pulling Beth with her.

I shake my head for a moment at their antics. I know whenever I have Avila in a group there won't be a dull moment. I'm so busy working through whatever *that* was with Avila and Beth that I miss the sound of footsteps coming down the path behind me.

"Hey," a deep voice rumbles right behind me. I, being a sane woman, alone on a path in the woods, do the only logical thing possible in response to being startled: I scream, turn around, hold my hands up and karate chop whatever the thing is that startled me. Unfortunately, my hands chop into a very solid chest.

Once my brain registers that this is a human person who is *not* out to get me, I raise my gaze and meet Connor's bright eyes twinkling with laughter. He puts his hand over mine, which is still on his chest but now grasping a fistful of his Camp CGO t-shirt. "Were you going to chop me to death?"

My brain is still not fully functional because I don't back away. "What? Oh. No. I was…startled."

"And you karate chop when you're startled?" he teases while his thumb rubs circles on my hand.

"No. I…I don't know. It was spur-of-the-moment thing."

"Hmmm," he hums. "So what was going on with those two? Why did they take off running like that?"

It takes a moment for my brain to catch up, but it finally does. I reluctantly let go of his shirt and take a step back. "Oh…uh…they were talking about you."

He leans down toward me. "Why?"

"They think you're cute."

He whistles. "That's new."

"Ehhh," I say. "Don't read too much into it. They also said you're cute like a grandpa."

"Grandpa-cute. I never thought I'd be in that category at the age of twenty-five, but I guess I'll take it."

"Yeah, and then they may have gotten an idea about me and you being together."

Connor's eyebrows arch. "How would that have happened? I know Chet's rules are ridiculous, and I will be talking to him about it, but with the new baby, it didn't seem like the right time."

"Ember had the baby?" It's more of a shriek than a question. "And you didn't think to tell me?"

Connor's mouth contorts into an expression that can only be described as 'oops.'

"I'm sorry." He clenches his hands into fists. "Chet called me right after our run, and then things have been busy, and I thought maybe Ember would have told you, but that's silly because she's with Samwise—"

"Hold up, hold it. They named their baby *Samwise*?"

Connor grimaces. "No. Kinda?"

"For someone with information that I would like to know, you are really *not* doing a good job at communicating it!" I shove his chest lightly to make my point. He catches my hand and traps it there against his heart.

"I'm sorry, Paige." His tone is so sincere that I almost feel bad for lightly shoving him, but it led to him touching me and me touching him, so I can't regret it too much. "Chet called me right after we finished running. Ember had a healthy baby girl named *Samantha Elizabeth*, but when I talked to Chet, he was running on no sleep, coffee, and a *The Lord of the Rings* movie marathon, courtesy of the hospital movie channel. He accidentally told me the baby's name was Samwise, and now I can't think of her as anything but a baby hobbit."

I snort. "That's perfect. Do you have a picture?"

"Yeah. I'll send it to you. But you can see it first."

He pulls his phone from his shorts pocket and extends the screen to me. Ember is there, looking a little puffy and swollen, but she's looking down on a tiny bundle in her arms with such love and tenderness that I want to cry. I bite back the tears.

"Here's another one of just Sam…gah. I can't do it. She's Samwise always and forever in my mind now." Connor laughs as his thumb swipes the screen to the next picture.

It's an image of a beautiful baby girl with a soft pink ribbon bow across her head. Her nose is crinkled, and her eyes are closed, her long lashes fluttering out over her alabaster skin. She's wrapped in a cream-colored blanket with her little feet sticking out.

"She's beautiful."

"Yeah. I'm an uncle again." Connor shakes his head as he puts the phone back into his pocket. "Well, since I'm *grandpa-cute*, I best be on my way to go see my admirers."

I roll my eyes but walk with him to the campfire. My fingers itch to take his hand, but I ball my hands into fists in my sweatshirt pocket instead.

36

CONNOR

Campfires with forty preteens are not for the faint of heart. Lucas brought his guitar and he strums popular melodies while the kids talk. There's a lot of squealing. I notice that the boys and girls are intermingled now.

This is both a good thing and a bad thing. Good because the kids are making friends and bad because now I have to be on the lookout for inappropriate behavior. All it takes is one poorly executed truth or dare to make a *big* problem for me.

Avila sees Paige and me coming up to the camp circle. "Hey, Connor!" She grins and bounds over with a bounce in her step the Energizer Bunny would be jealous of. The light of the flames reflects the mischief in her eyes. It's not fully dark yet, but it will be soon.

I glance at Paige's eyes and find them narrowed while she shoots Avila a warning.

"Soooo, Connor." She draws out the *o* so for so long it makes the one-syllable word at least six. "Do you have a girlfriend?" She bursts into giggles and runs away back to sit by her sisters and her friends.

I rub the back of my neck. As much as I'd love to proclaim Paige's and my fledgling relationship, I can't. The most truthful thing I can say that still offers a substantial deflection is this: "I don't know what that has to do with leadership camp."

I catch the barest trace of hurt in Paige's eyes as I turn to face the culprit of the question. I will myself not to react.

"But you've *had* girlfriends, right?" Aleigha presses.

My heart drops. "Yes."

"So, girlfriends are good, right?"

Prickles erupt on my neck. "Yes. Girlfriends are good when you're older. There's none of that happening with campers at this camp though." I clap my hands on my thighs. I don't have to dig too deep to find a way to direct this conversation elsewhere. "We have a special evening planned for you tonight," I say, speaking louder so that the entire circle of campers can hear me. "Lucas is going to play some songs and we're going to learn some lyrics."

Lucas begins strumming the tune of an incredibly popular and catchy preschool song.

As expected, a chorus of complaints assaults me. "Not this *again!*" and "We're too old for this!" and "There's *no* way! I'm not singing *this* little kid's song!"

I hold my hands up. Lucas stops strumming for a moment. A subtle nod at the counselors has them ready for the next part.

Lucas begins playing the song from the top, but this time, each counselor sings the lyrics. The counselors are getting into the song, making hand motions and dancing. Paige's red hair keeps catching the reflection of the firelight as she moves. Matt is completely uninhibited, making a fool of himself but also obviously having the time of his life. The kids look on, confused, as the counselors finish the song and sit down.

Lucas plays a soft melody in the back.

"That was *awesome!*" Matt exclaims, offering Lucas a pat on the arm.

Brooke stands next to her much taller twin. "I had a great time, but I wish I had more friends to join me. Sometimes, being a leader means that you don't care about looking silly, or being too old for something wholesome and fun. You guys missed out."

Matt leans down and whispers to Brooke, "What? No way. They won't do it."

She shoves his shoulder lightly.

He leans down again.

"Fine," she huffs and rolls her eyes dramatically. "My brother here—"

"He's your brother?"

Brooke nods. "Yep. Twins, but I'm still older."

Then, without missing a beat, she continues. "My brother has suggested that I invite anyone *brave* enough to be a little silly to join me." She shrugs. "But I told him you won't do it. I'm going to close my eyes and Lucas is going to start again, and when I open my eyes, I'll see who's brave enough to have fun."

Lucas begins the opening notes of 'Baby Shark' and I watch as, one by one the kids stand. There's varying degrees of participation, but by the end of the last shark, each camper has a huge smile on their face.

Brooke hops onto one of the log benches and yells, "That was *awesome!* Who had fun?"

The campers roar back in approval, and I have to laugh at her. This campfire song evening is part of our curriculum, and Brooke loved the idea so much that we gave her full reign over the lesson.

"Ok," Brooke continues from her perch on top of the log. "So you know how to have fun and how to be silly. But do you know how to help other people join in the fun? Being a leader is all about having your own fun but being sensitive to others too. You have to find a balance between the two."

Matt hops onto the log next to Brooke. Stephanie and Paige stand off to the side, surrounded by their own groups of campers. "I have an idea, but my sister would *never* go for it."

Brooke fixes Matt with a glare. "Them's fighting words, Matthew."

"Fine. Let's have a competition."

Brooke grins. It's all part of the lesson, but they pull it off so seamlessly that the kids have no idea. "You're on. How should we do it."

"Ok. We will split the campers into groups of four, each group will be with a counselor and each group will need to choose a silly song. Then, they'll need to perform it and get everyone involved."

"But Matt, how will we win?" a boy calls out.

Brooke raises her brow. "An excellent question, George! Whichever group gets the most people involved will be the winner!"

The kids roar their approval, and Brooke begins separating the campers into four groups.

I pull my phone out and begin snapping pictures for the CGO parent emails. Parents love to see pictures of their children, and while I've taken a few this week, I haven't taken as many as I should. The parents loved the privacy of a secure email, and no one had any issues with sending photographs of the activities this way.

Lucas comes to stand by me. "It's going really well."

I resist the urge to do something superstitious like knock on wood. "Yeah. I hope it stays that way. You good with all the music? Sorry if they put you on the spot."

"Nah. It's fine. These are preschool songs, and they really don't have that much variety. It's nothing compared to Stephanie and Brooke's usual selections." Lucas grins. "I'm going to see what songs they've chosen."

I'm not sure how he got to be so unflappable, but I appreciate his steadiness as he walks off.

Stephanie and Jorge have formed a group, standing too close together for normal friends. I frown. There's clearly attraction between them. I'm going to have to separate them. But also, I'm the pot and the kettle then.

Paige has her own group, as do Brooke and Matt. I walk around the campfire taking pictures of the groups as they whisper-sing their songs. Paige's group is the last one I meander over to. I stand behind the group, and Paige's back is to me. I try to pretend that I stand a little too close to her because everyone's whispering, but even I don't buy it.

Paige's red hair is scooped up on top of her head in a giant messy bun. I can see the slender column of her neck, and just barely make out the dusting of freckles there. I have the insane urge to kiss them. I push that down and lock that urge tightly away.

Paige's campers are laughing.

"What song did you decide on?" I ask.

Paige's body instantly turns and I put my arms out, craving her touch, wanting to draw her in. But she steps back instead of forward, and I let my arms fall awkwardly to my side.

Allison steps forward. She's the most reserved of the three Button sisters, but I've gotten to know her a little because she's done a few activities with me. Whenever I'm in charge of a group, I do my best to spend a little time with each kid. Swimming, hiking, and paddle-boarding have been a great way to do that.

"'The Alphabet Song.'" She giggles.

I stare. Out of all the options, Paige's group chose that? I must look as confused as I feel because Allison snorts.

"But backward. We're going to play on the competitive nature of the other campers and challenge them to the alphabet song, but backward."

I laugh. It's actually an ingenious idea. Wholesome fun. It's perfect. My admiration for Paige just keeps growing. Her sense of humor, her beauty, the way the firelight illuminates her eyes…

"TIME!" Lucas calls across the campfire. "Let's see what you got!" He looks around and sees me standing near Paige. The faintest flicker of a smirk passes over his features. I am not doing a good job of *not* showing that I'm attracted to her.

"Matt, let's do your group first!" Matt's group is settled on one of the four logs around the fire, and the campers begin a rousing rendition of "The Ants Go Marching." Next, Brooke's group is up. They perform "BINGO" but add a few extra letters, so instead of BINGO, it's "CAMP CGO." Stephanie and Jorge's group made their own song up to the tune of "This Little Light of Mine." The lyrics are funny and don't really rhyme, but everyone is laughing and singing and having a great time.

Finally, Paige's group is called. Allison takes the lead. "We present to you," she says with a flourish and a small bow, "'The Alphabet Song,' but in reverse, and I bet you can't do it as well as we can."

To quote Brooke from earlier, 'Them's fighting words,' and the other groups rise to the challenge in spectacular form. It is obvious that Paige's group has run away with the challenge and won.

I click record on my camera and film a video of the entire camp crew singing 'P, O, N, M, L, K, J…" When the song ends at 'A', a camper from Stephanie and Jorge's group jumps up.

"That was awesome!" he shouts. "Let's do it again."

Lucas laughs and starts strumming again while Paige's group belts out the beginning of the end of the alphabet.

Everyone is laughing, happy, and content. Stephanie pulls the tote bags over from where she stashed them earlier. She opens the bag of gluten-free marshmallows, and Jorge passes out roasting sticks to any camper who wants to make a s'more. I settle on a log bench next to Lucas. I try to put distance between Paige and me, but I can't stop myself from looking at her.

Lucas elbows me. "You know, you don't hide it."

I frown. "Hide what?" I regret the words the moment I say them because I know exactly what he means.

Lucas inclines his head toward Paige and purses his lips in an exaggerated kissing face. I roll my eyes.

A girl walks up to Paige, holding her stomach and whispering something in Paige's ear. Paige hops up and says something to the girl. They walk around the group and begin the path up to the main camp buildings. I'm on my feet, following behind them so fast that I almost don't hear Lucas' laughter as I click on my flashlight.

"Hey, Paige?" I call as I lengthen my strides to catch up to them. "Is everything ok?"

The girl standing next to Paige flushes beetroot red.

"Yes, of course." Paige takes one look at the girl and meets my eyes. "Tina and I are just heading to the infirmary for something."

"Oh? Are you sick?" I ask Tina.

Tina shakes her head no.

Paige's eyes shoot lasers at me, and I am suddenly reminded of the time a tampon hit me in the face.

"Oh." Understanding dawns. I'm not sure who's more embarrassed, Tina or me at embarrassing her. Periods are nothing to be embarrassed of, but I hate that I drew attention where she didn't want it.

"I'll, uh, let the campers know it's time to turn in. Let me know if you need anything else, Paige. Tina."

I head back to the campfire, disappointed to not get to spend more time with Paige today. Stolen moments and quick texts aren't enough. But what about long ones? What about a real conversation with her?

Suddenly, the idea of sending forty preteens off to bed doesn't sound overwhelming, it sounds like the best part of my day.

Whistling, I hurry to do just that.

31

PAIGE

It's supposed to be a quick visit to the infirmary with Tina, where I supply her with feminine hygiene products and some medication from her parent-approved list to help with her cramps, but when Tina starts crying, I know it won't be.

She tells me about how money is tight, and she's always worried about asking for supplies. She's twelve and doesn't have a job, but she's trying to think of what she can do to earn some money to contribute and how she's only here at the camp because she got a scholarship.

My heart breaks for her. I knew that feminine hygiene products are difficult necessities for lower-income areas, but I didn't realize how much it would hurt her to see my fully stocked tubs.

My phone has buzzed at least six times while I've been in here with Tina, but I haven't flipped it over or picked it up from where it sits on the shelf. I want to give Tina my full attention. She deserves my full attention.

Tina clutches the small brown bag full of supplies to her chest. "Thank you, Paige." She wipes her eyes with the back of her hands.

"Of course," I say, resisting the urge to cry along with Tina. She doesn't need pity right now.

She tosses her two long braids over her shoulders and fidgets. "Would you..." She bites her lip and looks at the ground. "Would you please come with me to the bathroom to get ready for bed? I don't like to walk from the cabin to the bathhouse by myself at night. I'm afraid of the dark."

Just like that, I'm twelve years old again, and my mom left, and I hate the dark. I hate it because it hid her leaving. I don't know what horrors Tina sees in the dark, but I know they're there.

I shove the thoughts of my mom away and say, "Sure. I have to brush my teeth and get ready too." I pick up my flashlight and my phone, and on an impulse, grab one of the emergency flashlights I keep on a shelf in the infirmary.

I say a silent prayer of thanks for Connor's insistence that there be extra flashlights everywhere on this campus. I click it on and hand it to Tina.

We trudge down the path to the cabins and the bathhouse together, our flashlights bobbing twin patches of light ahead of us.

It's late when I finally get into my bed. I tuck myself in under the covers and burrow down in the soft warmth. It is the dog days of summer, but still cold at night. The sweet breeze of Lake Superior rolls through the window screen and I catch a glimpse of my phone with a bunch of notifications. I remember the buzzes in the infirmary.

Curiosity gets the better of me.

I throw the covers over my head so as not to disturb the soft snores of the sleeping campers and punch in the passcode.

I have six texts from Connor.

Connor

I'm sorry I didn't tell you about Samwise.

I was very impressed by your group's backward alphabet tonight.

Ok, I haven't been very good at the texting stuff, but I wanted to tell you that you looked beautiful tonight.

And that my mom is a dentist, but I think it's gross when kids lose teeth.

Wow, you've been in the infirmary for a long time. I hope everything's ok. Let me know if you need anything.

I'll see you in the morning, Paige.

I bite back a laugh at Connor's texts. He's so boyish and sweet. And also I'm not sure where the confession about teeth came from, but I love that he's telling me random things.

I'm not sure if I should text back. It might be eleven forty-eight p.m. and entirely too late to text, but I do it anyway.

Paige

I'll forgive you about Samwise, but only if you promise to let me meet her first. Vampire teeth don't gross you out, just kid ones? Glad weird things from my childhood could make the campers laugh. I never imagined it would be a positive thing to know, but it worked. And you didn't look so bad yourself today...and every day. Goodnight, Connor.

I hit send and then lie there wide awake as I worry I implied entirely too much about my childhood. It would be better if he didn't know, but there's no way for me to unsend the text. I hope he'll just breeze over my comment about the backward alphabet in my childhood. Maybe he'll think it was just something silly all the kids in Viewport did for entertainment when we were eight.

I am groggy the next morning. It's an 'I tossed and turned all night, feel run down, kind of want to throw axes' type of day. It is also my turn to be on kitchen duty.

Tom is already in the kitchen when I arrive. He's practically taken over as chef and handyman, and I'm grateful he's there. Two people can handle making an industrial-sized breakfast much easier than one.

Tom takes one look at me before he sets down the giant spoon he's using to stir a vat of pancake batter. "You look like you've got something on your mind."

"Don't we all," I mutter to the griddles I'm placing on the giant stove to heat.

"Paige," Tom says. "What's bothering you? Is it Connor?"

I meet his blue eyes and am amazed at how this man, with his disheveled appearance, is so much more than he seems. He's intuitive and kind. "Uh. Yeah." I scratch the back of my neck. "Or no, I just said something I think he wasn't ready to hear."

Tom stares at me expectantly.

"It was about my childhood."

Tom continues staring.

"My mom is an alcoholic who also struggles with gambling and other substance addictions. She left when I was twelve, but when I was little, she taught me to sing the alphabet."

"The alphabet?" Tom questions.

Shame heats my face. "She taught me to sing it backward because it would help her with a sobriety test when she got pulled over. I didn't realize until I was about fifteen why she did it. And it ruined the happy memory I have of that day. And then yesterday, I taught the campers the backward alphabet song, and I shouldn't have told Connor about my childhood."

Tom blinks, then begins scooping cups of pancake batter onto the griddle while I stand by with the spatula. "You keep yourself folded as small as possible. Compact. Like being rolled into a tight ball means nothing will ever hurt you."

The pancakes sizzle merrily and tears sting my eyes. Tom has just explained who I am in less than four sentences. "Yeah," I say. "I do."

"What if Connor wants to know all about you? What if he's not going to hurt you? He has his own troublesome memories he's working through."

I shrug. "I know, but most people don't have the kind of baggage I do."

"Connor might have something different to say about that."

I scoff. "Please. I know Chet was a fool, but Connor's not like that. He learned from his brother, and he certainly doesn't have a son he never knew about."

Tom shakes his head and spoons more batter on the griddles while I begin flipping the earlier ones over. We work in silence as I move the finished pancakes to the warmers and Tom retrieves the cut fruit from the fridge. I start the sausage sizzling as Tom washes the pancake dishes. It's a simple breakfast, but it's plenty for the kids and the counselors.

"Good morning, Connor," Tom calls across the mess hall. He tips his head in my direction, and Connor, rubbing sleep from his eyes and looking adorably boyish, changes his course.

"Good morning." He walks over, his voice gravelly and low. It's closer in timbre to Chet's voice than I've ever heard, and all I can think of is that Ember's description of a 'weighted blanket' voice fits Connor too.

"H-hi," I stammer.

"Did you sleep ok?" he asks, concern lining his face.

"Uh…" I search for words because my mind is creating visions of a cozy moment between the two of us and I have to stop that train of thought immediately. "Yeah, sure…it was fine."

Tom announces loudly, "I'm going to go back to the freezer to get some more sausage patties."

Connor reaches out and touches my arm. "You weren't up too late attending to the needs of campers, were you?"

"No."

"It was late when you texted."

"Yeah."

"What did you mean about your childhood? And the alphabet?"

"Oh…" I breathe. I bite my lip and don't know what I want to tell him. "My mom… I don't have a lot of happy memories of her."

Connor's blue eyes look like Lake Superior this morning, endlessly deep as he watches me. The intensity in them scares me but also thrills me. It pushes me to go on.

"She taught me that—"

"Connor! Hey, Connor, you in here, man? We've got a problem." Jorge comes darting through the mess hall entrance. His eyes land on Connor, and relief smooths his furrowed brow.

Connor faces Jorge, and I'm ready to throw my apron off and run to the infirmary and grab my first aid kit.

"Jorge? What is it?" Connor's voice cracks slightly, and I remember how important this job is to him. How he doesn't want to mess anything up for Chet and Ember and Blaze and baby Samwise.

"We were leading a group of the early rising campers on the loop for a morning hike and we saw…*sign*."

"As in animal poop?" Connor asks. "That's normal for the woods."

Jorge shakes his head. He lowers his voice to a whisper. "Fresh *cougar* sign."

Connor's jaw firms. "Did the kids see? Did you tell them?"

"No."

"What other counselor was with you? Did they see?"

"Stephanie, and yes, she's the one who saw it."

Connor's eyes flash with worry. "Where was it? Can you take me to it? Are all the campers off the trail?"

"The farthest point of the red loop trail. Yes, and yes, all campers are back. We stuck together as a group and returned to the cabins."

"Ok. I'll need to pull trail cam footage and see if we can spot it."

Tom walks back in, his brow creased. "Connor? Jorge? What's wrong?"

"Cougar."

"Ahh. What do you need from me, boss?" Tom says.

Connor's Adam's apple bobs as he swallows. "I'm not sure yet. But would you come with us to the spot? I think you know these woods better than anyone else."

Tom shakes his head. "Sure thing. Paige, you good serving breakfast on your own today?"

Jorge meets my eyes. "I can get Brooke or Stephanie or…Lucas to help."

I wave them off. "I'm good. Please go. This is an easy breakfast."

The three men before me nod and hurry off. On the way out, Connor calls, "Paige, please don't say anything to the campers, but of course the counselors need to know. I'll have a protocol in place once I know what we're dealing with, and then we can tell the campers."

I nod, a tight-lipped smile on my face. A pang of guilt that I am resentful of the stupid cougar for interrupting my conversation with Connor crashes over me.

I shake my head. The safety of the campers is more important than anything I could have said at that moment.

I blow out a breath and watch as a stray strand that escaped my Camp CGO hat dances in the stream of air.

I tip the last of the sausages into the warmer and head to ring the mess bell.

As the campers eat and I keep an eye on the food, refilling as needed, I make a note to say something quietly to the other counselors. Stephanie approaches the pancakes with her tray.

"Eventful morning?" I ask.

"Yeah. You know?" she says as she slides two pancakes onto her plate.

"Yes. What do you think we do now?"

Stephanie shrugs. "I don't know, but it scares me that it was so close to the cabins."

"I thought it was at the farthest point of the red loop."

"That's not that far from the cabins. I mean, they're dangerous animals and they have huge territories. It's not like it would just stop right there and not venture farther."

"Maybe it was just passing through," I suggest.

"Paige." She drops her voice to a low whisper. "It was *fresh*-fresh."

"Oh." Understanding breaks over me and slides down my body. "So it's a problem today more than anything."

"Yeah."

Lucas sidles over with his tray. "Whatcha whispering about, ladies?" He's teasing, and I'm grateful for the way he breaks the tension.

Stephanie turns to him. "Jorge and I took the early-rising campers for a hike this morning. And we saw fresh cougar signs."

Lucas's eyes widen. "Here? I know they can be in these parts, but they have, like, a two-hundred-mile radius for their territories. What are the chances?"

Stephanie shakes her head. "I don't know, but I don't like it."

"Connor asked us not to tell the campers until they understand more about what we're dealing with and have a safety protocol in place."

"Connor asked us not to tell what?" Matt slides his tray along the rail and butts into our conversation. Brooke isn't far behind.

"Yeah, what are we keeping from the campers right now?" Brooke asks.

I look out at the group of kids sitting around the tables, laughing, joking, smiling, and feeling safe. I know that telling them there's a terrifying forest creature out there without giving them a plan for staying safe is a terrible idea, but I feel…weird about it.

"Uh. Stephanie and Jorge did the early risers hike this morning and saw fresh cougar poop on the trail."

A whistle escapes Brooke's lips. "That's not good. What are we doing about it?"

Stephanie's shoulders droop. "I don't know. They're investigating it now, right?"

"Yeah. Connor said they need to check trail cams and things too."

"Are you *sure* it was what you thought it was? It couldn't have been…a black bear?" Matt asks Stephanie.

She rolls her eyes. "Matt. Didn't you study the field guides?"

"Uh…" He holds his pointer finger and thumb together just a fraction of a space apart. "This much."

Brooke smacks his shoulder. "C'mon, Mattie. You're disgracing the family name. You *know* black bear and cougar poop would look nothing alike."

"Hey!" Matt exclaims, rubbing his shoulder. "It's all just so… poopy."

I roll my eyes at his immaturity, but stop midroll as Connor strides back through the mess hall with Tom and Jorge on his heels.

"Connor!" Several of the campers jump up when they see him.

"What group are you leading today?"

"Will you play frisbee with us again today?"

"I think I figured out how to do the paddleboard, I want to try it again!"

He slows his pace and smiles at the kids, listening to the ones calling out his name and fist bumping others. I know in my core that Connor is a good man, and I want to laugh at the way he's become a camp celebrity. I guess being the only adult who isn't always present but still manages to do fun activities makes you a hot commodity.

He finally excuses himself from the campers, sees the group of counselors standing by the pancakes and waves before disappearing down the hallway to his office. Jorge brings a tray over while Tom disappears in the same direction as Connor.

"So?" Stephanie asks, nervous. It occurs to me that she wants to be wrong.

"You were right," Jorge says. His shoulders deflate.

"I was hoping it was a mistake." Stephanie rubs a hand over her face and snorts. "I hate being observant."

Matt surprises me by stepping up to Stephanie. "Hey, you did exactly what you were supposed to do. You noticed something and now we can adjust. The kids are going to have a great time. We're going to keep them safe. And you are the reason for that." He slings an arm around her shoulder and she quickly leans into it before leaning away. "Now, let's go eat. I'm starving."

Matt grabs his tray and heads to an empty table. The rest of the counselors follow him. I'm struck with the sinking sensation that I've misjudged Matt.

The campers are finishing their breakfast when Connor purposefully strides back into the mess hall. Tom sidles over to me and begins removing the warmer trays and cleaning up.

"You should go sit down and listen to this," Tom whispers as he passes me.

I meet his eyes and see the earnestness there. Tom is an enigma, but he's never steered me wrong. As I approach, Brooke and Stephanie slide apart to make room for me.

A sharp, piercing whistle splits the air and every eye in the room is on Connor.

"Hey," Connor says, a little nervously. Usually the campers call something out, but they all remain silent as they look at him. "I know we've all been here for a week, and we've settled in, but we have to make some changes to our routine for today, and possibly the next few days. I..." He runs his hand through his curls, and I watch in amazement as they spring right back into place. "I need to tell you why first. Northern Michigan is home to cougars. We found evidence of one on a trail today. Cougars are very dangerous, especially if encountered alone. The best thing is to remain in a large group and to know that if you see one, you should back away slowly. Do NOT run, and do NOT turn away from the animal."

There's a buzz as the campers all begin talking at once.

Connor whistles again and the room falls silent. "Cougars have massive territories, and it's likely this one is just passing on by, but we still need to be careful. We'll follow protocol for the next week and continue to evaluate the situation."

"But, what about...like going to the bathroom at night?" Beth calls out.

"Sure thing," Connor replies. "You'll need to go in a group and have a counselor with you."

"I've contacted the Cougar Conservation Group, and they're coming out to do some things this afternoon. We'll be just fine, but for today, we're having a lawn game day on the green outside the mess hall." There's a groan from the boys, but Connor cuts them off. "Girls versus boys frisbee football."

That gets the whole group of campers on their feet, stamping and cheering. I laugh at their enthusiasm while silently thanking the heavens that I'm on kitchen duty today. I won't be forced to play an entire game. I'll be able to duck out and start lunch prep with Tom around 10:30.

"You're. Going. Down," Brooke yells to Matt, and I take that as my queue to begin cleaning up after breakfast.

"Ok, everyone meet on the green by the bell in thirty minutes. Stay together as groups. One counselor with each group, please."

I shake my head as I pass through a variety of well-meaning taunts being volleyed across the aisles.

The kids clear out, and it's me and Tom and the dishes. I'm humming a song with my earbuds in and loading the industrial dishwasher with silverware when a hand circles my wrist. It's not tight and not threatening. I know who it is before I turn and find myself in Connor's gentle grasp. An earbud falls out, hanging on the string.

"Sorry," he says, letting go. "I didn't want to startle you and end up karate chopped. I tried calling your name, but you didn't hear me."

"Oh." I hit pause on my phone.

"I have to go start the game, but what were you saying earlier about your mom? And the song?"

Tom leans casually against the sink, a dish towel over his shoulder and a spatula in his hand. He's not even trying to pretend he's drying it.

The weight of what Connor's dealing with here, the sincerity of his voice and interest—I can't burden him right now. He's got enough on his plate. The CCG people will be here, and the safety of the campers rests on his shoulders. "Oh. Uh. Nothing really." I shrug. "It's not important right now."

Connor frowns and I look away. I catch a glimpse of Tom's eyes and the flicker of disappointment in them.

"Are you sure? It seemed important to you."

"Nah." I push my worry away. "It's not important right now. Don't you have a frisbee football game to begin?"

"Well, yeah…but I was hoping for something first." He opens his arms and I don't hesitate. I step into the circle of his embrace and lean my cheek against his shoulder.

I listen to the steady thump of his heart under his plaid flannel shirt, relishing the feeling of safety. I have no doubt that if anyone could keep a group of forty children safe from a prowling cougar, it's Connor.

He whispers something that sounds suspiciously like "I love the way you smell" against my hair, and then he lets go.

As he leaves, Tom calls out, "That was a lot longer than 2.5 Mississippis!" He looks at me and adopts what is clearly a faux reprimanding look. Connor is close with Tom, and I'm sure he told him about Chet's extremely specific and strict rules.

I jam the earbud back into my ear and laugh, confident that being here today is exactly where I should be.

38

CONNOR

I wouldn't recommend telling forty preteen campers that a cougar is actively roaming the woods they're starting to love. In fact, I hope to never repeat it. This morning, zero out of five stars.

I stand on the lawn by the mess hall, with Brooke beside me. Of course Brooke takes over as coach and competitive leader for the girls. A few are laughing, and some are looking at the boys in a way that can only be described as ogling.

I'm explaining the rules and think I'm doing a great job of it until Paige walks into my view. She hangs back behind the group, trying to catch up on the instructions. Lucas is in the back as well, and he says something to her that makes her face light up and laugh.

"Uhh. Connor?" Aleigha sits crisscrossed on the grounds and draws my attention back to the campers.

"Sorry, what?" I say, shaking my head to clear whatever just happened.

"You said 'there are no tack…' and then you just stopped. Did you mean there are no tackles?"

I clear my throat and glance away, catching Brooke's bemused expression before she hides a smile behind her hand. "Yes. Sorry, lost in thought for a moment. No tackles."

Brooke saves me from further awkwardness. "We all good, Camp CGO?" she shouts.

A resounding chorus of "YES!" comes back.

Brooke gets the girls situated on the lawn while I find Matt doing the same for the boys. I breathe out a laugh at the siblings. Brooke and Matt live to compete.

The game gets underway. We decide to have one counselor from each side on the field at all times. Paige declined playing, saying she needs to go start lunch prep in a bit. I need to burn off some steam after the stress of the morning, and since the girls are down an adult, I head to their sideline.

"May I be an honorary lady today?" I ask the line of campers waiting to sub in. The girls giggle. "You need to wear something *pink*, Connor."

"Ah…" I look at my shirt. "Anyone have anything pink?"

Paige has a pink buff rolled into a headband holding back her red hair. In moments of not-so-subtle judginess, Kaleigh said that redheads should *not* wear pink. Paige pulls it off just fine.

"Paige does!" A few girls point at her with a giggle.

Paige rolls her eyes, but slips it off her head and says, "Here you go, m'lady," in a teasing tone.

I give an exaggerated curtsey and respond in a high-pitched voice, "Thank you."

The entire line of girls erupts into laughter while I unroll the buff and slip it over my head. I don't use it to hold back my hair; I place it like a sweatband. I am a pink warrior.

Jorge calls out, "Sub time!"

The kids all leave the field.

Brooke comes over and plops down, slightly out of breath. "It's a battle out there," she says. "Good thing we're winning, ladies! Connor?"

"He's an honorary lady today," one of the campers supplies.

Brooke raises her eyebrows. "Well are you going to sub in or just stand here looking pretty?"

"Oh, I am *in*." I gather the girls subbing in with me for a huddle. "Ladies! On three. One, two, three…" The girls all shout, "LADIES!" And we're off.

The fact that Paige is sitting on the sidelines, watching, and cheering me (ok, actually, she's cheering the girls on) has me playing my hardest. I want to impress her.

And I'm so busy trying to impress her that I don't notice when one of the boy campers jumps up to catch the frisbee and accidentally elbows me in the nose. He doesn't even catch the frisbee, which I know because I crumple to the ground and curl my head to the grass against the blinding pain. Instead of soft grass against my forehead, I'm met with the hard plastic of the frisbee edge. It hurts. A lot.

Black spots swim in my vision.

Cool hands land on my arms, then on my face. Paige is gentle as she tips my head up to look at her. Concerned blue eyes. Pink full lips. Bright red hair.

"You're not Kaleigh." But it comes out sounding like I'm underwater.

"Connor?" the woman before me says. "Can you stand? Let's try to stand and get you cleaned up."

She pulls my arms and I stand, more than a little grossed out by the stickiness on my shirt. It's blood.

"I'm taking him to the infirmary!" she calls. "You guys should keep playing."

Paige leads me by hand through the mess hall and into the infirmary, where she gives me something to put in my nose, tips my head up, and then shines a flashlight in my eyes. "Connor?"

The pain has subsided enough to register her voice. "Paige?"

"Are you ok?"

I groan. "It really hurts. He got me right in the nose." The dazed feeling has left, and now I'm alert because, heaven help me, Paige's gloved hands are on my face and she is so close I could kiss her. Her hands rest on my cheekbones as she peers deeply into my eyes. It's entirely too intimate for this infirmary setting.

I really want to kiss her—that's what I'm going to do. I lean in, angling my head toward her lips.

She abruptly takes a step back and tilts her head at me, looking at me like I'm crazy. "Your nose has stopped bleeding, but I think you need to keep your head up for a little longer. Here's some fresh gauze." She holds out her hand and I take the gauze, my fingers grazing her gloved palm a little. "You need to replace that gauze," she says, her hand still outstretched with her palm up.

I change out the gauze and she throws the first one away in the medical trash.

"If you have a headache, I can get you some pain relievers."

"I'm ok," I say stupidly, because my face hurts a lot; it's just not the blinding, stinging pain it was at first.

"Here." She hands me a small capsule and a paper cup of water. "Just take it so you're not in a ton of pain when the CCG people come. That was an intense hit to the nose."

"Oh." I forgot about the Cougar Conservation Group. I forgot about the cougar. I forgot about camp. I forgot about the campers. I forgot about Chet and his stupid rules. Suddenly, I realize what I almost did.

Paige deserves more than me breaking the code of conduct in the infirmary.

She turns to open the door and, I presume, leave. "Paige." I reach out and touch her arm. She turns back to me. "I'm sorry. I was dazed, and you're very pretty."

I'm rewarded with a blush. "Ah. I was checking you for a concussion…and you thought I was…"

"Setting things up for a kiss," I finish for her.

She laughs lightly. "That would *not* be good."

"Yeah," I say, my eyes drawn to her lips like metal to a magnet. "You deserve a better first real kiss than something stolen and against the rules."

She flushes even deeper red and I hope she's thinking about what a kiss with me would be like.

A knock sounds on the door.

"Hey, guys!" It's Jorge. "The Cougar Conservation people are here."

Paige cracks open the door and busies herself with wiping down the table as I pass by her.

"Thank you, Paige," I whisper before opening the door fully and meeting the CCG people with a fistful of gauze shoved up my nostril.

I spend the next few hours with the CCG representatives. We hike to the sign. They take samples, then they ask to see trail camera footage.

It takes a long time to review the entire week's worth of footage, but one thing Tom and the counselors helped me with prior to the campers' arrival was to install a robust trail camera system.

We watch the footage from last night first. At one point, the giant cat stops right on the trail and faces the camera directly. It's almost like it's studying it.

"That's a big 'un," the slender woman with gray hair tucked under her official hat says.

"I don't know, Miranda, might be a record. Have we seen this one before?" This comes from the portly man who could probably be a Santa Claus impersonator.

"Well?" I say impatiently. "What do you think?"

"We need to see more footage, see if we can figure out its patterns. It might just be passing through." Miranda sinks into one of the chairs I brought into my office.

"Or it might be a denning female," Santa Claus responds.

"Well, what does that mean for us if it is a denning female?" I ask.

"Claude?" Miranda passes the verbal baton to him.

"It's good for the animals, but not so good for your camp. We can't tell if this one is male or female, so we'll watch more footage to see if we can find out. But from what it looks like on here, I'd guess it's a male, or a heavily pregnant female."

The rest of the trail camera footage yields no sightings of the cougar.

Miranda stands up, slapping her hands on her thighs. "Welp." I stifle a laugh. It's the old Midwest goodbye. "It's time for us to get going. We'll let you know what we discover from the sample, and you let us know if you see any more sightings, but I'm betting that big cat was just passing through. I'd be careful for the next week, and really monitor the footage. If you don't see anything for a week or so, it's gone."

Claude nods his agreement. "Yep. They have huge territories, and you're doing the right thing. Keep the kids in groups and don't do any hiking at dawn or dusk for the next week."

I push my lips together in a tight-lipped smile. "Yes, sounds like a plan."

I walk the two officials out to their car while they make small talk about the camp.

"Yeah, it was my grandpa's property. He had the infrastructure, but it needed updates. Yes, it's up to code. Yes, it's owned by my brother. Yes, the kids are good. Yes, it's Christian-based."

Miranda leans against the driver's side of the parked car. "Keep us posted," she says as she gets in.

Claude climbs into the passenger side. "Good luck!" he calls before shutting his door.

Miranda gives a wave, and the two drive off down the road.

The next week is a whirlwind. I'm kept busy checking trail camera footage every morning, and the counselors adapt the options for the campers to include things closer to the main buildings. At the camp circle the next Friday evening before mess hall time, I'm beat but happy.

The campers sit around the bell in a semicircle as I stand before them. Paige sits off to the side next to Stephanie, and my eyes involuntarily find her. Stephanie shakes her head and gives a sharp jerk toward the campers. I haven't had many interactions with Paige this week. The ones I did have were far too brief, and instead of texting her in the evenings, I've been helping with the campers, or chatting with Tom about the cougar, or texting Chet and Ember updates about the camp. I also had to email every parent to notify them of the situation. I've fielded phone calls from several very concerned parents each evening this week.

My heart pangs with a twinge. I miss Paige, but as Stephanie's vehement gesture reminds me, I have a camp to care for.

"Camp C…" I wait for the campers to call out the rest of the letters. They do, with gusto.

"G-O!"

"It was a great week here!"

The kids nod.

"And I have good news! After the cougar sighting last week, enough time has passed that we are certain it has moved on from the area. We still need to be alert, but we can resume breaking into smaller groups and doing some of the activities you've loved."

The kids all cheer and I give them a moment to call out their suggestions for activities to add back into the week. I chuckle at their ideas, which include things we have *not* offered nor will offer as options. Free climbing the Lake Superior cliffs is not going to happen.

After a moment, I hold my hands up. "We'll let you all know." I settle them down, trying to gently remind them that the adults are in charge of the activities. "We'll still need to use a group policy for bathroom use at night, or a counselor can accompany you. But other than that, we can relax the protocol a bit. I do have one other announcement: Tuesday is August fifteenth, so Paige, Tom, and I will be taking the Catholic campers into Marquette for the Holy Day of Obligation. Brooke will be acting as the camp manager while Tom and I are offsite. Now, who's hungry?"

The campers cheer.

"Let's say grace and then head in for some food. I'm sure whatever Jorge and Tom cooked up will be delicious."

I bless myself with the sign of the cross, bow my head, say the prayer, and then ring the bell, signaling that the campers are dismissed. They leave in a flurry of activity and excitement while I lean against the bell, letting myself feel the weight of the past week as I stand in the sun with a gentle breeze lifting the curls from my neck.

I close my eyes and focus on the smell of the dirt and the unique watery lake smell that fills the air.

I am settled.

39

PAIGE

I am unsettled. I can't figure it out. But something about the words *Holy Day* and knowing that tomorrow Father Matthi will be here for the Saturday vigil Mass and that I'll sit with the Catholic campers, feeling part of something and not part of it at all has me all shaken up inside. I want to be a part of it.

My stomach is lurching, and I feel anxious, tense, and on edge. I've been putting it off for too long. I know what I need to do, but I don't know if I have the courage to do it.

I've been leaning back against my forearms on the green grass by the mess hall, my head tipped back to the welcome warmth of the sun on my face as I close my eyes. I inhale the scent of this place and know in my heart of hearts I love it here.

When I open them again and look around, I see that Connor is standing by the bell, his own eyes closed. I feel for him. While I was dealing with worried campers all week, he was dealing with adults worried about their kids. I desperately want to hug him, but I know that would be strange if any of the campers saw, and I don't think I can manage a 2.5 Mississippi count right now.

I push off the ground and head to the mess hall, ready to eat some dinner. Connor must sense as I pass by because his eyes flick open and lock with my own.

"Paige?" He's so tentative in the way he says my name, it breaks my heart a little. I stop and stare at his own blue irises.

He steps closer. "I'm sorry." He runs his hand through his hair. "I know this week was a lot, and I'm having trouble managing all this." He spreads his hands and gestures around the camp. "I…feel bad about my ability to spend time with you."

I shrug. "It's fine." I soften my words with a smile. "It was a busy week, and you had a lot on your plate. We all did. We were operating in crisis mode."

He bobs his head in agreement. "Yes, but still…when we're in Marquette on Tuesday, I have a plan."

I blink. "A plan?"

He shifts on his feet but grins. "Yes, a plan. Tom helped me think of it. The campers are all going to spend time on Tuesday doing a service project as part of the leadership curriculum. We have service projects for the campers that remain here, but the ones that come to Marquette for Mass will have a service project at the church. And Father Matthi said he, Tom, Teddy, and service coordinators from the church will oversee it. Which means, we get a chance to go on a proper date."

A swooping feeling erupts in my stomach. I'm not sure if it's good or bad, but I'm suddenly even more nervous than before. "It was Tom's idea?"

Connor's smile gets bigger. "Yes. He suggested that we take a moment away from the campers for a nice dinner."

"Why would he think of that?"

Connor draws in a breath. "He's interested in how things are going for you and me. He helped me make sense of some things in my past. He's a good friend. He helped. A lot."

I swallow. "Oh." The words stick in my throat. I force them out in a whisper. "I was wondering…Father Matthi said I could talk to him anytime…I, umm, was wondering if I could talk to him before Mass here Saturday."

His eyes search mine, and I see something deep and caring in his gaze. It makes me shiver. I wish I had his black zip-up jacket, but I left it at the cabin. "I can ask him." He pulls out his phone and begins typing.

"Thanks, Connor," I say, feeling parched and in need of water. I slip away into the mess hall for dinner prep before he can say anything else.

Saturday dawns bright and clear with a tantalizing breeze blowing off Lake Superior. I wasn't able to run for the last week, so slipping my feet into my running shoes feels heavenly. I opt not to run with music—I'm still spooked a little about the animals that might be on the trails—but I know I need to face the lingering fear and get back to my routine. It's good for me.

Still, I decide to do something that will keep me closer to people than I usually would for my early morning long run. The dirt track from the cabins to the main buildings is only about a quarter mile, but that works perfectly for me today. I'll do speed work and heart rate zone training along the path

What I don't expect when I finish my first interval is to find Connor standing at the edge of the trail in his own running gear and watching me so intently it makes my breath catch in a way that has nothing to do with the exercise. I slow to a walk and press the pause button on my watch. Connor wordlessly holds out a water bottle. When I see that he has two, I gratefully take it.

The water is refreshing, even after a short leg of a run. "I thought you might like company on your run today." He's almost shy in the way he's asking, and it sends a small thrill through my heart. When I don't answer right away, he continues. "I just thought with the cougar, I'd feel better if you weren't alone, but if you'd like to do this, I can go. I know how important running is to you, and you didn't get a chance to do it this week."

The idea of spending time with a man who likes me as much as Connor clearly does, even if he's been limited in the way he can show it, is appealing. And there's nothing wrong with two people enjoying a run together, especially after the cougar issue. Safety in numbers and all that. Chet couldn't have any concerns, and the campers who will undoubtedly see us when we return can't argue that anything is going on between us either.

I haven't said anything for too long, so Connor starts to back away, looking at the ground. I put my hand on his arm to stop him.

"Connor." His head snaps back up. "I'd love to do a longer run with you today."

His smile is infectious, and we stand there staring at each other and grinning until Steph walks by. "Aren't you two going for a run? Or has that type of cardio been replaced by staring at each other with goofy smiles?"

I give her a good-natured eye roll before starting my watch and taking off to the main drive and the trail along it.

Connor and I are well-matched as running partners. My legs feel wonderful; they crave the exercise, and Connor is able to keep a slight conversation going through this easy-paced run. By the end of the run, I learn that Connor spent a lot of time at his mom's dental office in California. His oldest brother, Evan, is taking over the dental practice. When he was little, Connor thought the dentist office was the coolest place ever. The swishy spit basins, the chairs you could ride on, the shiny tools, the minty toothpaste, the putty for making molds, it was all amazing and wonderful in his eyes. He regales me with the story of the time he got into the putty and used it as playdough. It caused a big problem for his mom's next patient, and he got in more trouble for that than for the things he did as a teen. As he got older, he realized he had no interest in actual dentistry. I'm grateful he keeps things light but still gives me a glimpse into the person he is.

When we pull to a stop back at the main cabins, we're both sweaty. My muscles burn in the best possible way and my heartbeat is steady according to my watch, despite the erratic thumps it gives whenever I notice Connor looking at me.

Before I can walk away, Connor brings up the one thing I was hoping he wouldn't. "Father Matthi said he can't meet with you before Mass today, but he can meet with you after for as long as you need."

A pit forms in my stomach, but I am brave. I shove the fear down and give Connor a small smile. "Thanks." I stand there for a moment wanting to tell him what I wanted to talk to Father Matthi about and also wanting to not say a word.

We can hear the raucous chatter of campers heading our way for breakfast. "I'm going to go get cleaned up before breakfast. I'll see you later?"

I notice his fists clench at his sides as if he wants to hug me, or touch me, but is dissuaded because of the campers. I love it here, but I hate Chet's rules.

"Sounds good." And then I speed walk as quickly as I can toward the cabins because I am entirely too close to throwing myself in Connor's arms.

I take my place in the back row of the small chapel where we have Mass with Father Matthi on Saturday evenings. The knot in my stomach is even more pronounced now, but I try, really try, to focus on the words of Scripture, the prayers, and the meaning of each action. When it's time for Communion, I long to go, but I know I'm not ready. At last, the final blessing is given and everyone files out of the chapel. Connor gives me a small nod of encouragement as he passes by. That simple gesture reveals his understanding. He knows what this means to me, how hard it is for me.

When Father Matthi is ready, he sits a few folding chairs down from me. "Paige, how can I help you?"

Inexplicably, I break into tears. Father Matthi says nothing, just offers me a soft smile that exudes kindness. When my tears slow enough that I can talk, I lay out everything. How my mom left when I was twelve. Her alcohol and drug and gambling addictions. How angry I am at God that He let her. How angry I am that I don't know what to do with my life or where to go.

Father Matthi listens, and when I'm done, he asks a simple question. "Have you told God how you feel?"

I cringe. "Doesn't He already know?"

"Yes, but doesn't He want to hear from you?"

"I guess." I pick at my thumbnail, a habit I dropped long ago but find myself picking up now.

"Just because He knows doesn't mean He doesn't want a relationship with you. He is the Father, after all."

At the word *relationship*, I pale. "I don't know how to do that. My dad tried, but he wasn't the most present after everything, and I don't know…what it's like to have a strong parent relationship."

"Many people don't. And many people have parent wounds. Are you willing to let them be healed?"

His question surprises me, but even more surprising is the way the answer to that question comes unbidden. *Yes. I want healing.*

"There is grace and mercy for all things." His words are soft, but I hear the intensity of truth behind them, and I know I'm ready.

"Father, it's been a long time, but would you hear my confession?"

The look that passes over his face tells me he truly would like nothing more. "Of course. Now?"

"Yes."

"Then let's begin."

When I've humbled myself to confess my sins and receive absolution, I say goodbye to Father Matthi and leave the chapel to complete the penance by singing my favorite hymn. I head down to the shore by myself, marveling at grace, mercy, and forgiveness. While I have a long way to go to forgive my mom, I'm trying. The notes of "Amazing Grace" drift over the Lake, and I revel in the untethered freedom of letting the past go for the first time in twelve years.

40

CONNOR

When I step out of the mess hall on Tuesday morning, I'm greeted by a flock of geese on the lawn. They honk noisily, and I cannot stop the groan that escapes my lips. Canada geese are the *worst*. Actually, maybe I'd rather deal with geese than a cougar, but I'm not sure. Geese can do some damage with their mob mentality and their sharp beaks.

I try shooing them away with just my voice, but when that doesn't work, I know I'll have to improvise. A metal spoon and a metal pot from the kitchen are the closest weapons of choice. Beating the spoon and pot together like a drum, I stand on the edge of the porch and watch as the geese start to move away from the awful noise. But not by much. It's clear I'm going to have to follow the geese with my terrible 'music' just to get them to leave the mess hall area.

I take a step toward the geese and they waddle just a little farther. Another step forward for me, another tiny waddle back for the geese. These birds are persistent, and I'm going to have to be louder, and hopefully annoying enough that they leave.

I begin banging on the pot harder and decide I might as well do it faster too. Perhaps the geese are sleepy this morning because they aren't as aggressive as I'd expect. I get bolder, marching around closer to the geese as I bang on the pot and do something akin to a yodel and a song.

"Are you doing a rain dance?" The words shake me from my purpose, and I look up to find Avila, Allison, Aleigha, Beth, and Stephanie standing on the other side of the flock of geese, amusement on their faces.

I straighten. "Absolutely not. I am trying to move these foul birds though."

The four campers laugh. "Can we help?"

I look at the flock of geese who haven't attacked—yet. "Ok. But you have to stay far enough away that they can't hurt you."

Aleigha hunches over, opens her arms like she's pretending to be a monster, and roars while running toward the geese. There's a honk of alarm, and then, as the other girls join in, the geese finally understand they are not welcome here and take off.

I stand there staring at my pot and spoon with an exaggerated scowl. The campers and Stephanie laugh at my expression.

"What are you doing this morning?" I ask Stephanie.

"Headed to the beach," Stephanie responds. "The early risers were up earlier than usual. I think some people are excited about today."

Avila, Allison, and Aleigha giggle.

"We've never been to Marquette!" Avila says.

"It's a great city," I say. "Have fun at the beach this morning." I turn to put away the pot and spoon and help Tom with breakfast preparations. I can't help the grin that spreads over my face as I think about heading into Marquette and finally being able to go on a date with Paige, like a normal person. Stephanie's smirk tells me she knows exactly what I'm thinking, but I'm too excited to care.

Whistling, I walk back to the mess hall while drumming the pot and spoon in tune with my song. It's going to be a great day.

After breakfast, I call all the campers who are headed into Marquette with us for the Holy Day to the parking lot. The eight campers who are Catholic include Avila, Aleigha, and Allison, another girl camper named Edith, and four boys, Tony, Louie, Evan, and Paul.

We split the kids into two, the boys unsurprisingly opting to ride with Tom. That leaves the four girls and Paige with me. Toting around a car full of girls isn't what I had in mind when I thought of a romantic date opportunity in my twenties, but I'll take it.

I give a quick rundown of behavior expectations while off camp property and reminders to stick together, and then we're off. I climb into the driver's seat of my SUV, noting with satisfaction that Paige is already buckled and looking expectantly at me. She's gorgeous sitting there in a soft green sundress, with thick straps, while she holds a light brown cardigan on her lap. Her hair is in a braid over one shoulder, and I can see the flutter of her pulse in her throat.

"So." Avila pops her head over the center console between me and Paige and leans her chin on her hands. "What is going on with you two?"

Paige visibly stiffens and the relaxed mood vanishes.

I scramble to intervene without lying. "We're friends. Taking campers into town for the holy day of obligation."

"Yeah, but it's obvious," Aleigha joins in.

"So obvious!" Edith and Allison chime together from the back seat.

"You two are, like, *grown-ups*, and you two *like* each other." Avila looks from Paige to me.

I flail for a response, but Paige surprises me. "Yep. I like Connor. I hope he likes me too. But we're adults and have obligations to our jobs, so don't get your hopes up about any romance. That won't be happening at camp."

"Awwww." The girls groan.

I start the car and begin driving off the camp property and into Marquette while the girls sing every Taylor Swift song ever known to man as they're played on the Taylor Swift satellite radio station. I laugh when Paige joins in on a few of the older songs.

She turns to me, a teasing lilt in her voice. "Do you know any of the lyrics, Connor?"

It brings me back to the time Kaleigh made me buy her every Taylor track and study the lyrics. I haven't stayed up to date the past two years, but I know a fair amount. My favorite is "Mean." I shove the discomforting thoughts of Kaleigh away and break into the lyrics, even though the song is not on. By the time I get to the word *knives*, the campers all know exactly what I'm doing and join in.

We arrive at the church just as "Fearless" plays the final notes. I park the car and the girls giggle. Paige's crinkled nose and gentle laugh make me feel like I'm on top of the world.

"That was *awesome!*" the girls exclaim before piling out of the car to wait on the sidewalk. Tom pulls into the spot next to mine. As the boys climb out of his ancient truck, I catch snippets of a discussion about longbows, crossbows, and hunting rifles.

Paige stands next to me, shrugging her cardigan over her dress. "Sounds like Tom had a very different experience than us on the ride here," she says.

"Yeah," I respond, "but I bet the boys loved every moment of Tom's wisdom as much as the girls loved my Tay concert."

Paige puts her palm on my bicep and pushes lightly. "Oh my. Connor, who calls her *Tay?*" she teases.

I grin, catching her hand and squeezing her fingers before I drop them. "I do."

She shakes her head good-naturedly.

When we get to the church, the girls slide into a pew after Paige. The boys and Tom are next, but suddenly there's a reshuffling of seats and Avila stands next to me. "We need to switch seats, Connor. I might have to go to the bathroom during Mass. Your seat is over there." I look at the direction she's pointing, the one next to Paige.

"You shouldn't meddle," I murmur with a smirk as I pass by Avila and awkwardly scoot past the campers, who tuck their knees against their chests or twist to the side to let me through. I know exactly what Avila's doing, and I'm not mad about it.

Mass is beautiful as always, and when the last strains of the music notes drift into silence, I find myself turning to Paige with the most sincere desire to tell her how beautiful she is. I restrain myself because the campers are staring.

Teddy, the receptionist with the hot pink cat-eye glasses and the walking boot with the inappropriate stickers, sticks her head around the end of the pew. "Hi! Camp CGO campers, right?"

I shift to face her fully. "Yes." But Teddy isn't wearing the walking boot today. "Did your foot heal up ok?"

She smiles and bobs her head, gray curls flying. "Sure did. Now I'll have to display my grandkid's stickers somewhere else. I'm thinking of a clipboard for the front desk. A way to break the ice with newcomers since the boot won't be there to help anymore."

"As long as your infamous coffee pot head sticker makes it to the clipboard, I think it's a great idea." I flash her a smile, knowing she will absolutely have no problem breaking the ice with newcomers. I doubt Teddy has ever met a stranger.

"Campers," I say, "this is Teddy. She's going to be overseeing your service project today. Father Matthi and Tom will be there too."

"Come on, kids, we have a bunch of things we need help with. We need to stock our food pantry, make peanut butter and jelly for our sandwich ministry, and match socks for the clothing donation boxes we put together. It's going to take us *hours*. So come with me!"

Teddy gestures for the kids to stand and they do. "We'll be at the social hall, but we won't be done for at least four hours."

The campers follow Teddy as she marches off out of the sanctuary to the social hall. Tom follows the group, but before he leaves, he tosses an exaggerated wink over his shoulder at Paige and me.

I extend a hand to Paige, free from Chet's rules and burning with excitement. It shouldn't thrill me to my core when she places her cool palm in mind without hesitation, but it does. I've missed contact with her. I've missed casual touches and flirtations and conversations that aren't being eavesdropped on by forty preteens and multiple other adults.

When we get to my SUV, I open her door and shut it gently for her. I am determined to treat Paige like a princess this entire time, simply because she deserves to be treated that way.

Paige faces me when I climb into the driver's seat, her hands working through her braid. I realize she's taking out the braid and letting her red hair run wild and loose down her shoulders. My mouth goes dry as the sunlight turns the red strands to copper.

She must be oblivious to my longing to run my fingers through her hair because she asks, "Where are we going?"

I clear my throat. Once. It's not enough. Twice. I might be able to get a word out. The word comes out as a croak. She fixes me with a concerned look. "Lunch," I finally utter.

"Where?"

Her question gives me just enough time to recover.

"North Ore, of course. It's kind of our spot."

She quirks her brow at my phrasing. "We went there once."

"First of many times, I hope."

I run my fingers through my hair as the nerves start to kick in. *Will Paige ever realize she's too good for me? Will Paige leave me? Will Paige reject me? What if I can't make her see how amazing she is?*

I don't know what to say. I'm clamming up now, and an awkward silence fills the vehicle as I drive toward the restaurant. After such a long time of dreaming of being able to take Paige on a proper date, I'm suddenly lost. This isn't like me, but something about this feels big.

"Do you think we could do something before we go to lunch? I'd rather eat a little later today."

That's an easy yes. My stomach is fluttering with nerves and the sense that something big is about to happen. "Sure. Were you thinking of anything in particular?"

"Yeah. I was wondering if we could go to Little Presque Isle. The water didn't look too rough from the church parking lot and at camp this morning."

Little Presque Isle is a tiny island that's only accessible on calm days. You can walk across the sandbar and explore the area, but there's always a chance the water will be too whipped up by tides and winds.

"We can try it." I turn the car in the direction of the park where Little Presque Isle is accessible.

"So you're a secret Taylor fan?" Paige asks.

I don't know how much to share, and it seems silly to bring up Kaleigh on our first date, but I also should probably tell her a little about Kaleigh. I hesitate.

"Never mind," Paige says. "I didn't realize it was a sore subject."

I sense her shrink back into her seat, doing that thing she does where she makes herself smaller. I shake my head and she cringes.

"No, Paige." I inhale, exhale. "It was my ex-girlfriend who loved Taylor Swift, and also *Twilight*. Some very humiliating things happened, and I just don't want to dwell on that part of my life."

Paige breathes out an "oh" before she places her hand gently on my arm. "I'm sorry for whatever happened there."

"Don't be. I get to be here with you, and really, Paige, there is no place I'd rather be." I pull into the parking lot and stop the car. "Wait here," I say before rounding the car and opening her door.

"Connor, I can open my own doors."

"I know." I smile down at her. "But I like to open doors for you."

She breaks eye contact and turns to look at the water. "It looks calm enough, don't you think?"

I nod my agreement and we walk together to the sandy beach where we'll leave our shoes before walking across the sandbar to the little barrier island. Paige's hand is loose at her side, and I realize she's waiting for me to take it again. The thought that she craves our contact as much as I do nearly makes me pull her into my arms and kiss her, but not yet.

I search my mind for safe topics that will not bring up more of Kaleigh. "What's been the best part of camp for you?"

She bites her lower lip before she looks at me and grins. "Besides getting to know you, right?" Her tone is teasing and I understand I'm seeing Paige open up and be comfortable with me. That's a gift, because she doesn't do this easily.

"Obviously, I am the superior highlight of the summer," I tease back. It feels natural, easy, right.

"I have loved hiking, and I've also really enjoyed the rock wall."

"Ahh." I wouldn't have expected that.

"What about you, Connor?" The way she says my name sends tingles through my limbs.

We're at the sandy beach before the sandbar. I slip off my shoes as Paige does the same, leaving them close to the pine needle strewn path back to the parking lot.

The sand is soft and smooth under my feet, warm from the sun. I revel in it for a moment before tucking Paige's hand securely in my own and walking toward Lake Superior. "I think my favorite thing about camp has been the stand-up paddle boarding. Watching the kids grow their confidence and abilities has been really fun. And also, I've just enjoyed all the games. I love the enthusiasm the kids have."

Paige steps into the water before I do, a hiss escaping her lips. "I always forget it's going to be this cold, even in August when the Lake looks like a tropical postcard."

"Come winter, it's definitely not something you can forget."

Paige grins. "Exactly." She trudges forward. "Eventually you just lose feeling in your ankles and it's fine."

I laugh at her blunt retort. Paige's humor is something she keeps locked inside of her but lets out on rare occasions.

The sandbar shifts, and the water can throw someone off balance if they aren't paying attention. The waves are only ripples today. Lake Superior is nearly as smooth as glass, but we both know better than to take the Lake's power for granted. We cross the rest of the way in focused silence.

41

PAIGE

Connor is solid, warm, and good. He's loyal and kind. He's fun and really great with kids. He's attractive. So why on earth am I so nervous? The expanse of sand between Little Presque Isle and the park feels momentous, and yet it was my idea to do this.

Something about Connor makes me want to challenge myself, makes me want to see where we could end up together. But truthfully, I'm terrified of that.

I'm probably giving mixed signals, but I want him to enjoy time with just me. Will he, though, when we don't have the buffer of campers and counselors and the overbearing rules of campers-with-us conduct hanging over our heads?

Connor steps onto the small expanse of beach on the little island first. He lets out a low whistle of appreciation as he takes in the stands of aspen trees and the sandstone cliffs.

I spy a boulder perfect for lounging on, so I call "Race you to the top!" before I take off running.

Connor's footsteps pound behind me, but he's heavier, so it's harder to move through the sand. I reach the boulder first and begin attempting to scale the smooth sides, but I can't find a foothold and keep sliding down. Connor catches up to me, then wraps his arm around my waist and hoists me up. I'm able to get just enough momentum to slide onto the top of the boulder, even if the ascent isn't dignified.

I catch my breath as I pull myself into a sitting position on top of the boulder, looking out at the vastness of Lake Superior and its faux tropical blue. A moment later, Connor slithers onto the rock and sits next to me. He's breathing hard.

"Tough run?" I tease.

"More like a tough sprint. I had to get a running start to get over the top of this rock."

I let my eyes wander across the horizon. "It was worth it though, right?" When my gaze lands on Connor, I find that he's watching me.

"It's always worth spending time with you, Paige."

The way he says my name sends a feeling I can't name through my skin. Desire? Fear? Excitement? I don't know what it is, but it is new and unfamiliar. There's a tension between us that makes me want to run into his arms and also run away. *Is that normal?*

A lock of my wavy red hair flies into my face. Before I can move it away, Connor's fingers brush it back behind my ear.

"I have wanted to do that for a long time," he whispers as I sit completely entranced by the gentleness of his rough thumb. He lifts the strand and presses a kiss to it.

"You like redheads?" I try to lighten the moment because it feels heavy, and I am aware of how inexperienced I am.

"Just one." He breaks eye contact and looks out across the Lake. I know I want something more, but I don't know what *more* is in this instance. I shiver.

"Are you cold?" He frowns. "I don't have my jacket to offer you this time. A certain *redhead* never gave it back."

Words I never intended to say spill from my mouth. "You could keep me warm." The flush of embarrassment drops across my body, starting from my head and ending at my toes when I realize *what* I implied.

Connor chuckles. "One day. For today…" He trails off and wraps his strong arm around my waist. Instantly I relax, leaning into him, his strength, his kindness, his goodness.

We sit together for a few minutes, just enjoying this new closeness in silence. A freighter comes into view, but it's too far away to tell which one.

"Look at that," I say, pointing.

"So you really love ships?" he asks.

"Yeah, I do. They're modern marvels. And such a big part of our history, and also industry too."

He's silent for a beat before he says something, and for a moment I'm afraid my soliloquy about ships was too much. "Paige, I'm sorry. I haven't been doing this well at all. The truth is, I don't know how to do casual dating, and I don't know how to get to know you better when Chet's rules are in the way. I'm not really a texting-to-get-to-know-you type of guy."

I turn toward him, angling my body away from the sun in the sky and looking deep into his blue eyes. "But I feel like I do know you." I bite my lip. "I've watched you interact with the campers, handle a crisis, follow rules that your brother instituted, and be faithful, and I like all those things—a lot." I take a breath. "I know I told you I'd never had a boyfriend before, so it shouldn't surprise you that I don't know how to casually date either."

Relief washes over Connor's face as the arm around my waist tightens and he pulls me closer to him. "Paige, I…was in a serious relationship before, and it's been a long time, but I need you to know that I don't want to be casual with you. I want a lifetime."

I blink, because those words sound an awful lot like love, which would be insane to say, seeing as we've been on one not-real date and then this. But maybe not as insane as I think. Sometimes you just know things—that little glimmer of peace that sits in your heart and grows and grows until it's an undeniable and irrefutable fact. And I know in my heart that Connor is the one for me. So despite the fact that I have no experience, and the fact that I don't know what happens next, I trust the peace in my heart as I think the words and whisper back, "I want a lifetime with you too."

Connor's warm hands slide up my torso to my arms, up my arms to my shoulders, up my neck to my head. He angles his head down toward mine as his thumbs and fingers move through my hair, every motion a lingering caress. He stops just short of kissing me, meeting my eyes and silently communicating, *Is this ok?* with his gaze.

The only answer I have for him is to lean forward and close the distance.

Our lips meet in a tentative and soft collision, but as Connor's hands slide down my hair and over my back, the intensity increases. He pulls me closer to him as his lips move over mine with gentleness. Despite never being kissed, I know instinctively what to do, matching his movements with my own.

He moves away from my lips and presses a trail of kisses along my jaw and up to my nose.

He pulls back, his breathing ragged, but he keeps me tucked close to his chest where I can feel his heart hammering in a beat that I can only describe as *I. Love. You.*

I must be sinking into the most glorious, luscious, warm sandy beach as I sit there wrapped in his arms, claimed by his kiss. I must be home.

"Paige, I…" He blows out a breath. "Was that too much? I know you said—"

Bolder now, I lean up and press my lips to his, starting a new kiss.

He's soft and gentle, and his lips press against mine in the most delightful way. I want a lifetime of this.

"Connor," I say, breaking the kiss. "I could kiss you all day."

His lips claim mine again.

42

CONNOR

Paige has never had a boyfriend. She's never been kissed. And yet, that was the best kiss—kisses actually—of my life. She's beautiful, she's kind, and she lets me see the parts of her personality she's learned to keep locked away from the world. She is a treasure, and I am determined to prove that to her.

Despite her proclamation of wanting to kiss me all day—which, for the record, I would happily partake in—we do need to get something to eat and get back to our responsibilities with the campers.

"Paige," I say as I take a deep breath and fill my nose with her hair's floral scent. "I don't want to leave here, but we need to eat something and then go back for the kids."

She laughs. "You sound like a dad."

I laugh too. "I feel like a dad with forty kids."

"Quite a family size," she teases

I smile against the silk of her hair. "Quite."

She stands and stretches, and I'm sad to lose her closeness but grateful that she's mine. We'll go forward and date, and I'm calling

Chet the moment I get home tonight to tell him his rules can be thrown straight into the next campfire.

Our meal is uneventful, and after I finish paying for our food, we walk to the parking lot. The wind whips up waves on the Lake, and Paige starts running her fingers through her hair, twisting it out of the way.

"Stop," I say quietly.

"Stop what?" she says, confusion knitting her brows together as her hands drop.

I take my hands and scoop up a fistful of her hair before I bring it to my nose and inhale. It is my favorite scent.

I let it drop and she laughs lightly. "You really like my hair?"

I grin at her. "You have no idea." I swallow, solemn at the thought that we need to go back to the church and return to our responsibilities with the campers. "Paige...'"

She turns her blue eyes on me and waits expectantly.

"I'm going to talk to Chet. And I'm going to tell him his rules are not reasonable. And I don't want to hide our relationship, not from the campers, not from anyone."

Paige finishes her braid and then throws her arms around my neck, nearly knocking me off balance. "Thank you," she whispers against my neck.

"You're worth it, Paige. You don't need to be hidden."

She tightens her hold for a moment before stepping away and gesturing to the car. "I think we need to go get the kids."

I don't have a response for her because my mind is churning up images of a future with her, where we climb into a car at the end of a date and return home to a houseful of children.

We're quiet on the way back to the church, but she keeps her hand on my arm as I steer. When we park the car and head to the social hall to pick up the campers, I tuck her hand into my own.

She looks at me, startled.

"I meant it, Paige," I say. "I'm not hiding this anymore."

"But what about the campers' parents?"

I shrug. "We'll figure it out. We'll make sure things are proper, and that there are other people around. We won't be in any rooms with closed doors, or have big public displays of affection. We can keep it PG."

Father Matthi and the campers greet us at the door of the social hall. The room is full of boxes of clothes, trays of sandwiches, and bins of handmade cards.

"Woah," Paige breathes, looking around, her hand still in mine. "Did you do all this?"

"Yes!" the campers respond.

"Tony makes the best cards!" Avila shouts.

Tony looks at the ground, embarrassed, but I catch the glimmer of pride on his face too.

"It's true," Father Matthi adds. "You have a real gift for drawing and art, Tony."

"Can I see some of the cards?" Paige asks.

"Here!" Allison brings over a bin of cards, and I reluctantly release Paige's hand so she can look through them.

"Wow! These are amazing. What are you going to do with everything?" Paige asks, her question clearly directed to Father Matthi.

Tom and Teddy duck in through a side door, each gathering a bin and carrying it out again.

"The cards are going to go to our Hot Meals on Wheels program for shut-ins. People who are sick, unable to get out. It's nice to know people are thinking of them. The clothes are going to our local shelters, and the sandwiches to the soup kitchen."

"It looks like they did a lot while we were gone," I respond, surveying the organized piles.

"Yes, they were great. They definitely spent the afternoon doing service for others."

"Do you need help moving the bins?" I ask as Tom and Teddy come back through the door. This time, Tom says something to Teddy, then pulls her into a side hug, waving as he crosses the expansive room and stands by me.

"No," Father Matthi responds. "Teddy and Tom took care of some of it, but we have our youth group helping move them this evening after the evening Mass."

Father Matthi holds out his hand to me, and I shake it. He has a knowing twinkle in his eye as he cocks his head ever so slightly toward Paige. She's putting the bin of cards on a table and doesn't see his subtle question, but I can't stop grinning in response.

A look at the clock tells me we have to leave quickly if we're going to make it back to Camp CGO in time for dinner.

I slap my hands on my thighs. "Ok," I call to where the campers have drifted, doing some sort of hand-clapping game while they wait on the adults. "We have to head back to camp."

We all head out, and smiles and waves abound from the children and the church staff. I open Paige's door for her, and Avila pipes up. "Awww. You said there wouldn't be any romance."

Making a point, I open Avila's door for her. "It's called manners, m'lady." I bow exaggeratedly to a chorus of giggles. After the girls are all in, I shut their door and climb into the driver's seat. I need to talk to Chet immediately.

I start the car and Paige cues up the Taylor music. While she's doing that, I send Chet a text.

Connor

FYI, I'm done hiding my relationship with Paige. We'll keep everything PG, but these rules were absurd for two adults.

I huff a sigh of relief as the text sends and I begin the long drive back to Camp CGO.

The next day dawns crimson. I stand on the porch of the mess hall looking at the redness of the sky with a cup of tea sending tendrils of steam heavenward. Thoughts of yesterday cause a smile to spread over my face, stretching my cheeks taut. The campers didn't say anything at all about Paige and me. I kissed her on the cheek before she left with the campers for the night, and no one so much as batted an eye.

Chet didn't respond to my text yet, but that's hardly surprising with a newborn at home.

Tom joins me on the porch, leaning against the rail with clasped hands. "It's going to storm today." He inclines his head toward the rising sun. "It'll be a bigg'un."

I frown. I check the weather every morning as a safety precaution. "Why do you say that? There's nothing on the weather sites."

"Just looks like it to me."

I shrug. "We can keep the kids off the water today."

He nods. "Probably a good idea."

"I'll make an announcement."

43

PAIGE

Connor is in the middle of an announcement about safety for the day. It sounds like he's going over storm protocol. I slide onto a bench next to Brooke with my tray of food.

"What's going on?" I whisper.

Brooke shrugs. "Maybe a storm. Nothing's on the weather sites, but Connor said no water activities today."

"Oh, so what can we do then?"

"I'll lead a hike with you."

I smile. "That sounds good."

When we're done with breakfast, all the counselors stand in a line on the porch of the mess hall, looking at the brilliant sky. There's a hard edge to the blue, as if it's made of glass or even diamonds.

"Not a cloud in sight," Matt says.

"I don't know, I trust Tom," Stephanie says, her eyes narrowed. "I'm staying around here with the campers today."

"There's nothing there." Jorge gestures to the horizon.

"We can do a small hike, stay closer to the camp today," Brooke suggests. "Paige and I will go. Anyone else?"

"I'll go," Jorge volunteers.

"Great, let's get the campers who want to go and begin in thirty minutes." As usual, it's Brooke who takes charge. In half an hour, we're standing by the mess hall with a group of fifteen campers who want to hike.

"Take your weather radios," Connor reminds us before we leave. He stands next to the big brass bell on the lawn, his hands clenched at his side as he scans the sky.

There are still no clouds, and we'll only be gone for an hour at most. I wave as we walk away.

The hike is a simple loop, two miles in total. In the worst case, we could run back to safety in fifteen minutes or less. On impulse, I walk to Connor and hug him, not caring that I'm in front of the campers.

"It's going to be ok," I whisper.

"I don't feel good about this but...I might be being overbearing." He lets go, stepping back from our hug. "I'll feel better when you're *all* back."

Brooke turns on the weather radio and two-way radio before dropping them into her over-the-shoulder backpack. I click on my own before storing them in my backpack. Jorge waves, and we begin marching down the path to the trailhead, the campers laughing and joking with the counselors. Jorge is telling the campers about his favorite way to mess with his family. Instead of setting out cups or glasses for water at dinner, he fills up measuring cups, bowls, or things that hold water, but don't make sense to drink out of. We're all clutching our sides in laughter at his comedic telling when a sharp wind picks up, blowing across a field and buffeting us with dry, hot air. Just as fast as the wind arrives, it dies down.

"Oh," Brooke says, pointing to the sky.

I look up and discover a thick bank of black clouds in the distance. Lake Superior is still blue, and while the waves are a little choppier, it's not like the storm is right here, right now. We have time. We're nearly at the halfway point, and since the trail is a loop, we might as well complete the hike. Despite the logic, a heavy weight drops suddenly into my stomach.

All that laughing, coupled with the sudden anxiety, means I need to use the bathroom. "Hey, Brooke!" I call. "I'm going to take a second." My phrasing is universal among the lady counselors for *I need to pee in the woods, please don't make a big deal about it.*

"Sounds good," she calls back.

I duck off the trail into a thicket, nervously scanning the woods around me because something does not feel right. The hairs on my arm stand straight up, and my ears ring with the sudden quiet of the woods.

I hear the softest whisper of a branch moving. There is no wind here. My head snaps to a tree several yards away, and I find myself looking at the terrifying form of a mountain lion.

The cougar isn't gone.

Slowly, I straighten, backing away as calmly and quietly as I can. The cougar moves forward just a bit, its tail swishing. I need to get back to the group.

As quickly as I can while backing away, I try to step onto the trail, but when I do, no one is there. My weather radio crackles a warning.

Severe weather imminent. Seek shelter now.

The cougar continues moving forward, and I continue moving backward. My foot lands in something.

I look down. It's cougar sign.

The counselors saw it and hurried the campers away from here, especially with the weather warning. They assumed I'd catch up. It's protocol for this situation. But they didn't think the cougar would be actively stalking me.

It's doing it lazily, but it's still advancing. I can't run. I won't out-run it. All I can do is make myself as big as possible and throw my bag at it.

A huge boom shakes the earth. The thunder is the epitome of a startling, loud noise, the kind that leaves my body shaking no matter where I am. The tremors in my body are so forceful, I can't control them. Another boom and my hands fly to my ears, trying to lessen the roar of the wind that now whips around me. I lose sight of the terrifying animal.

The only thing I can do is back into the middle of the field on the other side of the trail. I'll be able to see it coming and have enough time to throw my bag at it if it attacks. I can't think about what I'll do if I miss.

44

CONNOR

The weather radio crackles staccato beeping warnings. The campers who stayed here sit quietly inside the mess hall in a circle as Stephanie, Tom, Matt, and Lucas keep an eye on them. I stand on the porch, willing the hikers to return.

Brooke leads the group down the path at a jog, Jorge at the rear. I count fifteen campers and breathe a sigh of relief.

"Connor," Brooke says, her voice strained as she ushers the campers into the mess hall. "We found more cougar evidence."

I feel the blood drain from my face. The cougar is back. At least all the kids are back. I do a quick mental tabulation. "Wait." My voice comes out harsh. Thunder crashes overhead like cannon fire. "Where is Paige?"

Brooke swallows hard. "She went to the bathroom in the woods, around the halfway point, and then we saw the sign, and then the weather radio said to find shelter immediately. We were just trying to get the kids to safety. We thought she'd catch right up to us. But she never did."

I clench my jaw. "How fresh was the sign?"

She whispers, but I hear it. "Very."

I reach into my pocket and pull out the key to the heavy duty gator UTV we keep on campus for emergencies. It looks like a golf cart, but has more power, and this is an emergency if there ever was one. Paige is alone, on a trail, with a cougar somewhere out there in the middle of what is suddenly being called the 'storm of the century' by the previously silent weather forecasters.

"I'm getting her," I yell as the sky decides it's the perfect time to dump sheets of rain to the earth.

I'm in such a hurry that I leave my phone on the railing of the porch as I sprint to the UTV and start the ignition, pressing the gas pedal to the floor and not caring if it ruins the engine.

The rain makes it impossible to look farther than a few feet ahead and around. *What was Paige wearing today?* Bright green. I focus on driving along the trail, looking for flashes of bright green.

The thunder is relentless, a constant shaking of the earth. A small scrap of green fabric waves in the downpour from where it's stuck to a bramble. The trail is a muddy sludge from the pouring rain. I turn my attention away from the woods and scan the field that lines the other side. Paige stands completely drenched in the middle of it, clutching the red backpack she wears on outings to her chest. I can't make out her face through the driving rain, but her fear is evident.

I climb out of the UTV and begin running toward her. "Paige!" I yell over the wind and thunder.

I get closer and can see her eyes moving frantically from side to side. A hand is pressed to her ear and she's shaking. She's also the tallest thing in the middle of the field during an intense thunderstorm.

I run to her, expecting some sort of reaction, some sort of recognition, but she doesn't give any sign of awareness that I'm standing in front of her. "Paige?" I grasp her arm, but she doesn't move.

She's in shock. A clap of thunder sounds practically on top of us, and she shrieks, dropping the bag to the ground. I have to get her out of here. I tug her arm and try to spur her into running to the UTV with me, but she doesn't move.

I can't overthink. We're both in danger and she's not ok. Without hesitation, I scoop her up and begin jogging to the UTV, carrying her bridal style in my arms.

I place her into the UTV, then slide in after her.

I weigh my options as I start the UTV. A flash of movement in my periphery makes my decision. We could drive as fast as possible back to the mess hall with a cougar on our tails, which would take around five minutes, assuming the trail isn't completely impassible because of the storm, or I can drive us straight across the field, to the far back edge of the property and take shelter in my grandpa's old hunting cabin. If it's still standing.

I floor it just as the cougar lets out a scream and charges out of the field and back into the woods in front of the UTV.

When I pull up directly next to the old cabin, I punch the machine into park. I know the cabin hasn't been cleaned or used in years, but it's standing, it's dry, and it's safer than being out in the open. I slide Paige across the seat and tug her inside. There's no lock on the door, so it opens easily, letting me into the musty cabin.

I slam the door shut and look around the dim for provisions. I know this cabin from when I went hunting with my grandpa. The small table with a drawer contains a pistol, matches, and a flashlight.

I click on the flashlight and take in the single room. There's a bed in the corner, and a fireplace on the opposite wall. A small table with chairs sits close to the fireplace, a thick coating of dust on top of it. I'm relieved to see a stack of old wood in the fireplace, and a stack of more in a rack next to the hearth.

Paige stands, shivering, dripping just inside the room. The cougar ran into the woods, but I don't like that the door doesn't lock.

I grab a rickety wooden chair from the old table and jam it under the door handle. We're as locked in as we can be.

I turn my attention back to Paige. Her face is ghostly white, her red hair a shock of color on top of her skin. Even her freckles have blanched. Her shivering intensifies, and it's no wonder. She's freezing.

I slowly approach her.

"Paige?" I say her name softly. Her eyes snap to mine, sheer terror in her gaze. "Paige, sweetheart, you're safe now."

Her only response is to ball her hands into fists at her side.

I place a gentle hand on her arm and she pitches forward into my arms. She is soaked to the skin.

"Paige," I whisper, hating the insinuation of my words but knowing that her safety is more important to me than anything right now. "We need to get you dry. I'm going to light a fire. Can you take off your shirt? We'll let it dry by the fire." With trembling hands, she starts to lift her hem higher. I turn away, bending to light the fire with the matches. They ignite immediately after years of drying out.

My flannel is drenched, but the undershirt I'm wearing is relatively dry. I'll give her my shirt. She deserves the dignity of clothing. I remove my shirts and turn back to her, holding out my undershirt with my eyes closed. Her shirt hits the ground with a slop, the sodden fabric slapping the rough wood floor.

"Paige," I say as calmly as I can despite my hammering heart. "I need you to put this shirt on. You'll feel better once you're dry."

The fabric slips out of my hands. I wait a moment, then ask, "Are you dressed?"

"Y-y-yes," she stammers. I open my eyes to see her standing in the middle of the room, looking exactly as stunned as she did in the field. She's not soaked anymore, but she shivers violently.

"You need to get warm. Can you get into the bed?"

I watch as she starts toward the bed, but her legs buckle and she crumples. I lurch forward and catch her just before she hits the floor. I cradle her to my chest as I move a few feet to the bed and lay her down.

The bed is covered with my grandma's old quilt, and more quilts hang on a ladder against the wall. I pull the quilts off the ladder and spread them gently over her. She looks so small and helpless and terrified.

My heart breaks in two seeing her like this. The thunder continues its relentless assault as the rain pelts the old roof. There's a small leak in the corner opposite the bed, but it's a slow drip down the wall.

An eerie howl that could be the cougar prowling or the wind surrounds the cabin, and Paige's tremors grow so forceful they shake the bed.

I gather the sodden clothing from where it lies on the floor, spreading it out on the back of the remaining chair near the fire. When that's done, I take an old, moth-hole-riddled crochet blanket from the edge of the bed and use it to soak up the puddles on the floor.

The wind continues shrieking, the thunder continues booming, and Paige continues shaking. I leave the wet blanket spread out on the floor to act as a rug. I grab the pistol from the table by the door before I walk to Paige. I lay it on the nightstand next to the bed, where it's within easy reach. If the cougar barges in…I shake my head to clear that thought.

"Paige?" I ask as I sit on the edge of the bed. Her blue eyes blink furiously at me. "I'm going to sit by the fire."

She shakes her head *no* and continues her tremors. Her voice, when it comes, cracks and breaks. "Hold me?"

I need no other words. I climb into the bed. She adjusts the quilt a little so that I can cover my bare torso. She rolls toward me and I wrap my arms around her. I can feel the frenetic pattering of her heart, but after a while, her breathing slows. I tighten my hold on her as I kiss the crown of her head.

"You're safe, Paige. I've got you."

I stay awake a while longer, worrying about the campers and the counselors, especially since I have no way to contact them. Paige's backpack is in the middle of the field, and quite possibly destroyed by lightning, or at the very least drowned in rain, and I didn't grab anything in my rush to the UTV.

The crash of the thunder, the whipping of the wind, and the rain pelting the single window in the cabin eventually drives me to sleep, holding Paige in my arms.

The storm rages for hours and hours. Eventually, it moves out, but Paige and I are asleep. A huge thud against the door wakes me. I try to determine where I am and what I'm doing, but all I can hear is the sound of something crashing against the door.

The chair moves slightly back, and whatever it is will have the door open soon. I sit up, holding the pistol in my hand and staring hard at the door, knowing I'll only have one shot if it's the cougar.

The door flies open, and to my relief, it is not the cougar.

It's my brother. I lower the pistol and leave it on the table.

Chet. Why is Chet here?

His eyes scan the room wildly, his face contorted, red, and pinched. "Are you serious, Connor?" he hisses.

My mind can't catch up fast enough. Why is he angry? We're safe.

Chet's eyes sweep the room, seeing the burned-out fire, the clothing hanging on the chairs, and I realize how bad this looks. Paige is in the bed, her body completely rigid. She's frozen.

"Chet, we're safe. There were a lot of safety issues, and we did the best we could."

"Only to not contact anyone at camp? You two disappear for an entire afternoon and night after you send me *that* text? What am

I supposed to think? Tom called me," he shouts, his voice growing louder.

I cross the room and shrug my flannel on. It's stiff from drying by the fire. "Not everyone is as stupid as you."

The moment I say the words, I regret them, because the ire flashing in Chet's eyes is more intense than the fury of yesterday's storm.

Chet reaches into his pocket and pulls out his phone. Slowly, deliberately, he clicks a button and turns the screen so I can see it. The volume is turned all the way up because suddenly the soft sounds of the California woods fill the air.

I watch in horror as I see myself on the screen. There I am, down on one knee, looking like I've been dropped in a vat of glitter. Kaleigh's in a short blue dress with her long blonde hair dancing in the whisper of the breeze.

"Kaleigh, will you marry me?"

Silence, just the chirping of birds, and then…

"No, no, no, no, no, no, no, no, no, no, no, no… Oh, no."

"Kaleigh?" I'm still kneeling.

"Connor—" she starts, then looks directly at the camera. "No. We want different things in life. You're so…" She thinks for a moment, then lands on exactly the right word to suck all the air from my lungs then and now. "Bland. I need spice. I need someone with aspirations that match mine."

She turns and runs off screen while the camera pans close to my face. The video shows my dropped jaw, and the hurt in my eyes is unmistakable.

"It's gone viral, Connor. It has thirty million views, and it's titled "Tries Too Hard: Boyfriend Fails With *Twilight* Proposal." There's an interview with a man named Marvin from Marquette saying that you threatened him. The media hasn't figured out you're here at camp, but it's just a matter of time. So, who's stupid now?"

Paige lets out a whimper, and Chet snaps his attention back to her. "You're fired," he barks.

She shrinks into the covers. "But the cougar?" she whispers.

Chet ignores her. "I can't believe you, Connor. You're making the same mistakes I did and throwing everything away on a girl—again. Only this time, you have to clean up your mess. I'm not cleaning it up for you."

"Fine!" I roar. "I'll leave. I'll head back to California and never see you again. It was better that way!"

I am so angry, steam pours from my ears like a tea kettle. I am exploding.

"Let's go," Chet snaps at Paige.

My rage at Kaleigh leaking the video, Marvin doxing me, and Chet throwing it in my face has me seeing everything in crimson. I shake with anger and all I can hear clearly is the sound of rage billowing through my veins, boiling, bubbling, hot fluid.

Paige's voice sounds in the distance, but I can't hear a word she says and I can't look at her and see her disgust at my elaborate proposal gone wrong.

I turn away from them as they leave.

My burning rage could consume an entire forest if left unchecked. I pound down the path back to the mess hall.

Chet isn't there when I arrive, but the campers and Tom are. I walk past the kids with as much dignity as I can until Avila calls out, "Connor, where did Paige go?"

I can't answer that, so I hold my hand up to indicate I heard, but also continue my march to my living quarters.

I storm through the door to my private space and fling myself down on the couch. The door bangs so hard behind me that it ricochets open again. Tom leans against the door frame.

"What?" I snap. His long, braided beard and his faded blue jeans annoy me today.

"Chet told me what happened."

"Yeah, well then, what do you need me for?"

"Are you leaving?"

"You'd like that, wouldn't you? Chet offered you the position of camp manager, didn't he?"

Tom shakes his head. "He did not, and I would not like that. You two have got to cool off before things blow up."

I snort. "Blow up, like making sure the woman I love is safe in the middle of the worst storm this area has seen in one hundred years, and then getting her fired while I've become a viral sensation?"

"Ahh." He rubs his hand down his beard braid. "You love her."

"Of course I do," I growl. "But Chet ruined that, and Kaleigh really ruined it."

"Why do you think that?"

"She had to be the one who shared the video. It's something she'd do. Boost her Hollywood credibility while applying for some movie role. Probably needed a little internet fame. Stupid." I punch a pillow. "I was so stupid to be with her for so long."

"You need to clear things up with Paige, and Chet, and Kaleigh. Son, your life is a mess right now."

"You're right," I say, springing into action. "I'm leaving. I have to deal with this." I stomp around the room, throwing my belongings into a travel bag.

I storm through the mess hall as I load the first round of my possessions into my car. Chet sits in his idling truck in the parking lot. He scrubs his hand over his face, but I don't care at all what he's feeling.

After I've gathered all my stuff, I rap on Chet's truck window. He rolls it down.

"I'm leaving," I say. "I'm done. You can run your own camp for the last three days."

He starts to say something, but I ignore him. I peel out of the parking lot and drive to the closest small airport.

I have to get to California and deal with Kaleigh and this video.

45

PAIGE

Chet slams the door to the cabin behind him. He gestures me into the UTV outside the cabin. Connor left the key in it. I sit as far away as I can from him on the bench. I don't know what to say or what to do. Connor mentioned a serious relationship in his past, but he didn't mention he *proposed*.

Chet drives quickly down the waterlogged trail. Muddy water flies up and coats my skin. Along the side of the trail, trees have fallen. Pinned under one tree is the still form of the cougar. I bite back a scream and clutch the edges of the seat as hard as I can. The plastic fabric rips.

The cougar's death shakes me, but it's nothing compared to what Connor said. He said he'll leave. Tears well up in my chest, hot and heavy, but I can't let them fall, not with Chet driving the UTV. His anger radiates off his body. I know about his past with Ember and the way that Blaze came to be, and I understand he's making assumptions about Connor and me being alone last night, but we didn't do *that*.

But after seeing Connor's same brand of O'Malley anger directed back at Chet, I don't know what to think. All I can do is make myself smaller and hope the humiliation evaporates.

Chet parks the UTV outside the cabins. "Get your stuff. You have three minutes. I'll be following you to ensure you're off camp property."

I hurry into the cabin. Brooke pushes a mop through a puddle of water.

"Paige?" she asks. "What's wrong?"

I can't talk without crying. I can't tell them Chet fired me, and Connor went viral, and creepy Marvin told the internet he was in the U.P., and that Connor has no interest in me and is leaving.

I shake my head and gather my things.

"Paige? Are you leaving?"

I nod.

Brooke comes over with tentative steps. "Why?"

"I have to go," I croak, then bundle only the things I can carry. "Can you send the rest of my stuff back when camp's over?"

"Yeah." Her eyebrows knit together. "But aren't you coming back?"

"No."

And then I turn and run out of the cabin. Chet revs the UTV and flies down the path to the parking lot. He stops outside his car. "Get going," he growls before stomping off and shouting Tom's name. A group of campers stands open-mouthed at the brass bell, watching the spectacle that is *me* being fired.

My hands shake so much as I open the driver's door of my old car that my bundle of belongings spills to the ground. Larry Mr. Beary rolls under Chet's truck. I lay on my stomach in the mud and try to reach the teddy bear, but I can't.

Chet's heavy footfalls return. He gets in the driver's seat of his car and calls out, "Time to go. Now."

I can't not listen, and I can't ask Chet to get the bear that's under his car.

Larry Mr. Beary, Connor, the cougar, Chet, the storm, the *Twilight* proposal—I'm burned to an emotional crisp.

I slam my door shut and let my own rage fill me. "FINE!" I scream as I steer the car down the driveway to the main road. Chet's pickup truck stays too close to my bumper as he ushers me off camp property.

I turn off camp property, and Chet parks his truck across the bottom.

I make it one mile before the tears fall. They don't stop until I'm back at my dad's house in Viewport.

"Paige?" Dad greets me at the door. "What happened?"

I don't answer, I just shove inside past him and march directly to the shower. I take the longest, hottest shower of my life. I do not care if I look like a lobster when I'm finished. All I care about is scrubbing the past few months off me. While I'm letting the cleansing heat destroy every nerve ending in my skin, I formulate a plan.

I haven't had any expenses this summer, except for the gas and snack I bought on the way home today. My paycheck has been regular, and my bank balance is higher than ever before. I can't live here in Viewport and see Chet anymore. I can't. I've always wanted to drive across the Mackinac Bridge and go somewhere else. Now I don't have a choice.

When I venture out of the shower, I'm surprised at how hungry I am.

Dad stands in the kitchen, a plate with meatloaf and potatoes and green beans loaded at the ready. He passes it to me, and I gratefully accept before sinking into the chair.

"Paige?" he asks softly. "What happened?"

I tell him the whole story. We've never been particularly close, but I have no tears left, so I might as well be blunt about it. He'll find out from Chet and Ember eventually.

"Oh, honey," he says, his voice scratchy. He reaches out and touches my hand. "What are you going to do?"

"I can't stay here," I mutter around a mouthful of food. "I'm going to Detroit. I'll figure something out."

He nods solemnly. "You're an adult, and if you think this move is the best thing for you, then I'll support it. But are you sure?"

I let my eyes meet his and see the wrinkles around the edges. The pain loving Mom put him through is evident in the lines of his face. "Yeah. I need a fresh start."

"Ok. When are you leaving?"

I frown. "I'll figure out an apartment tomorrow, then go."

Dad frowns this time. He stands up and reaches into an old coffee grounds canister, procuring ten one hundred dollar bills. He lays them down next to my plate. "Stay in a hotel first, find where it makes sense to live, then you can worry about apartments."

"Dad," I croak. "I can't accept this, it's too much."

"Paige, you take my money, or…"

I stare at him. "Or what?"

"I don't know, but you need to take it. Let me help you. Let me be a dad to you." The hurt in his gaze makes me stop short, and I know he's thinking about all the ways Mom failed me.

"Thanks, Dad," I say. "I want to leave tomorrow. I don't want to see anyone."

"Even Ember?"

I shake my head. "I can't, Dad. Not after what Chet did. I need a fresh start, and that means cutting them all out of my life."

His shoulders slump. "I'll miss you, Paige."

I get up and wrap my arms around his neck from behind. His hands clasp my own, offering comfort. "I'll miss you too, Daddy."

When I slide back into the chair, I block all of the O'Malleys' numbers, and it hurts with each one. But nothing hurts worse than when I hit the button to block Connor O'Malley.

46

PAIGE

Early November in Detroit isn't as frigid as the Upper Peninsula. It's almost pleasant, if a little brisk. I've spent the last few months working at the various sports stadiums selling concessions. Detroit is definitely a sports city.

I found a small apartment quickly because one of my concession coworkers needed a sublease in order to move in with her husband after they married. I took her up on it. It's a great location. I can walk to work. The crowds and police presence after a big game are always so big that I don't worry about safety much, but I still carry pepper spray.

Dad and I text every few days.

I cut everything to do with Connor out of my life. I have zero social media. I don't want to ever see that proposal video again. Brooke sent a package of my things to Dad's house, including a washed and worn and newly mended Larry Mr. Beary. Her mom fixed him, and that made me cry. It was another reminder of what I don't have. Of what I'll never have. Honestly, I'm weepy about everything these days. She included letters from some of the campers and a letter from each of the counselors. Dad mailed everything to me.

Brooke's letter asked a lot of questions while telling me Connor left shortly after me to go to California, and Chet had to step in and run the camp for the final few days. They told the campers an emergency came up for both of us, and the counselors tried to play it off as much as possible, but everyone felt the change.

Stephanie reminisced about fun times and jokes and her favorite part of the summer camp season with me. Lucas's letter was a song he wrote. The lyrics don't make a lot of sense, unless you were at Camp CGO, because each verse is about a different memory from when we worked together with the campers. It won't be on American Top 40, but I appreciate the thought just the same. Jorge's was a simple note saying he missed me. Matt's was surprisingly heartfelt, and he apologized for his behavior earlier in the summer, told me he thought I was a wonderful person, and hoped that things would be ok. He shared a little bit about his hopes for the future, and I was shocked to see this different dimension of him, even if it was on paper.

The campers' letters were sweet, confused, and worried. Disappearing like that wasn't how I'd ever planned to leave the kids, but Chet made it so I didn't have a choice. He didn't listen, didn't want the truth. He pinned a scarlet A to my chest and couldn't recognize that *he* was in the wrong.

I put all the letters in a shoe box and read them when I feel that I should. It's a good reminder of my new life and why it has to be this way when I feel melancholy.

Because I do feel melancholy—often. Despite everything, my heart still aches when I think of Connor.

I think of leaving Blaze and Ember and Brooke and Stephanie, and my heart twinges, but it is nothing compared to when I think of

Connor and the time we spent on Little Presque Isle or the way he cared for me in the storm but still left to go back to California. I'm leavable, and his huge fight with Chet meant he couldn't stay.

I grit my teeth as I step through the apartment building door into the brisk morning.

In the last month, I finally had enough money saved to replace my old car. I opted for practical, a four-door, small SUV with five seats and all-wheel drive. Detroit might not get nearly as much snow as the U.P., but the idea of not needing to put chains on my tires while still having control on slippery roads is appealing.

It's November tenth today, the sun is shining, and although the sky is pale with hints of dark clouds on the horizon, it's not raining. I walk the cracked and pitted sidewalk to the Old Mariner Cathedral. There's a memorial service for the wreck of the *Edmund Fitzgerald* today, and I've always wanted to see it. I shove the thoughts of telling Connor about this particular dream of mine and the accompanying discomfort deep down. Feelings about Connor in the bottom of my heart? Forget it. They've been shoved so far down they've consolidated in my ankle.

I slip into the church and sit in a pew among the crowd. It's full, shoulder-to-shoulder, and all I can see as I look around is men who look like they could be Connor at first glimpse. I hate my traitorous heart for wanting to see him everywhere because a longer glance shows that these men are not Connor.

I settle in for the service. By the thirtieth time the bell is rung in honor of all sailors who lost their lives on the Great Lakes, I'm a snively, puddly, crying mess.

I let the tears fall because no one here knows me and no one will. I do just enough to fit in. My personality is that of a chameleon, blending in as needed. I don't get close to people; they all leave. A knife twists around my heart as the thought *I left them all too* comes unbidden into my mind.

The crowd stands, and I follow the throng of people out the doors and into the streets. It's busy today, and noisy. I shoulder my way past the congestion on the sidewalk, noting the way the sky has changed from blue and sunny to gray and dark. For a moment, I think I hear my name, but then a horn blares and I'm sure I imagined it. I cross the street just before the police officer gestures that the people still on the curb should stop. Once across, most people turn to find their cars parked in the many garages along the main road. I continue straight, grateful for the day off from work and hoping to get home before any possible storms. As I walk, I mentally formulate a grocery list, getting lost in thoughts of my meal planning.

I reach for the building door to my apartment when I hear my name again. It's unmistakable, as is the voice calling it.

I spin around and am confronted with my greatest dream and worst nightmare. My brain can't process the emotions fast enough. I freeze.

"Paige!" Chet yells.

He jogs along the sidewalk, and seeing him makes me want to run away, but he's not alone. Connor jogs next to him. His hair is cut short—so short that I can't see the curls, only the wave of texture. He wears a black jacket and jeans, and I can't drag my eyes away from the intensity in his blue ones.

I am a woman starved for water in the desert, and seeing him again is like stumbling into an oasis.

Chet's voice sounds from in front of me, and I startle backward, bumping my back into the heavy metal handle on the door. It hurts.

"Paige," he says. "I am so sorry."

My mouth drops and all common sense goes out the window. The words I have to speak aren't kind. "You humiliated me. You fired me in front of my friends and a bunch of kids, and you didn't even let me defend myself."

"I know." Chet frowns. "I know that I was wrong. I know that what happened with you and Connor was nothing like what happened with me and Ember. I know that I have to stop thinking that way. I was wrong to assume the worst and not hear you out, and I hope you can forgive me. But at the very least, please don't hold my stupidity against Ember and Blaze. They miss you." He swallows. "We all do. I can't change the past, but if I could, I would."

I nod, mute, because there are tears in Chet's eyes and I'm not sure I've ever seen him have that much emotion, let alone emotion directed at me.

Connor coughs just as a low rumble of thunder sounds and the first pitter-patter of raindrops splash the ground. Chet stares at me for a moment but then walks away, leaving me alone with Connor. My heart begins racing as he takes slow, deliberate steps toward me.

"Paige?" he asks, his voice low and hoarse. "Can I come inside and talk to you out of the rain?"

I nod. He opens the door to the lobby, and my feet take me through the door. I turn to face him in the lobby where Antonio stands behind the service and security desk.

"I—" His voice trembles and he holds out a hand. I grab hold of it on instinct and he relaxes slightly. "I'm so sorry, Paige. I am so sorry. I was stupid." He shakes his head. "I can't believe I ever thought dealing with that video was more pressing than being with you. Kaleigh wasn't…isn't…she's the past, Paige. That entire thing was years ago."

I swallow as he grips my hand tighter.

"I have been completely lost without you these past few months, Paige. I knew as soon as the plane was in the air on the way to California that I had made a terrible mistake. I tried so many times to call you, to text you, to find you online, but you disappeared, and your dad wouldn't tell Ember or Chet or me where you went."

I sniffle. "You talked to my dad?"

His Adam's apple bobs as he nods. "Yes. I had to find you."

"What happened at camp?"

"Once Chet cooled off, he realized what an idiot he was. Everything about our relationship was fine and normal and right." His voice cracks and tears form in his eyes. "The only thing is that when you weren't there and I couldn't find you, I knew I'd never recover from that far more than I'd ever care about being a laughing stock for the entire world in a viral video. Paige, I am so sorry for my pride. I am so sorry that I lost you, and that I did the one thing I swore I'd never do when I left you."

Tears stream down my face as I look into his eyes and see the sincerity, the pain, the regret there. My feet move forward of their own accord, and I fling my arms around him, burying my face into his strong shoulders and feeling the rhythmic thump of his heart.

His lips brush the top of my head and I tighten my arms around him. He squeezes me back, then leans down and whispers in my ear, "Paige, I had no idea it was you when I was with Kaleigh, but I can tell you that *it will always be you from now until the day I die*. I will spend a lifetime trying to be worthy of you, and I'm begging you, please give me a chance to do better. I never want to hurt you."

I turn my face toward his, and after a long, searching look where he waits for me to tell him what I want, I know. I've known all along that all I wanted was *him*. I stand on my tiptoes and press my lips against his, letting the warmth of his kiss unlock everything I've kept frozen for so long.

Antonio's sharp "Ahem" breaks our kiss after seconds, or minutes, or possibly hours. I start to step back, embarrassed that I forgot where we were, but Connor keeps his arm protectively around my waist before smiling softly down at me.

"Would you like to show me your apartment, and could I please take you on a proper date as soon as you're ready?"

I bob my head and lead him to the elevator. Connor waves to Antonio as we pass him. He doesn't let go of my hand the entire ride up to the eighth floor. When I open my apartment door and he steps inside, I turn to him, closing the door. He reaches down and places his palms on each of my cheeks before he kisses me. If I wasn't leaning against the door, I would fall. Honestly, I already have.

When he steps away, I'm breathless, but his hands find the curve of my waist, and he whispers, "I love you, Paige." And the peace in my heart as I hear those words assures me that I love him too.

Connor tucks my hand in his before opening an umbrella and stepping into the pouring rain. The storm has let up a little, but I still hate them. At least it's not thundering. I hesitate a moment and he looks back at me, concern filling his eyes. "You're safe, Paige. But if you'd rather stay in, I can cook something, or order take out, or..."

I shake my head and blow out a breath. "No, I want to go out. I just still don't like storms much."

He tips his chin in understanding. "We can wait until you're ready."

The look in his eyes says it all. I am completely safe with him. I lean on his bravery and step through the door.

47

CONNOR

I pull Paige's chair out for her as she sits down at the small farm-to-table bistro. Her smile pinches my conscience. I can't believe I left her. I can't believe I went to Kaleigh instead of defending this beautiful woman with a heart of gold and silver and all the precious metals of the world combined.

I chastise myself for my idiocy. It's not the first time.

The waiter pours water into our glasses, takes our orders, and leaves.

Paige looks at me keenly, questions evident on her face. I know what she's going to ask, and I'm going to answer anything because she deserves answers.

"Connor?" she asks softly. "What happened?" She lowers her voice further. "With the video?"

I keep my face neutral when all I want to do is grimace. "Uh. I found out when I went to California that Kaleigh was trying to break into acting. I thought as much, but I kept getting stopped and asked if I was 'that guy from that proposal video'."

Paige's eyes drift to my hair. "Is that why you cut it?"

I nod. "Yes, after the tenth person asked me, I walked into the first barber shop I found and told them I needed to look entirely different. I think the man who cut my hair knew about the video because he raised an eyebrow and didn't say anything. He definitely did his job though. No one asked me if I was 'that guy' after."

She frowns. "I liked it long." Then she shakes her head. "I mean, I like it like this too. I just always wanted to…" She stops looking horrified. "I'm going to stop talking now."

I lean forward. "Paige." I hold my hand out palm up on the table and she places hers in mine. "What did you always want to do?"

She looks down and mumbles, but there's a twinkle in her eye. "Wanted to run my hands through it and see if the curls would bounce back."

"I can grow it back out."

She shakes her head. "Only if that's what you want. I think I would much rather not have anything to do with that video ever again."

I sober. "It was messy, and it was underhanded of Kaleigh to leak it. She is…not the nicest person. Or at least definitely not considerate. And then Marvin—the creepy guy from the phone store—he showed the media a picture of me and said I threatened him."

She tucks her bottom lip under her teeth. "Why would he say that?"

I sigh. "The day you got your phone number changed in Marquette, I went into the store to see if you were still there. You weren't. He had…words about you. And I told him to leave you alone."

Her eyes grow wide and her shoulders slump.

"Hey." I squeeze her hand with mine. "What's wrong?"

"It's a mess. I miss home. But I couldn't stay there, and I'm still mad at Chet and what he did and how everything happened and the way I had to leave the campers."

Tears bead the corners of her eyes.

"It was awful, and it was wrong. You didn't deserve to be treated that way by anyone. Paige, I didn't defend you then, and I should have. I will regret that until my dying breath and then into eternity." I send up a silent prayer that when she looks into my eyes she sees the sincerity there.

"You didn't deserve to be put in that position by…" She scrunches up her nose. "Kaleigh, or Marvin either."

"I knew there was always a chance she'd do something like that. I just wish I wasn't so blind to how wrong we were for each other for so long. Ultimately her saying no was the greatest gift she ever gave me."

Paige snorts. "Some gift."

I lean forward across the small table and pick up her hand, placing a kiss on her knuckles while keeping my eyes fixed on hers. "Definitely a gift. One I'd like to spend forever with."

She shivers and I sit back, satisfied that she understood what my gaze meant.

"And Marvin is currently in jail. He was arrested for running an illegal goods ring."

Her eyes widen to comical proportions and I stifle a laugh.

The waiter delivers our food and she bows her head briefly in prayer. I smile at her quiet gesture. It's not meant to draw attention, it's meant to be reverent, and I join her in a quiet moment where I ask God to bless our food.

When the meal is done, we walk back to her apartment. She's quiet, but just before the exterior door, she broaches something that makes me laugh.

"So…forever?"

I lean down and, despite the fact that I'm holding an umbrella over us, loop my arm around her waist. I drop a kiss on her temple.

"That's probably not long enough." I wink at her, lightening the mood.

She laughs. "I like the sound of that. But maybe no video proposals?"

"Definitely not." I take a breath. "You'd really consider saying yes, even if it means you have to see my ridiculously over-assuming brother again?"

She rolls her eyes. "You can't help your family any more than I can help mine. I'll have to work through my anger at Chet, and I don't think we're anywhere near ready for something as big as an engagement, but if we date like normal people for a while and decide it's right, then yes."

I squeeze her tighter and place a kiss on her lips. "Just give us time," I murmur against the velvet of her skin.

SIX MONTHS LATER

"Connor! It's time!" Chet calls from the side door into his kitchen. He leans against the door as soft snowflakes fall. Yes, it's May, and yes, it's snowing. The big flakes are probably the last ones we'll have all year, but it makes the perfect backdrop for what I'm about to do. "Are you ready?"

I stand up from where I've been playing a video game with Blaze. I am terrible at this one, and it only took him thirty seconds to beat me. The truth is, the solitaire diamond on a thin gold band has taken all my attention, and I couldn't care less about Blaze's teasing.

The boy has shot up over the past nine months, and when he stands, he's nearly as tall as I am. His voice is deeper, and he smacks me on the shoulder in a playful way. "Can't believe you're going to marry my babysitter."

"She has to say yes first," I say yet again.

"She will," he says before turning back to the TV and plopping back down on the couch.

Ember holds a giggling baby Samwise as she comes down the steps.

"It's *time!*" Ember exclaims. "Oh my gosh, Connor, I'm so excited for you. I can't wait to see you at the party after."

Nervous butterflies explode in my stomach. "She has to say yes first," I find myself saying yet again.

"Connor." Ember draws out the *r*. "Come on. She will. Now, *go*."

I make a silly face at baby Samwise, who is now called Samwise by Ember, Chet, and Blaze. Samwise makes a face back at me and giggles as Ember bounces her on her hip. The joy and peace and contentment on their faces makes me flash forward a year or two, and I envision Paige holding our own baby. That thought is enough to put my feet in gear and walk to my car.

I pass Chet on the way, where he stands on the stoop in all his snow gear, and as I walk by, he claps me on the shoulder. "You couldn't have found a better person. I don't know what she sees in you."

I roll my eyes. "I wonder the same thing about Ember and what she sees in you," I quip back.

"Touché," he replies. "I'll see you at the party."

I firm my jaw, feel in the pocket of my jeans for the thousandth time, and then march off to what I really hope is the most successful proposal of my life.

PAIGE

Connor is picking me up from my dad's house today. When my sublease ran out at the end of December, I decided to move back to the U.P. I resumed working at Dr. Gartinen's office, and he offered me a full-time position when another one of the phlebotomists moved to Florida.

Connor has taken over managing the Lodge, a rustic hotel a few miles from Viewport. He bought a small house just outside the limits of Viewport proper, directly between Chet and Ember's house and the Lodge. His house has a wood-burning fireplace, a view of Lake Superior from the picture window in the living space, and three bedrooms. It needs work and love, but Connor and I have been fixing it up room by room. The only room I haven't seen is the upstairs bedroom. Like most bungalows, the bedroom spans the entire upper floor. When I asked to see it the first time, Connor looked me right in the eyes and said, "Not until I've married you." Those words proceeded to hatch an entire kaleidoscope of butterflies in my stomach.

Connor and I may have had an unconventional relationship start, but after the past six months of real dating, I know that I want to spend my life with this man, and only this man. I've had time to see Chet and Ember and Blaze, and work through my anger with Chet. Father Matthi comes to visit occasionally, and his words and counsel about grace, mercy, and forgiveness continue to make an impression on how I want to live my life. I spent far too long being mad at my mom for her addictions. Chet apologized, and while I won't ever forget the pain he caused, I can move forward and be the best person I can be. I know he's trying to do the same.

I am completely bundled up in my winter parka, hat, gloves, and snow pants. Connor told me to dress warmly because we'd be outside. I keep thinking he's going to propose, but then he doesn't. I shove down the thought that maybe today will be the day. It's the middle of a Saturday morning, and it's snowing. This is just a date.

Connor knocks on the side door and I fling it open, eager to see him. Dad leans against the kitchen counter, watching me and shaking his head. Connor laughs as I fall into his arms. "Easy there, tiger. Are you ready?"

I step back a bit and hold out my arms. "I think so. I look like that kid from *A Christmas Story*."

"I love you," Connor says as he looks me up and down. There's not much to see as far as my figure goes because I look like a marshmallow, but when he stops at my face and locks eyes with me, I feel like I might melt.

He walks me to his car, opens my door, and closes it for me as I situate myself. He's quiet while he drives, and I catch a glimpse of his hand nervously twitching on his thigh. It's unusual because he always holds my hand when we drive. Granted, I do have snow mittens on.

He pulls to a stop in the parking lot of a local trailhead and hops out of the car. "Just give me a minute to get my snow stuff on. I'll be right there."

I turn to the back of the car and find two sets of snowshoes. The snowfall creates a magical winter landscape with evergreen trees dusted in shimmery white and thick fluff on the ground.

He comes around the car in his own snow gear, bundled up with a brown Carhartt hat and zipped into his snow pants and coat. He pulls the snowshoes from the backseat and lays them on the ground. We both step into the shoes, and once I'm ready, he takes my mittened hand in his gloved one.

We walk for a while and listen to the soft sound of snow falling, looking at the tracks of sweet woodland creatures who belong here. Animals like rabbits and deer, and definitely not cougars—much to my relief.

We enter into a clearing surrounded by magnificent evergreen trees. The sun is tucked behind clouds, but the snow is so pure and white, I don't miss it. A cardinal sits on a branch of one of the pines across the clearing.

"Oh!" I breathe. "Look at that, Connor." I point in its direction, but Connor doesn't respond.

I turn around to show him, but when I do, I find him down on one knee.

I breathe out another "Oh!" But this time, it's for an entirely different reason.

His gloves and snowshoes lie on the ground next to him, and he holds a forest-green velvet box. It's open, and a solitaire princess-cut diamond on a gold band sparkles at me.

"Paige," he says as my own mittened hands fly to my mouth. "I love your kindness, your goodness, and the way you care for others. I love your forgiveness, your faith, your humor, your athleticism, and your ability to help young children get answers with their medical care. I love all of that, but most of all, I love *you*." He swallows and I watch as his Adam's apple bobs. "I know it's a lot to ask you to marry me, but Paige, would you please be my wife?"

I stare down at him, his eyes so full of tender love they're brimming over with tears.

I kneel down in the snow in front of him and throw my arms around his neck to compensate for the awkwardness of kneeling in snowshoes before I angle my lips to his. "Yes," I breathe between soft kisses. "I will marry you."

I feel him smile against my lips, and there is nothing I want more in the world than to be this man's wife. "Can it be soon?"

"As soon as you want." I lean in to kiss him again, but he pulls back.

"I hate to say it, but there are some people who want to celebrate with us, and I am really ready to put this ring on your finger."

I laugh as I slip off my left mitten. "You were confident I'd say yes?"

He slides the ring onto my finger and throws his hands up in a mock 'surrender' pose. "I wasn't the only one." He ticks names off on his fingers. "Your dad, Tom, Ember, Chet, Samwise, even Blaze, Brooke, Stephanie, Jorge, Matt, Father Matthi, Teddy. They were *all* confident, and also…" He fishes into the pocket of his winter coat and extracts a large manilla envelope that's folded and crumpled along the edges. "I emailed all the campers' parents and asked them to tell the kids about how I was going to propose to you, and if they wanted to, they could write back to you."

I open the clasp and see the thick stack of letters. Tears well in the corners of my eyes. "You did this for me?"

"I know you didn't get to say goodbye."

I shake my head. The gesture is so sweet. I launch myself back into his arms, and he reels back a bit from the force of my impact.

"You're happy?" he asks as my tears wet his cheeks.

"Can we invite them to our wedding?" I whisper.

Connor pulls back just enough to look me in the eye. "Whatever *you* want, we can do for our wedding." He stands, pulling me to my feet against the awkwardness of my snowshoes, while I clutch the envelope of letters to my chest and admire the way the snowflakes reflect light around my engagement ring.

"Come on, love." He takes my left hand. "There are so many people who can't wait to share our good news."

I smile as belonging and family and safety and goodness and love all settle into my chest, branding my heart with peace.

Epilogue
PAIGE

Father Matthi stops by the room in the back of the church where I'm getting ready. I can hear the people filling up the church, the joyful hum of anticipation like a living thing. Ember bustles in along with him. She's my matron of honor, but it's been Brooke who's called the shots all day. Stephanie quietly suggests things to Brooke and Ember, and then it all magically happens.

Stephanie should probably be an event planner. Or a teacher. She's good bringing order out of chaos.

"I'd ask if you're ready, but I've learned to *not* ask a bride that question," Father Matthi says, his warm brown eyes meeting mine.

I swallow and smooth the front of my white dress. It's an A-line with a simple square neckline that extends into cap sleeves. Teddy the church receptionist custom-made it when I couldn't find anything that felt beautiful and modest enough for the occasion.

"So I'll ask you this instead: How are you doing?"

I think about it for a moment. "It's a big day." I'm getting married and my mom won't be there. That part stings. But also...I'm getting married.

"Connor is a good man," Father Matthi says. "He's anxious to see you. We are set to begin in ten minutes. Can I pray with you?"

My mouth is dry, but I manage to nod. Father Matthi bows his head and begins to pray, asking for courage, peace, and the joy of the day to fill both me and Connor. When he says 'Amen,' I'm surprised that I do feel peace.

Brooke pulls her phone from the pocket of her bridesmaid dress. "Thanks for the pockets, Paigey," she says. "I need to go check on something real quick."

"As long as it's not Matt making trouble," I grumble, even though I know Matt isn't that sort of person anymore.

"Nah, Matt wouldn't ruin your wedding day. I think he's enjoying his job seating the little old grannies who walk through the door too much. He texted me a picture of all the butterscotch candies he's gotten today. I counted thirteen."

I laugh. Matt has matured so much in the past year. He's opening his own personal training business and gym in the spring, and I have no doubt he'll charm all the old ladies who want to train with him.

Brooke slides through the door, closing it softly behind her. Ember takes her hands in mine and looks deep into my eyes. Unwavering support from the woman who's been like my sister makes emotion claw its way up my throat.

"Paige. I am so happy." Tears start to form in her eyes.

"Ember..."

"No, I need to tell you this. I am so happy you're going to be my sister-in-law, but you have always been a sister to me. And I am so grateful you have Connor. He won't leave you. He's loyal to a fault. You can let that worry go. Please, he deserves that, and you deserve to let that worry go too."

Tears start forming in my eyes.

"Nope! No crying! You cannot ruin your makeup!" She passes me a tissue and pulls me into a warm hug.

A man stands outside the door, I can see his silhouette through the frosted glass. He taps gently, once. "Paige." It's my dad. "We're ready."

At my single nod to Ember, she gathers up the bouquets of pink stargazer lilies and opens the door for me. I follow her across the threshold where my dad meets me. The bridesmaids are all disappearing down the aisle as Pachelbel's "Canon" in D major plays, but Chet, who is the best man to Ember's matron of honor, catches sight of me before the two of them walk together.

He places a kiss on Ember's cheek, then waggles his eyebrows at me suggestively. I can't help but laugh. The two of them disappear through the doors, and then suddenly it's my turn.

I feel like I want to vomit, but also like I want to run to Connor as fast as I can. It's as if I'm being pulled toward both the South and North Pole at the same time.

"Paige," Dad says. "I know that…I haven't always been what you've needed. But I'm so proud of you. You're marrying a *good* man. Every marriage has its problems, but you won't have the same ones as your…mom and I." Words stick in my throat and all I can do is bob my head in acknowledgement. Dad doesn't seem to mind.

The music changes, and now the bridal march begins. Ember's words about Connor not leaving burrow into my soul. Twice today, different people have told me that Connor is a good man. I know that. I'm not afraid of him. I have nothing to fear about a life with Connor.

My dad gives me his arm, and together we begin the agonizingly slow walk down the aisle. I try not to let myself look at Connor until I'm close enough to really see him, but I can't help it. My eyes are drawn to him like magnets.

He stands there in front of the altar and all our friends and family in a black tux. His bowtie is just the slightest bit crooked, and I love it. His hair is neatly gelled and styled, but it's still short. I'll always be a little sad about the curls, but I understand why he doesn't want to wear his hair like that again. He's clean-shaven, and his eyes sparkle even across the distance between us.

My dad whispers, "I'm proud of you, baby girl," before he passes me off to Connor's arm.

I meet his eyes with a watery smile of my own as Connor slips his hand in mine and leans down to whisper in awe. "You are so beautiful."

Father Matthi begins the ceremony, and I manage the proper responses. When he says "You may kiss the bride," I turn to my husband.

Connor's thumb brushes over my cheek as he wraps his other arm around my waist and pulls me to him. He presses his lips down on mine and applause breaks out around us. He lingers a moment, whispering against my lips, "I love you, wife."

He pulls away and Ember passes me my bouquet. I'm holding Connor's hand, and he's walking with me down the aisle, and we're headed to our future together.

Want to know what's next for Paige and Connor? Find out in the newsletter exclusive bonus scene!

dl.bookfunnel.com/f926vay661

Preorder *Superior Hearts Winter: Chet and Ember's Story*!

a.co/d/illoYvU

Acknowledgements

All glory and honor to God!

Writing a book is a team effort and I am so grateful for the community of authors who has continued to uplift and support me.

Caitlin Miller—I adore working with you. Thank you for being the world's best editor and supporter of em dashes. Your feedback and commentary is the most fun part of writing.

Benita Thompson—how you took my haphazard ideas and turned them into this masterpiece of a cover is beyond me but I am so grateful. Your cover designs never cease to amaze me!

To my online friends, Paige, Andie, Madelyn, Rachel, Lainey, Ursi, and Leah—your expertise is incredible. Thank you for sharing it with me!

To my in person crew—Mary, Lily, and Julia—thank you for making me a better writer and especially for helping me brainstorm pranks for this novel.

Amanda, Judith, April, Mary Kate, Nicole, and Beriah—thank you for being you. You ladies continue to inspire me each and every day.

To my family—Patrick for never even considering proposing to me as a vampire and also for supporting me in every crazy venture. I love you.

Gabriella, Maria, Pascale, Blaise and Paxton—you are my greatest joy and I pray you never lose your faith and always know my love for you.

Olivia Hope McCarthy loves uplifting love stories where characters grapple with real life issues. It is her greatest hope that her books encourage readers in daily life while still pointing to something higher.

All of Olivia's romantic comedies contain some elements of Christian faith.

You can connect with Olivia on Instagram:
@oliviamccarthyauthor